Never Waste a Second Chance

JANICE M. WHITEAKER

Run, Book 1 of the Never Waste a Second Chance series

Copyright 2016 by Janice M. Whiteaker.
www.janicemwhiteaker.com

All rights reserved. No part of this publication may be reproduced, stored in a retrieval system, or transmitted in any form or by any means electronic, mechanical, photocopying, recording, or otherwise without the prior written permission of the publisher and copyright owner except for the use of brief quotations in a book review.

First printing, 2016

Cover design by Robin Harper at Wicked by Design.
Editing by Laura Seroka.

For the two most supportive women I know, my mother and my sister. I couldn't have done this without you.

ONE

"FOR THE LOVE of God Mina, be careful. My insurance doesn't cover your ass."

"Throttle back Paul. This isn't my first rodeo." The ladder barely moved as Mina readjusted the positioning of her right foot. Her building contractor had it in a death grip as if his substantial weight parked on the bottom rung wouldn't suffice. She looked down at the thick hedges, their branches sticking like giant fingers between the rungs. "Those damn bushes made it impossible to get any closer." If she didn't like the way they made the front of the house look, she'd have them chained to Paul's bumper, yanking them out of her way.

"Just don't break your neck." Beads of sweat dotted his forehead as he squinted up at her. "Damn it Mina. I don't understand why we have to do this. There are people you can call for this you know?"

"Calm down. It will be fine. Just give me a second." For a big strong man he was turning out to be quite the baby today.

Bracing her left foot on the trim framing the top of the picture window below her, she leaned as close as possible without losing her balance and aimed for the papery honeycomb dangling from the soffit.

"You better get it on the first shot or they'll be mad as hell." Paul swiped at his sweaty forehead, the ladder shaking as he moved. "Jesus Christ why did it have to be wasps? Why not spiders or roaches? They can't come near me Mina." Paul's voice got a little higher and his words a little faster. "I can't be responsible for my behavior if they get near me."

"Stop moving. I'm shooting lefty and I'll miss if you can't stay still." Bracing herself in preparation for a speedy decent, she squeezed the trigger on her can of chemical death.

"What's happening? I need to know what's happening."

"I'm trying to blast the shit out of them. Calm down." She kept her finger firmly on the trigger, completely coating the nest and anyone who dared try to escape her wrath. As she was stretching to inspect the fallout of her attack, the ladder jerked under her foot.

"Paul!" Grabbing the gutter above her head for a little added stability, Mina looked over her shoulder toward the bottom of the ladder. Paul was gone. Great. Testing the ladder, she decided it was probably stable enough without him. Hopefully.

"Wimp. Should have waited for Maddie to be out of school." At least her daughter wouldn't have abandoned her.

Mina slowly straightened and started to lean her weight onto the ladder, keeping her grip on the gutter just in case. Getting both feet in the same place would be the tricky part. After that she should be fine.

The little bit of momentum it took to push her left foot off the trim was enough to send the ladder slowly leaning away from her. As she scrambled to get a better grip on the gutter she tried desperately to use her right foot to steady the toppling ladder. Mina's mind raced while she tried to think of a way out of her predicament. Was the gutter strong enough to hold her weight? Maybe she could pull herself up on to the roof and wait for Paul to come back. Then he could help her down so she could kick his ass.

She tested the gutter, putting a little more weight on the flimsy aluminum. The gutter groaned under the added weight. She eased back off before it could pull free and she landed in those damn bushes she just had to keep.

There she hung, holding onto a gutter that could give out at any second, left foot dangling, right foot barely keeping the ladder from completely abandoning her and falling to the ground. "Damn it Paul." Suddenly, the ladder pushed back under her foot and held steady.

"About time. What the hell happened?" she yelled down as she planted both feet on the now sturdy ladder.

"Didn't know you were expecting me," a smooth deep voice teased below her. Paul's voice was many things, gravely, strong, well-worn, but definitely not smooth. She knew that voice. *Damn it.* Fate was dishing out some shitty luck today.

"Sorry. I thought you were Paul." Mina scrambled down the ladder as quickly as possible almost feeling the singe from eyes burning their way up her legs to settle on her ass. Reaching the bottom she had to hold back a shudder at the arms caging her between a necessary evil and the ladder that did it's damndest to betray her.

"Hey Don. Paul was helping and disappeared." She tried to force a friendly smile knowing it didn't matter how sincere it looked. She pointed up at the nest that started this whole fiasco. "He's allergic to wasps."

"That would explain him running around the front yard swatting and screaming like a little girl." Don grinned at her, a gleam in his icy blue eyes as his biceps flexed beside her ears.

Mina struggled to maintain her composure, finding the situation at the bottom of the ladder even harder to deal with than the one at the top. Keeping what she hoped was a congenial smile plastered on her face she edged under the vein-y, overly tanned arm on her left. If she had to be that close to him much longer, there's no telling what would come out of her mouth and explaining to the slimy building inspector just how unwanted his blatant advances were, would be the kiss of death for any future project she attempted in the city limits.

Don's smile didn't waver as she tried to put a more comfortable distance between them. It really was too bad he was such a schmuck.

She'd consider his face handsome if she didn't want to punch it on such a regular basis. He had a great body he obviously worked very hard to maintain. She'd been able to appreciate it for the five minutes it took to squelch any consideration she might have given him. There were probably more than a few women who had fallen for his good looks and over the top charm. There was a time she might have too. Unfortunately for him, that time had long passed.

"What brings you by?" She needed to direct the conversation until she found Paul. Surely he saw Don pull up. Knowing her extreme distaste for the man who, judging by the look on his face and the tent in his pants, was currently imagining her naked, Paul should be coming around the corner of the brick house any second. Unless he was so distracted by the kamikaze wasp he missed their unwelcome visitor.

Shit.

Resting his arm on the ladder rung above his head, Don flexed his considerable bicep and winked at her.

Double shit.

"Just doing some rounds. Checking out some jobs in the neighborhood." He brought his hand up to his hip and adjusted his stance, pushing his obvious interest in her front and center.

Refusing to look at what he must consider one of his proudest accomplishments, she took a few steps back and pretended to look for Paul. The extra distance from him and his sad little pants teepee made her feel incrementally better. Just as she was about to suggest they find Paul and do a walk-through together, Don began slinking her way, closing the small gain she made with a few determined steps.

"I feel like you don't like me Mina. It hurts my feelings."

"Of course I like you." She bit the words out, trying to keep her cool, but he was pushing her limits. Don didn't seem to notice her growing annoyance as he continued to slither her way, his eyebrows low over his crystal blue eyes. She needed to smooth this over.

"You have been really helpful on this project. It has been so difficult and Paul and I appreciate your expertise." She tried to give him just enough to pacify his ego without giving him any more reason than he already thought he had, to believe she might be interested in him.

He paused and cocked his head. "You and Paul?"

It was only a momentary reprieve. He began coming toward her again, this time faster, forcing her to back up or deal with his body against hers. Just the thought of it made Mina careless and before she knew it, her back bumped into something hard and unmoving.

Oh God.

The house. She had her back against a wall, literally.

Stupid. So freaking stupid. How could she let him corner her like this? She was not the kind of woman who backed down when a man pushed her. No. She pushed back. And right now she wanted to push Don. Right off a cliff.

Unwanted advances were nothing new. Normally she would make it very clear she was not interested, but he had her stuck between a rock and a hard place, no pun intended, and he knew it. Not being able to deal with him the same way she would any other asshole had her scrambling. She either had to figure out how to handle this guy or pick another profession and that wasn't an option. Construction was all she knew.

Her mind raced as she looked for an escape route. Then she noticed Don was stopped dead in his tracks annoyance smeared across his face.

"Hey Don."

Mina closed her eyes and breathed a sigh of relief. It wasn't the house that she'd backed into, but another equally immovable force. Obviously recovered from his earlier wasp debacle Paul had come to her rescue. Feet planted, standing tall and imposing behind her with his hands on his hips and a shit eating grin on his face he looked every bit the hero he was.

Having back up cleared Mina's mind and she picked up where Don left off. "Yes. Paul and I are so grateful for your assistance and support with this house. I can't imagine how hard it would have been without you as our inspector."

She gave him a genuine smile. He didn't have to know it was because she was genuinely ecstatic at Paul's timely arrival. "Didn't you want to do a walk-through? Paul and I would be happy to take you around."

There was no way Don would believe she and Paul were a thing. He was old enough to be her dad and treated her like a daughter, but maybe if she said "Paul and I" or "we" and "us"enough, it would make him wonder just enough to deter his advances for a bit. Maybe long enough to be done with this house and if she could come up with a plan B, him.

There were plenty of foreclosures and distressed properties around here to choose from, so she might just avoid buying places in his jurisdiction for a while. Let him cool his jets. Hopefully he would find a new love interest. No. She couldn't wish that on anyone. Maybe he could just relocate... or become impotent. That would probably save the members of her gender a lot of hassle.

Don didn't hide his annoyance at Paul's interruption any more than he hid his earlier boner. "I have other places to be." He looked Mina's way, his eyes serious and almost threatening.

"Good thing I stopped by when I did to catch that ladder or you'd be in an ambulance right now." He nodded Paul's way, not taking his eyes off her, "No thanks to him." A smug grin spread across his face. "Maybe sometime you can return the favor."

Before she had a chance to spit a snarky retort in Don's face, Paul saved her once again, this time from herself. Stepping casually between them, he put his arm around Don. "I should be the one to make it up to you man. She would have had my ass in a sling if she hit the ground. Let me take you out for a beer as a thank you for saving me from the boss." Paul threw her an affectionate wink over his shoulder.

"I don't drink beer. Too many carbs. Doesn't fit in to my macros."

"What the hell's a ma-crow?"

Don eyes brightened and he immediately perked up as he proceeded to educate Paul on his ridiculously strict eating plan. That explained the body. Paul did his best to seem engrossed in the explanation of portions, ratios, and grams of carbs, fats and proteins, as he took one for the team. Looked like she would be making a batch of his favorite brownies as an offering to honor his sacrifice, albeit an ironic one.

Twenty minutes later, Don was belted in his white city issue truck, waving out the open window and promising to bring Paul more information about his fitness plan at their next inspection.

"He seemed real happy to tell me all about that food stuff he does." Paul rubbed a big calloused hand in a circle over his six-pack-a-night belly. "I think he's tryin' to tell me something."

The pent up emotions of the day, the fear from her almost fall, the stress of dealing with Don, the irritation of those damn wasps, all decided to release simultaneously. Paul standing there, rubbing his pooch and looking down at it like he wondered where it came from, sent Mina into a laughing fit. She bent over at the waist, put her hands on her knees and just let it all loose. She laughed until her stomach hurt and her eyes watered sending tears running down her face. The look of indignation Paul tried to give her only made her laugh harder.

Sitting down in the grass of the front yard she gulped in deep breaths as she tried to get it together. "I'm sorry. It's been a really long afternoon."

"I'm glad I could provide you amusement." He sat down beside her on the lawn and slung a hefty arm around her shoulders. "Too bad you missed me running around screamin' like a sissy, waving my hands around my head like a lunatic," he gave her another wink, "you'd of wet your pants over that one."

That set her off on another laughing fit, and this time Paul joined her. After a few minutes more of laughter at his expense, Paul turned to her, suddenly more serious.

"What's up with Don?"

"His dick for starters." She told Paul about the ladder tipping and Don trying his best to trap her into— She shuddered not really sure she wanted to know what he was trying to do.

"I figured as much."

"I wish I hit the ground. It would have been a more enjoyable experience than his exceedingly inappropriate attempts at seduction."

Paul busted out in a roaring laugh. "No way! He would have insisted on personally checking every part of you for broken bones. Probably would've tried mouth to mouth too."

The thought of his hands or even worse, mouth on any part of her body made Mina want to gag. "Sick Paul. Just sick." She tried to shove him over in the grass, but his big body didn't even move under her push.

"You need to work out more little girl. You're seeming a little weak." He chuckled as she kept pushing so she landed a punch on his shoulder.

"Ow!" He rubbed the spot where she hit him. "Better. Still needs work though."

"If you hadn't saved me from the twat, I'd punch you again."

"You do owe me for that." He paused as he looked thoughtfully into the quiet, tree lined street that ran in front of the house. "What are we gonna do about him?"

Mina sighed. "I have no clue. He's just so cocky and dense. He wouldn't realize a woman wasn't interested until he was in the hospital bent over an eye wash station trying to get the pepper spray out."

"Don't you dare pepper spray him Mina." Paul wagged a big finger in her face. "We are almost done with this God forsaken house and if you screw us by pissing off the building inspector, I will tan your hide." With his serious expression and raised brows, it was almost the same look her father had given her so many times growing up. Thinking about her father brought the sudden urge to cry. Being so far away was awful.

She threw her arms around Paul's sweaty neck and squeezed him tight. "I won't. I promise." Paul was one of the best men she'd ever known and she'd sort of adopted him as her surrogate dad. No matter what, he would always have her back and she would have his.

"It's alright kiddo." Paul stroked her hair and hugged her back. "We just gotta get this house done and move on to the next one. Preferably one far away from his sorry ass."

"I was thinking the same thing." She leaned her head back and looked at him, staying in the comfort of his embrace. "Thank you."

Paul smiled and gave her an affectionate wink.

This was their sixth house together. When she first moved here, Mina went through a number of contractors trying to find someone who would treat her like an equal. Paul didn't treat her like an equal necessarily, but he respected her ideas and recognized her abilities when it came to remodeling. He never assumed she was incapable of something just because she was a woman. As a bonus, he never tried to hit on her which was more than she could say about the majority of the other men she worked with.

He was actually recommended by one of the guys she fired. As the no-longer-employed contractor was packing his tools and grumbling about never working for a woman again, he suggested in a not so nice manner that Paul might be the only one around here who could deal with her... crap. Apparently the guy was better at referring than remodeling and she and the big burly construction worker hit it off right away and became fast friends.

They made a great team. She was motivated and goal oriented, always worried about money and time. He was laid back and careful, making everything as perfect as humanly possible. She kept him on track, he kept her grounded.

"Well, I'm starving. I think I'm gonna go grab some lunch. Wanna come with me?"

Mina stood up, dusting loose grass and a couple ants off the butt of her pants. "Nah. Thanks anyway. I'm gonna go do a walk-through and start a checklist. I want to be done in time to get the kids from school and not have to come back. I think I want to spend the evening with them and just relax."

"I'll believe that when I see it. Relaxing isn't in your skill set." Paul fished his truck keys out of his jeans pocket. "In that case I might just head out for the day too. I need to pick up a part for my baby and give her some attention."

His baby was a shiny orange 1969 GTO. He'd had it forever and was more than a little attached to it. He hadn't been married as far as she knew and didn't have any kids so she guessed the car filled a void for him. A dog might make more sense, but who was she to judge?

"We can meet back here first thing tomorrow and go over that list you're starting. Try to knock out as much as we can. Get this thing on the market and put it far behind us."

"Agreed."

She stood on the covered porch of the brick two story and waved as Paul pulled away from the curb. She grabbed her notepad and started her list.

Remove wasps.

TWO

"FIGURES." TRY TO sleep in one day past six. He should've known better.

Thomas rubbed one hand down his face as the other stretched to grab his phone off the TV tray he had moonlighting as a nightstand.

"Yup."

"That's how you greet your mother?"

"Good morning Mother. How can I be of service to you?"

"Why do I have to want something to call my son and be sure he's okay?"

He almost laughed. She called him every day and it was never for a well check.

Instead, he waited silently, pulling the bed sheet up and tucking it firmly under his chin to block the scruff abrading the skin of his chest. After enough seconds of dead air she stopped expecting a response, Nancy gave a sigh of defeat.

"Richie is sick. I need someone to help me at the market."

He wasn't surprised. Worried, but not surprised. He'd been trying to get a hold of his cousin all week with limited success. A few words in a text here and there. Nothing to explain his sudden flakiness. Nothing besides history.

"Okay. What time?"

"It starts at 10, but it takes a couple hours to get loaded and then set up..." she paused, "then it's over at 7."

"So you need me to load your stuff, drive it there, unload your stuff, then come back, load it again, drive it again and unload it again?"

"I'll make you pancakes."

"You should have led with that."

* * * *

Three hours later, standing on his mother's deck surrounded by piles of freshly picked produce, Thomas decided a stomach full of pancakes and all the coffee he could drink was a bad deal.

They'd been picking, bundling and crating all morning. It was 9:15 and they still had to band and crate the beets before loading the truck and heading out to spend another hour unloading and setting up. Rich was either crazy or a saint for doing this every week.

"I really appreciate your help. I knew I was going to ruin your day. I promise to make it up to you." She paused. "Maybe I can help you decorate your house a little this winter. It's... um... sparse."

The image of his large brick two story dripping in the same lace and floral she'd filled her father's house with would make any self-respecting man gag.

"Nope. It's fine." He glanced sideways at his mother as she worked beside him twisting rubber bands around bundles of leafy topped beets and loading them into crates. She was quiet for a few minutes. Too quiet.

"What about when you bring a girl over? She will think she walked into an issue of *Utilitarian Farmer Weekly*."

He closed his eyes and took a deep breath. Talking about his social life, or lack thereof, was at the bottom of his list of favorite pastimes. Unfortunately, it was quickly climbing to the top of his mother's list and she was more than happy to dish out advice she never took herself.

For years his dad ran around behind her back, bedding any woman who'd have him. By the time he was killed in a car accident when Thomas was five, everyone in town knew what he was up to, including Nancy. As far as he knew, she hadn't dated since.

He never understood her decision to remain single. Not until two years ago when he found himself on the receiving end of an unhappy divorce. Unhappy for him anyway.

After that, her choice made more sense. Single was better than the alternative.

Better, but lonely.

However, his mother recently decided what's good for the goose was not good for the gander. It was okay for her to be single but he was a different story. After nearly thirty years she must have forgotten the kind of damage a failed marriage inflicts on a person.

"... my friend. She's new to town and maybe you could show her around."

Thomas' attention snapped back to his mother. "What did you say?"

"I said you should meet my friend. She's new in to- "

"I heard the rest. I am not at the point of considering cougars."

Nancy's eyes shot wide as she covered her gaping mouth with a beet stained hand. "I would never suggest you take up with a woman of my... my... " she struggled. "...generation."

A smirk tugged at his lips. His mother was always mentioning her customer's single daughters, the niece of an acquaintance, but she had yet to suggest one of her friends. I guess desperate times called for desperate measures.

"I guess I don't understand what you're suggesting then."

"She is much younger than me for starters. And she's beautiful. And she's successful. And she likes kids."

Thomas raised an eyebrow. "And you know all of this how?"

"Like I said, she is my friend. I met her at the market and we just hit it off... I guess you could say we're kindred spirits in a sense."

"What sense is that?"

"Turns out we're both bad at picking husbands." She looked thoughtfully at the fistful of beets clutched in her hand. "I might even say she's worse at it than I was."

Thomas stopped what he was doing and looked Nancy's way. Suggesting this woman's husband was worse than his dad was a big statement for her. The virtually nonexistent interest he had in this conversation two seconds ago was now replaced by mild curiosity. What had this guy done to qualify as such an awful husband?

"I mean, at least your dad never tried to kill me."

Nancy dropped that bomb and left it there to detonate. She waited, allowing the impact to blow that small curiosity up by epic proportions. She had him. Hook. Line. And sinker.

"Why?"

"Why what?" She glanced up from her bundle. "Why did he try to kill her?"

"Yes." Thomas grabbed his coffee off the rail of the deck and took a long pull.

"I guess she found out he was involved in drug trafficking and he knew she'd go to the cops." Nancy snorted. "Found out real quick she was meaner than he thought. So he ended up in prison for trafficking *and* attempted murder." She shrugged her shoulder, a devilish grin on her face. "Of course that was after a stop at the hospital to repair the testicular damage."

The surprise of that statement stopped his coffee halfway down his esophagus and launched it immediately back up. Back up and back out, scorching as it climbed his throat and invaded his sinuses. His eyes watered. His throat seized up not letting air in or out. He wheezed trying desperately to suck in anything he could get.

"Jesus Christ Thomas! Sit down." Nancy shoved a metal patio chair at the backs of his knees knocking him in the seat. He bent forward, head between his knees, coughing coffee out of his lungs.

"You just hurled coffee all over the damn beets. I'll be right back." A few seconds later, she was back and wiping at the coffee covering the better part of his face with a towel and handing him a fist full of tissues. "What the hell happened?"

Between nose-blows, Thomas managed a few good chuckles and finally, "She a bit of a pistol?"

Nancy folded her arms across her chest and leaned back against the deck rail. "Well that's what you need. A woman who can handle you and your," she waved a hand in his direction, "ways."

Thomas rolled his eyes and turned his back, going back to work on bundling beets. It wasn't worth fighting about. If and when he started dating again, he wouldn't be relying on his mother to play matchmaker. Especially if her choices were going to be based on what she thought she knew about him and his 'ways'.

* * * *

A couple of hours later, Thomas pulled his truck out of the farmers market parking lot and onto Main Street. By the time he finished getting his mom situated and chatted with a couple customers, both old enough to be his grandmother, and both trying to set him up with their daughters, it was after 11:00 and the place was beginning to fill up with white haired ladies doing their weekly shopping before the after work crowd hit.

Over the years, Nancy had grown the original small market into a large, booming business with a waiting list of vendors eager to snap up a spot. Everyone in town came for their produce and homemade items from spring through fall. So much so, the local supermarket had to scale their stock back while the market was in season.

Thomas had eight hours to kill until it was time to pick Nancy up and haul her and anything she had left back home. That left him plenty of time to go see what exactly his cousin was up to. It wasn't like him to leave Nancy high and dry. Something was up.

Thomas wasn't happy about the possibility that Rich was doing things he swore off no more than two years ago, but at least it gave him something else to occupy his mind. Lately it seemed to be stuck in the same place he was. The past.

Thomas rolled down the window as he headed out of town, the smell of farmland flooding the cab. Taking a deep breath, he let the familiar scent wash over him as he tried to relax.

Normally, he enjoyed spending time in town and catching up with everyone, but today the commotion of vendors setting up at the market only added to the aggravation building inside him.

His mom meant well and only wanted him to be happy, but pushing him wasn't going to accomplish anything. His divorce was still a sore spot and bringing it up was like a punch to a bruise.

He didn't plan on spending the rest of his life alone. He just didn't know how to get over this hump. How do you learn to trust someone else? Hell, how do you learn to trust yourself?

Maybe you don't. His mother hadn't. Maybe he wouldn't either.

Hopefully he was wrong. Maybe one day he'd find someone. Someone who would have his back, be his partner. Love him the way he would love her.

He pulled his truck down the long, winding driveway, hoping he would find Rich well and simply wrapped up in his own life. If not...

Parking in front of the four car garage, he made his way up the steps to the stone alcove surrounding the carved mahogany double front doors. He rang the doorbell and waited, listening to the gentle chiming it made on the other side.

Rich's house was beyond nice. After high school, Rich had gone on to get a degree in accounting while Thomas stayed and helped their grandpa on the farm. Farming was in Thomas' blood. He'd rather be in the field than just about anywhere else.

Rich's passion was a little more fiscally profitable. He seemed to have a knack for making money.

Even back as far as college, Rich was investing and playing the market. He did pretty well too. Made enough to pay for his education. Since then, he'd managed to turn the decent amount he made as the manager of the farm into a hell of a lot, if you went by the looks of things.

He rang again and held his breath, listening for the sound of anything other than the bell. Nothing. No footsteps. No voices. Nothing.

He headed back down the steps and crossed to the garages. He moved from bay to bay, jumping so he could look through the windows set high on the door. Cherry red classic Corvette. Harley Street Glide. Rich's custom extended cab cobalt blue truck. Only one was empty. The one that held the most modest vehicle they owned. Beth's minivan.

"Shit."

If Beth was gone that would explain a lot. None of it good.

Rich's wife had left before. After what Rich later described as a temporary lapse in judgment, she loaded their daughters up and took off to her parents. It had been enough to scare him back on the wagon. Maybe it wasn't enough to keep him on the wagon.

He pulled out his cell and found Beth's number. The chances of her picking up were slim, especially if his assumptions were correct, but it was worth a shot.

The phone rang once and went to voicemail. He ended the call without leaving a message. It would be a waste of breath.

He was going to have to figure something else out and come up with a way to keep his mother out of the equation. If Rich was back to his old ways Thomas wasn't sure she could handle it... again.

THREE

"YOU HAVE TO go potty?"

Daphne blew an excited puff of air through her floppy doggy lips and wagged her tail while making a bee line for the back sliding door. The big shaggy dog danced in place as Mina disabled the alarm and slid the door open, then shoved her way out into the still dark yard.

Mina stood and watched mindlessly for a second, her exhausted brain not quite up to the task of thinking yet. Daphne was taking her time, sniffing around the grass as she looked for the perfect location to deposit last night's dinner. Mina slid the door open.

"Hurry up."

Daphne raised her head from the area she'd been inspecting and stared.

"Go potty."

The dog turned her butt toward Mina and went back to sniffing the ground.

"Damn dog." Mina slid the door closed and headed into the kitchen. Daphne might have time to kill this morning, but she did not. It was almost 6:30 already and the kid's lunches still weren't packed. If she didn't get it together she would have to skip her run and nobody wanted that to happen.

By the time two lunches were packed and in the fridge, Daphne had made her way to the back door where she stood with her wet nose pressed against the glass adding one more print to the five hundred others already there. Cleaning the door went on her mental list of shit to do. The bottom of the list.

Big brown eyes watched pitifully as she crossed through the dining area toward the door. "Poor baby." Mina opened the door and switched off the flood light as Daphne sauntered back in the house and headed for the couch.

"Don't even think about it." The sheepdog looked back over her shoulder and flopped down on the floor... temporarily. The white puffy fur stuck in the chenille of the couch everyday gave her away.

Mina shot her the stink eye as she walked to the stairs leading up to the bedrooms, pointing her finger as she went.

"Stay off the couch." The dog wouldn't listen, but it was worth a shot.

Maddie was still asleep, curled up in her bed. Mina couldn't help but feel a pang of jealousy. How long had it been since she slept like that? Deep and peaceful. Waking up to the sound of an alarm instead of the twisting of her gut as her mind ran through everything it could find for her to obsess about.

Years. It had been years.

Three to be exact. The last time she slept well was the night before her ex-husband tried to kill her.

"Sweetheart." She nudged her daughter softly.

"Hmmmm?" Maddie adjusted the covers, tucking them tightly against her neck.

"I'm going to go run. You're phone is right here." She checked to be sure the alarm was switched on. "I'll hurry, but if I'm not back get up and start getting ready, okay?"

"Okay."

She brushed the hair off her daughter's forehead. "Call me if you need me." Almost fourteen was old enough to be left alone for less than an hour, especially with an alarm system and a hundred and twenty pounds of Daphne. But it was still hard.

Maddie jutted a hand from under the covers to swat at her. "Mom, go. I want to go back to sleep."

Ugh. Maybe not as hard as it was before she found her attitude. "I'll be back." She dropped a kiss on the blanket as Maddie pulled it over her head.

On her way back downstairs, she peeked into Charlie's room making sure he was covered and still sleeping soundly. The sight of his sweaty sweet face made her smile as she wrapped her phone holder around her bicep and plugged in her ear buds.

They were finally on the other end. It had taken three years and moving from Florida to rural Indiana for a fresh start, but it was over.

She activated the alarm, the steady beep timing her as she pulled the door shut. She stayed, stretching on the porch for a few seconds until the beeping stopped. Four years ago, she would have never given their safety a second thought. That was before she knew what kind of people were in the world. Awful people who would take you out in a minute to get what they wanted. The worst ones hiding in plain sight, right under your nose, or in her case, beside you in bed.

Switching on her running playlist, she skipped down the steps of the 1970's contemporary cedar tri-level she and the kids had called home for almost a year and headed down the driveway to the unlined road. Taking a deep breath to suck in a lungful of fresh air, her body begin to relax.

Running and long, hot baths were a Godsend these past few years. Probably the reason she held on to her sanity. Most of it anyway. Every morning, she pounded stress and frustration out on the pavement so she could get through the day without losing her mind. Every night she soaked her tired body until her skin was pink and prune-y so she could get at least a little sleep before her brain woke her up reminding her of all she had to stress about.

This morning there was no shortage of stress to motivate her run. After the summer off, she and the kids were trying to get back on schedule and into the swing of homework and after school activities. On top of that, she and Paul were struggling to finish the house they were working on. And she couldn't forget Don and his boner.

Of course this was all in addition to her normal list of things to worry about like laundry, grocery shopping, cramps, the last time she changed the oil in her van, how many sets of contacts she had left, Daphne's nose prints on her glass door. The list went on forever.

That was why she ran. The never ending list of things she could find to worry about.

Well, that wasn't the only reason she ran. Not recently anyway.

Watching the sun just begin to peek over the horizon, Mina slowed her pace a little so she could steady her breathing. She smoothed her hands over the hair around her face making sure everything was still well contained by her ponytail, then tugged at her running shorts so nothing was bunched up and weird looking.

She knew it was stupid, she just didn't care. It had been such a long time since she'd had butterflies for any reason other than nerves and it felt good. Her little crush was the perfect baby step into the world of dating. It was a place she'd never really been before. Marrying your high school sweetheart when you're eighteen and stupid didn't leave much room for experience in that arena and she was more than a little nervous about the idea.

Being in a male infested profession hadn't really helped her cause. For the first six months here she'd gone through contractors like cheap toilet paper, each one chapping her ass before she kicked him to the curb and moved on to the next. As much as she hated everyone knowing her business back home, at least they knew what she was capable of and it kept them in line.

Here, she was fresh meat in a small town where everyone knew everyone and no one ever left. She'd heard rumors there was a bet in the bar downtown about who would manage to get in her pants her first. She could give them a hint. None of them.

Paul seemed to be one of the only nice guys around here. Actually, he was one of the best men she'd ever met. In a dad sort of way. Too bad he didn't have a son.

Rounding the last corner, she straightened and made sure her gait was smooth and long, her strides even and consistent as she focused on not falling on her face.

Actually, that might not turn out too bad for her. It could end with the only man to strike her interest in years finally coming closer than half a field of soybeans away to make sure she was okay.

As good as that sounded, she wasn't ready to risk the end of her fantasy just yet. Maybe he was as wonderful as she'd made him in her mind, or maybe he was just a creep with a bet in at the bar.

Thirty uneventful minutes later she was jogging back up the driveway. The front door flew open and Maddie and Charlie stood staring at her with wide panicked eyes.

"What's wrong?" She picked up her pace.

Maddie's chin quivered a little. "Daphne's gone."

"What do you mean she's gone?" Daphne wasn't the world's most motivated canine and physical activity had never been a strength of hers.

"She had to go out and I was trying to get ready so I walked away and when I went back she was gone." The words came out jumbled and on top of each other as Maddie started to cry.

Mina wrapped one arm around each of her children and led them inside. "We will find her. She won't get far." She unhooked her headphones and dropped them on the entry table. "Get your phone and call me if she comes back. I'll go find her."

* * * *

Thomas leaned back against his tractor and picked at the pod in his hand. With the highlight of his day over there was no reason to stand in the field pretending to look at beans anymore.

It was a sad state when a man got up before dawn to check on perfectly fine beans just to watch a woman run past his farm. It was worse than sad actually. It was stupid. And pointless considering he would never try to talk to her. A strange man approaching a woman in a deserted place would probably end up with a face full of pepper spray. Or a kick to the nuts.

Thomas laughed out loud. He'd almost forgotten his mom's story about the woman with the wicked front kick.

What was her name? Shit. He couldn't remember. Ball-Kicker... Ball-Destroyer was more like it. Part of him wanted to meet her just to shake her hand. The other part wanted to stay the hell away. Far away. Any woman with that much spunk was certain to be a handful.

It was surprising he hadn't heard of her before now. Gossip ran rampant around here and personal business didn't stay personal long. He'd been on the wrong side of the grapevine twice now.

Maybe this time he could finally use it to his advantage. Ask around and figure out who she was. See if he could find something out without having to go through his mother. Just out of curiosity.

He tossed the mutilated soybean on the ground and was just about to climb back on his tractor when a noise had him turning around. A good hundred pounds of fur came tearing through his field, headed right for him. Before he realized what happened, he was flat on his back and getting more action than he'd seen in a depressing amount of time.

"Dammit Daphne!" Just as he was losing the battle to keep the big dog's tongue out of his mouth, she was being dragged off him.

"Oh my God. I am so sorry."

"It's okay. She just surprised me." Thomas leaned up on an elbow and started to stand. He glanced up to make sure Miss Daphne wasn't gunning for round two and almost fell back down.

"Do you need help up?"

He'd never been this close to her before, but he knew her in an instant. Her cheeks were still flushed from her morning run.

"No. I'm good." He tried to get on his feet as quickly as possible, but by the time he was up, Daphne was dragging her master back across his field.

"I'm so sorry." She waved at him as she struggled to control the big dog.

39

He waved back. "It's okay." By then, she was far enough away he was the only one who heard.

He wiped his sleeve across his face trying to get the dog slobber off before it dried on his skin. He wasn't sure if his little make-out session was worth finally getting to see her up close for less than five seconds.

Who the hell was he kidding? He would have let Daphne tongue kiss him.

*****

Thomas cut the engine of the John Deere just as his mom reached his side. "Where have you been this morning?" She squinted at him. "And why are you covered in dirt?"

"I went to check on the beans." In one quick, frequently executed move, he swung his large frame over and off the tractor. "Someone's dog got loose and I helped them catch it." There was no reason to give his mother any more information especially the part about the someone being a woman.

"And you ended up covered in dirt, how?" Nancy crossed her arms and raised an eyebrow at him.

"It was a big dog." He shook his hands through his hair, trying to knock out anything that might be hanging on.

Nancy shook her head and rolled her eyes. "Whatever. Do you have time to help me with something?"

The question was rhetorical. It always was. And until the weather cooled off and the fields dried up, he had nothing but time. He could find things to do, but why try when his mother was so good at doing that for him?

"You know I do."

"I know, but I didn't want to assume." She started to walk away heading to her back deck. "I mean, maybe you've found a woman to spend some time with."

Finding a woman wasn't the problem. And he could name more than a couple who'd be happy to spend a little time with him. But that wasn't what he wanted. He wanted something more. Unfortunately, history taught him he wasn't good at telling the difference between the two.

He followed behind, stopping behind as she pointed at the far corner of the deck. "Something shoved the lattice back on this side and gets up under there and scratches at the basement window."

"Maybe it's a secret admirer." He rounded the corner and crouched down. Little claw marks marred the dirt where the lattice used to meet the ground and, just as Nancy said, the lattice was shoved back far enough something the size of a raccoon or opossum could scoot through.

Nancy laughed above him. "I doubt that."

After his father's wandering eye came to light, Thomas' mother decided if one man didn't want her, no man would want her. Not only did her convoluted way of thinking not make a lick of sense, but it couldn't be further from the truth. She turned just about every male head in town, including some of the married ones.

He squinted up under the deck she'd tricked him into building for her last summer. "I think I need a flashlight. See if I can see anything up under there." If he hadn't had to rush when he put it up last year he would have dug the lattice down into the ground, but finding Nancy with a pile of composite wood, a circular saw, and a YouTube video on how to build a deck hadn't given him much choice in the matter.

The screen door slammed as Nancy ran into the house, returning less than a minute later with a heavy, metal flashlight. Thomas recognized it immediately. Over the years, he'd seen it countless times, gripped in his grandfather's hand. Now it was in his, bringing on a small tug of sadness. It was the same tug he felt every morning when he went into the barn in front of his mom's farmhouse and climbed onto the tractor, sitting in the same seat where his grandfather sat. Tilling the same ground he tilled.

"Can you see anything?"

Leaning on his elbow, he swept the beam of light toward the basement window where Nancy said she could hear scratching. "It's hard to tell. The ground is a little uneven."

"So what do we do?"

"We?" Thomas stood and handed the flashlight back. "I think you could use a pet. Give you something to do."

"Maybe you're right. I could get some goats. Start making cheese." Nancy leaned against the rail, a dangerous look of contemplation on her face.

Nancy needed more to do like she needed a hole in the head. Any dirt Thomas didn't plant in, his mother did. To the point she couldn't handle it herself anymore. What she needed was a man besides him helping her, but pointing that out would only invite her opinions on his own situation so he kept his mouth shut.

"No goats." Thomas headed to the side of the house where he'd parked the tractor. Looked like he'd be spending today with his mother too. It was a good thing he didn't have another woman in his life. This one took up all his time.

"Let me put this away and we'll go get some more lattice."

FOUR

THOMAS CROSSED HIS arms and waited. It was time for a come to Jesus talk and he wasn't leaving until he'd said his piece.

Rich had to know he was coming and he wouldn't be leaving until he saw the whites of his eyes. If that meant getting the cops out here for a well-check, then so be it.

Thomas pounded on the door. He would give him five more minutes. Calling the police was a last resort. This was family business and he wanted to keep it that way, but Rich wasn't leaving him many options.

He'd managed to get enough information out of Beth to know Rich needed his help. She wasn't very forthcoming. Probably just as tired of this as Thomas was. What he did get out of her made his heart sink. That's why he was here now, giving

Rich no other option than to face him. They could handle this. They'd done it before. Everything would be fine again.

Finally, the sound of footsteps. Loud footsteps, tromping through the house. Seconds later, the door jerked open.

Thomas was not prepared for the sight that confronted him. Growing up, he and Rich were almost always mistaken for the brothers they might as well have been. As kids, Thomas was always taller and a little leaner. Rich had dark brown eyes while Thomas had blue. Other than that, they were two tanned, tow headed boys running around the farm. They had the same wave to their hair, matching square jaw lines, and identical thin, straight noses.

In recent years, the differences grew as Rich suffered from the effects of a desk job. While Thomas was out working in the fields keeping his arms strong and his body toned and tanned, Rich was inside behind a computer eating crap and getting soft. Without the sun to lighten it, his hair was now two full shades darker than the wheaty blonde of Thomas'.

Those changes, crappy as they were, Thomas was used to. That was the Rich of recent years. The Rich who stood before him now, was nothing like either Rich. This was another Rich. One he'd hoped to never see again.

He was down thirty pounds, conservatively. He was unshaven and unkempt. His clothes were wrinkled and stained.

The worst part was his eyes, sunken and hollow, staring vacantly at Thomas.

"What the hell Rich?"

The question seemed to snap Rich out of his daze. He stood up straight and began raking his fingers through the hair wildly sticking out of his head, before trying to smooth down the front of his wrinkled shirt.

"Hey." He sniffed, rubbing his nose then wiping his hand down the leg of his pants. "What are you doing here?"

"I left you like five messages telling you I was coming." He nodded over Rich's shoulder. "Can I come in so we can talk?"

"Yeah. Yeah. Sure. Sorry. I wasn't thinking. Come on in." He stepped back and let Thomas slide past him onto the intricately laid travertine tile of the entryway hall. Rich closed the door quickly, locking the deadbolt.

"Are you alright?"

Rich shuffled barefoot past him down the hall and headed toward the back of the house. Thomas followed, waiting for an answer.

The house seemed so dark. As he passed the rooms at the front of the large house, Thomas glanced in. The living room on the right was filled with overstuffed beige furniture and a piano where Rich's daughters loved to plink out chopsticks. Every blind in the room was shut tight.

Across the hall, was a formal dining room Thomas had never seen used. A large, dark stained table was centered under an elaborate chandelier. Like the living room, each blind was closed. From what he could see in the dim light managing to slip through the tiny gaps between the tin slats of wood, both rooms were immaculate.

As the entry hall opened up into a great room with soaring ceilings and a two-story stone fireplace, Rich turned to him.

"Want something to drink?"

Rich was stalling, but since Thomas wasn't quite sure the best way to start this conversation, he let it slide. "Sure."

The kitchen sat directly to their left, open to the great room on one side with a butler's pantry at the other connecting it to the dining room. Like the two front rooms, this part of the house sat in darkness. Shades pulled and curtains drawn, the only light glowed from a small pendant above the sink.

Rich made his way to the French door stainless steel fridge, pulling out a bottle of cranberry juice and setting it on the grey and white swirls of the marble counter top. "This okay?"

"That's fine." Thomas watched as he retrieved two tumblers from an upper, open front cabinet and set them beside the juice, the glasses clinking softly as they hit the counter and each other.

Rich filled each tall glass half way with the crimson liquid. Thomas held his breath and waited, afraid he knew what was coming next. Rich opened the freezer and Thomas let his breath out in a long sigh as disappointment tugged at his gut. Pulling out the vodka bottle, he turned to Thomas and raised his eyebrows in question.

"No. I'm good."

Rich filled the other half of one glass with the icy vodka and tipped it against his lips, easily downing three quarters of its contents.

It was worse than Thomas was expecting. Past the point of hiding. Past the point of caring. Hopefully not past the point of no return.

"Where's Beth and the girls?"

Rich stopped halfway across the kitchen, one arm outstretched holding the virginal cranberry in Thomas' direction. He paused for a few beats, then continued on, stopping in front of Thomas and handing him the cool glass.

Taking a sip of the sweet tart juice, he watched Rich down the rest of his glass and set it on the counter, eyes fixed on the empty glass.

"Where's Beth?"

"Oh, yeah. She, um. She took the girls to her parents for a visit." Rich tried to take another drink from his empty cup. He was either already drunk or still drunk. It didn't matter which.

Realizing he was dry, Rich crossed back to the fridge, this time pouring a much higher ratio of vodka to juice, barely tinting the liquid pink. Again, it took him seconds to down most of it. His throat had to be burning from the freezing temperature of the vodka, but he didn't seem to notice.

Thomas took a step toward him. "What's going on Rich?"

This wasn't the first time Thomas had found him like this and as much as he hated it, it probably wouldn't be the last.

"I don't know man." Rich set his glass down and leaned both hands on the counter's edge letting his head hang to his chest. "Everything was fine."

He wiped his nose on his shoulder and straightened up. "It was better than fine. It was fuckin' great." He stared across the darkened room and seemed to sober up a little bit. "It just got out of control."

"Kinda seems that way." Thomas took the cranberry juice off the counter and slid it back into the fridge. He grabbed the neck of the two thirds empty vodka bottle. "Maybe getting rid of this would be a good way to start working your way back to fuckin' great."

Rich eyed the bottle in Thomas' hand. They had been here before. Rich teetering on the edge, Thomas dragging him to safer ground. Last time he came kicking and screaming. Thomas didn't imagine this round would be any different. To his surprise, Rich agreed.

"Yeah." He took a deep breath and rubbed his hazy eyes, swaying against the counter. "But it's probably too late."

"Beth will be okay. She loves you." He wrapped an arm around Rich's shoulders, trying to offer support, physical and moral. "I'll talk to her. She'll understand. She'll be back. She just needs to cool off."

Rich stared at him blankly. Maybe he hadn't sobered up as much as Thomas thought. It seemed to take a minute, but clarity returned. "Beth. Yeah. Maybe. I don't know."

"I do." Thomas patted his back. "Let me get rid of this and then we'll get you in the shower. It'll make you feel a hell of a lot better." Crossing to the sink, he unscrewed the lid and poured the rest of the bottle down the drain. As he pulled open the drawer holding the recyclables, the extent of Rich's problem stared him in the face. At least ten empty bottles just like the one he held in his hand filled the space to capacity.

He turned to find Rich leaned back against the counter with his eyes closed, beginning to snore. This was bad. Maybe worse than last time. And last time was bad.

* * * *

As Thomas drove away from Rich's house he ignored the ringing of his phone. Nancy was calling for the fifth time. It was the last day of the farmer's market and she'd asked him to come back early to help tear down her displays so she could take them home for the winter.

By the time she started calling, he was already late. He decided it was best to ignore her until he came up with a good excuse for his tardiness. He jumped in his truck and hauled ass for town hoping he could come up with something as he drove. So far he had nothing but the truth and he wasn't quite ready to divulge. Hopefully Rich would get it together before he had no choice.

He pulled into the nearly empty lot of the market and jerked his truck into a slanting spot beside a mini-van. She was going to kill him. Maybe she was too pissed to care where he was. He could only hope.

He half-jogged to the double doors of the building. Yanking one open, he heard a startled yelp from the woman on the other side as she teetered trying regain her balance. He reached out gently gripping her arms and helping her maintain control of the two full brown paper bags she held.

"I'm sorry. I didn't mean to surprise you."

His apology was met by light brown, almost gold eyes lined with black feathery lashes which opened wide in surprise. He froze. Long, shiny dark hair tumbled over her shoulders where it brushed softly against his hands.

He barely caught a glimpse of her this morning as he fought off her dog's advances. It was probably a good thing because if he had gotten a good look at her, he would have been too stunned to keep Daphne from having her way with him.

He'd been watching her run past him for months, imagining what she was like. Now, for the second time today, she was right in front of him and all he could do was stand there and stare at her.

After what seemed like an eternity, a slow, shy smile teased its way onto her lips. He drug his eyes from hers to a soft, full mouth almost the same peachy pink color as his mother's favorite peony. They began to move, offering glimpses of straight teeth the color of porcelain. She was talking. Oh shit, she was talking.

"-didn't even look. So sorry." She was apologizing to him.

"No. No, no. It was my fault. I was running late and... Just... *I'm* sorry." He wanted to kick his own ass right now. He was acting like a kid, stumbling over his words the second he saw a pretty girl.

She smiled making his heart beat a little faster. "Well, thank you. I think I'm good now."

Good now? Holy shit. He still had a hold of her. He released her arms and took a step back. "Good. Okay. Again, I'm really sorry."

"I'm really sorry. This is the second time I've almost had you on your back." She gave him another smile. Then her eyes widened. "I mean knocked you on your back."

She squeezed her lips together for a second.

"Technically I went down the first time."

She squinted her eyes. "I'm really sorry about that. She's not usually so forward."

He laughed. "She must have a thing for farmers." Maybe her owner felt the same way.

She nodded back at the door. "Hope I didn't make you too much later."

Crap. He almost forgot his mother was waiting. "Oh, no. The damage was already done."

They both stood for an awkward moment. "Well, have a good night." She gave a little finger wave and headed into the parking lot.

"Thanks." At the risk of appearing even weirder than he already did, he waited to be sure she made it safely to her car. She climbed into a minivan the same dark honey color as her eyes. The same van he'd parked beside less than five minutes earlier.

As she pulled away, he carefully pulled the door open again, shaking his head at himself. Damn he was rusty. He should have offered to help carry her bags. He should have let go of her before she had to practically ask. He should have introduced himself. He should have asked her name. He did none of those things. He was just weird. Awkward and weird.

Maybe getting his ass ripped by his mom would take his mind off how badly he'd just bombed with the woman he'd been secretly dreaming about for months. Suddenly the conversation he was dreading the last half hour seemed like a welcome diversion. He made his way through the emptying building ready for the lashing coming his way.

Seeing Nancy's face, he made his way toward her. A man about her age was clearly enjoying her attention as she bagged some of her last remaining vegetables and chatted about her plans for the winter. She was just handing him his purchase when she saw Thomas. She quickly shoved the bag into the man's hands, thanked him and headed her son's way. The look on her face was no match for the foul one the abandoned suitor shot his way.

"Where have you been?" She threw her hands on her hips and narrowed her eyes. "I have been trying to call you for an hour. You were supposed to be here early." A finger came up to stop a few inches in front of his face. "How are we supposed to get all this crap out of here before they lock the place up?" The finger swung away as she poked it at her displays.

Holy cow she was worked up. "We'll be fine." He tried to sound as calm as possible. "I had some business that I needed to get done and it took longer than I expected. I'm really sorry."

Her demeanor softened, incrementally. "It's fine. If we need more time I'm sure Mike will be okay with it." She leaned to look over his shoulder and gave a smile and a wave.

Thomas turned and gave Mike a nod he was sure went unseen, since the guy's attention was focused entirely on Nancy. The pudgy fifty-something man straightened up, tried to suck in his considerable gut and gave Nancy a wink and a wave back. "I'm sure he will."

"What's that supposed to mean? He's married you know."

"Yeah. I don't think he's too worried about that."

Nancy sighed loudly. "I am. Not that it would matter if he wasn't. I can't even imagine being underneath all that volume. I can't breathe just thinking about it." She began stacking empty crates into manageable piles.

"That's disgusting."

"I know, that's what I'm saying." She paused turning to face him. "It's your fault anyway. You're the one who says I should consider finding somebody. I just want you to know I'm trying. I'm saying I would consider him but he's married and fat."

Thomas followed her lead, helping stack crates. "Then let me be more specific. Try considering someone not married or fat."

"What about you? Who are you considering?" She crossed her arms and stared at him, her gaze boring into his back as he bent over to collapse one of the large wooden stands used to display the crates.

He shrugged. "No one to consider." That was a lie.

"Well that's your fault." She came to help him with the display stand. "If you were here on time you could have met Mina."

"Mina?" That name sounded familiar.

"My friend. Mina. I told you about her."

Thomas stopped what he was doing and stared at his mother. He swallowed hard. It couldn't be.

Nancy kept organizing her displays oblivious to the mind fuck she was bringing down on him. "You just missed her. Probably passed her in the parking lot. I sent her home with two big bags of stuff. If you were here on time, you could have helped her carry it all to her car."

Son of a bitch.

FIVE

MINA PULLED HER caramel colored minivan into the parking lot of Roy's, her favorite diner in town. She was fifteen minutes early for her lunch date, and needed the time to look over some recent sales. She and Paul were finally on the home stretch with the house from hell and it was time to crunch numbers and come up with a price. Hopefully one that would get them a quick sale and out of Don's jurisdiction ASAP.

Scanning the packed lot for a vacant spot to park her makeshift office, she caught a glimpse of a white city truck out of the corner of her eye.

"You've got to be kidding me." She fished her cell out of her oversized and yet still somehow overstuffed purse.

"We need to pick someplace else." She cruised through the lot and quickly headed back out the same way she came in. "Don is here and I really can't handle him today."

"Don't feel like an extremely unsatisfying lunch of a burger, fries and a beefcake who can't take no for an answer?" Her friend's contagious laugh bursting through the line made Mina smile in spite of the fact that she was going to miss out on the crispy edged burger she spent all morning anticipating.

"What about the deli? I can be there in two minutes."

"Excellent idea." Not quite the burger she was dreaming of, but fresh tuna on homemade bread didn't sound too bad either. She disconnected the phone and pulled the van back onto Main, hoping no one inside noticed her little detour.

It was beginning to feel like the harder she worked to get away from him, the closer Don got. All she'd been doing for the last week was avoiding him. He seemed to be everywhere. The grocery, the gas station, now the diner. She had to finish this damn house and get it sold before she lost her mind and told him where he could stick it. Every time she saw him it was getting harder and harder to resist the urge to stick it there for him.

The deli was only a couple of blocks away from Roy's. Two minutes later she pulled into the lot, finding Nancy leaning against her car with a smile that turned to laughter the minute she saw Mina's face.

"Rough day?"

"Rough week and I'm starving. Not a good look for me I guess."

"Anything is a good look for you. You even manage to make these look good." She reached over and picked at a cobweb tangled in Mina's hair.

"I probably should have checked myself over before I headed this way." She ran her hands through her hair, shaking it out. "I've got to get the house spotless so I can get it on the market next week." She followed Nancy through the glass door into the surprisingly empty shop. The aroma of freshly baked bread hung heavy in the air.

"I thought you had to redo that whole place? Where in the hell did you find cobwebs?"

"The attic." She was looking at the menu board when she heard a snort beside her.

"The attic?" It wasn't just a snort. It was a laugh and a snort. Nancy was snaughling at her. "Who in the world cleans an attic? That's like vacuuming a shed."

"Some sheds have carpet in them."

"Oh my God you've vacuumed a shed."

"Well how the hell else was I gonna get it clean?"

Nancy leaned into her, bumping their shoulders together. "This is why we're friends. You're as crazy as I am."

"There is no need for name calling missy. You-"

Their banter was interrupted by an impatient clearing of the throat that came from behind the counter. Both women turned their attention to the man waiting to take their order.

"Sorry Joe." Nancy gave him a big smile and he softened immediately. "Can I have my usual?"

"You can have anything you want." He smiled back and Mina was pretty sure he meant exactly what he said. Her friend however, seemed completely oblivious to the man's obvious interest.

"Thanks Joe. You're the best."

Joe turned five shades of red as he grinned at Nancy like a love struck teenager. He stood gazing for a few seconds more before he remembered Mina.

She quickly ordered her tuna on toasted rye, and after filling her cup with crushed ice and red cream soda at the fountain, joined Nancy at a two-seater by the glass wall that made up the front of the restaurant and faced Main Street. "How'd the last day at the market go?"

The older woman heaved a sigh. "Not as well as I would have liked."

Just then, Joe arrived at their table, a foam plate in each hand. He quickly plopped Mina's sandwich down in front of her, and then carefully placed Nancy's between the elbows she had gently resting on the table.

"Can I get you anything else?" he directed solely Nancy's way.

"No. This looks great as always. Thank you." Thankfully Nancy's praise didn't encourage him to stay and he made a hasty, almost embarrassed retreat to the kitchen.

"You probably make a killing with single middle-aged men." Mina took a bite of her tuna. It was always good here, but today her sandwich was loaded with creamy pickle-y goodness. She glanced down and noticed double the normal amount of chips were overflowing her plate and a cup of delicious looking pasta salad she didn't order was parked at her elbow.

"What do you mean?"

Mina glanced over her shoulder to be sure Joe was out of earshot. "I mean this." She waved her hands above their lunch. "I mean him." She threw a thumb in the general direction of the kitchen Joe disappeared into. "I mean," she dropped her voice imitating Joe, "You can have anything you want Nancy. Anything." She wiggled her eyebrows at her friend for emphasis.

"First of all, you just made poor Joe sound like a sexual deviant. Second, he and I have been friends since high school.

Third, I come here all the time. He just wants a satisfied customer."

"He wants to satisfy you alright." Mina tested a forkful of what turned out to be the most amazing pasta salad she'd ever had as she chose to ignore the eyeballs needling into her from across the table. "And maybe you should let him. You seem a little uptight lately. It would probably do you some good. Clean out your cobwebs."

"Look who's talking!" Nancy pointed her plastic fork right in Mina's face. "Your pipes could use a little cleaning of their own missy."

She was right. It had been *years*. "Ugh. The only man around here showing any interest is Don, and trust me when I say the feeling is not mutual."

"Donnie was so sweet when he was a kid. A scrawny little thing though."

Mina gave Nancy a skeptical eyebrow. "Well he's no longer scrawny or sweet."

"Oh honey, I've seen him. He definitely left scrawny in the dust a long time ago."

"Well hello Mrs. Robinson."

Nancy's eyes widened as she feigned innocence. "How could I not notice him? You could bounce quarters off his-"

"Satisfied?" Joe seemed to materialize out of nowhere.

Mina nearly choked on a bite of her sandwich. Nancy kicked at her under the table as she once again thanked Joe for their lunch assuring him it was wonderful like always. As he walked away with his chest puffed up Mina regained her composure.

"Missed opportunity. He probably would have taken you to the kitchen if you'd asked nicely."

"I have no interest in Joe or any plans you think he might have for me and my cobwebs in his kitchen." Nancy popped a chip in her mouth. "Besides, I'm sure the Health Department has regulations."

Mina laughed out loud. "Horny men tend to ignore any and all rules and regulations."

"Ain't that the truth. Don't forget commitments and wives." Nancy took a noisy, gurgling sip then shook her cup, the lonely ice rattling around. She went to refill, leaving Mina to happily devour her lunch. She had been going since five this morning and was starving.

Nancy slid back into the seat across from her and checked her cell phone. A cloud passed over her friends face as she poked at her pasta salad.

"Everything okay?"

Nancy sighed. "I don't know."

Mina wasn't used to seeing her friend anything but happy and upbeat. This sudden change was throwing her for a loop. Against her stomach's wishes, she pushed her lunch to the side and leaned forward against the table. "What's going on?"

Nancy rubbed her hands over her eyes and down her cheeks as she leaned back in her chair. "All the men in my life are absolutely driving me crazy."

"All the men?"

"Thomas and Rich. Both the men. Unfortunately that is also all the men."

"It is a little depressing when the only men in your life are biologically tied to you." Mina thought of her Charlie. "Plus they know you are way less likely to kill them and they use that against you."

Nancy sighed. "It's not even really like that. Something's going on with Rich and I'm pretty sure Thomas is trying to keep it from me." Nancy glanced down at the sizeable amount of lunch she had left. "I'm gonna need a box."

Mina began stacking the trash from her lunch into a pile in front of her while Nancy snagged a box off the counter and returned to the table. "Do you think it's something serious?"

"I hope not, but I just don't know." She began transferring the contents of her plate into the foam container.

"Why would he keep something from you? Especially if it's serious."

"He just wants to protect me." Nancy shook her head. "I think he feels responsible for me."

"I bet his wife loves that."

Nancy's brow wrinkled. "Oh, no. Thomas isn't married. Rich is the one who's married." She closed the lid on her food container. "I hope one day Thomas finds the right woman, but I can only imagine him with someone very special."

Nancy glanced up at her quickly. "He's a wonderful man and would need an equally wonderful woman."

Mina smiled. She would probably feel the same way when it came to Charlie. There was something about the mother-son relationship. All mothers thought only the best woman would be good enough for her son. It was probably why mother-in-law's got such a bad rap.

She helped as Nancy gathered the trash pile and tossed it in the can near the door. As the bell tinkled on the glass door when they left, Joe came running from the back.

"Have a nice afternoon Nancy."

Stepping out into the warm sun, Mina took a deep breath and closed her eyes, letting the glow warm her skin. She loved the fall. There was something about the lingering warmth of the sun mixed with the crisp edge to the breeze that made her feel cozy and calm.

Nancy stepped beside her, joining Mina in appreciating the beautiful weather. "I wish the weather was like this last week. Even with it being the last day for the season, the rain kept people home." She slid brown tortoise sunglasses over her eyes.

"Bad for you, good for me. I got a bunch of great stuff since everyone was still stocked when I got there." The market was one of Mina's favorite things about the town. It was one of the best she'd ever been to and she guessed Nancy had a lot to do with that.

"If you came earlier you would always get the good stuff."

"I know. I lose track of time. After the kids get out of school it's total chaos trying to get homework done, dinner on the table and run them to any activities they have going on." She dug in her cavernous purse until she felt the cold steel of her keys. "I promise I'll try harder next year."

Nancy shot her an unbelieving look.

She considered asking about the man she ran into last week as she left the market. The same farmer she'd been doing her best to impress by impersonating a gazelle as she ran past him every morning. It would figure Daphne would be the first one to get her lips on him.

Maybe later, when Nancy was having a better day she could see if she knew who he was. Maybe she'd get lucky and run into him again. Hopefully she'd be a little better at flirting by then. All her smiles and eye batting seemed to have him dumbfounded when she fell into his arms at the farmer's market. Could you Google flirting?

"Well, I guess I will see you when I see you then." Nancy reached out and gave her a short hug. "Sorry you had to listen to me whine."

"It's about time for me to be able to return the favor." Mina smiled and squeezed her friend back. "Sorry the boys are being boys."

Nancy gave her a smile. "Oh, I have a feeling Thomas will be just fine. He just needs a kick in the pants." Her face became serious. "Rich though. I'm afraid to find out what's going on there." She clicked the door locks on her remote, her horn giving a quick beep. "That boy might be the death of me."

"Is there anything I could do to help?"

"If it's what I am afraid it is I'm not sure anyone can help. Maybe take me out for a spa day. At least then I'll look pretty while I go crazy."

Mina rolled her eyes. Nancy was one of the most beautiful women she'd ever known. Inside and out.

"How about I take you out and find you a man instead?"

The older woman looked at her straight faced. "Just remember. Turn about's fair play young lady." Her seriousness faded and she gave Mina a bit of a wicked grin, making her wonder just what kind of man Nancy would like to pick out for her.

SIX

"DAMN."

Mina pulled into the crumbling driveway of an even more crumbling house. This was the tenth house she'd seen this week and it looked to be no better than the others. She got out of her van to take a closer look, hoping to be surprised.

She peeked through the front window, but the shingles strewn across the dead grass of the lawn made the sight of the living room ceiling on the living room floor anti-climactic. Roof leak.

Picking her way through the discarded flower pots and random trash, she made her way to the side of the house. She stepped on one of the overturned pots to peer into what she guessed was the dining room window. Oh, yeah. Major roof leak. That room's ceiling, while not yet on the floor, was bowed dangerously low and emitting a steady drip of water that would be quite useful in a torture chamber.

She ran her finger down the paper in her hand until she found the list price. She started laughing. No flippin' way.

She'd laughed a lot this week. It was either that or cry. The idea to move out of Don's jurisdiction for her next project was dying a slow agonizing death. If she went closer to the city, prices skyrocketed, even on properties like the one standing before her, in all its decaying glory. Farther out and the max value just didn't give her enough to work with.

She made her way back to her van, dried vegetation crunching under her sneakers. Flopping into the driver's seat, she tossed the paper onto the growing pile in the floorboard. Waking up her phone, she swiped her thumb across the screen and called Paul.

"Yes ma'am."

"We're screwed."

"That bad?"

"Probably worse. I'm not even sure this one has a roof. I think it used to but it's all over the yard now."

"Hmmmm. I'm not sure if I should tell you this or not."

"Might as well. Can't be any worse than this thing I'm looking at now."

"My buddy's folks just went into a retirement community and are lookin' to sell their place."

"Is it awful?" If it wasn't too bad, this day just might be looking up.

"No. Just, what's that you call it? Granny chic?"

Mina laughed into the phone. Hearing Paul describe a house as granny chic just made her whole day. Maybe even her week. "Looks like old lady?"

"Kinda. Old lady with very, uh vibrant, taste."

"Can we see it? Check it over?"

"I thought you might say that so I got him to meet us there in an hour."

Mina looked at the clock on the dash. The lined numbers glowed 10:00. She would have to hurry. "I can make that work." She fired up her GPS. "Where am I going?"

"Well, that's the bad news."

She let her head fall to the steering wheel. "You're shitting me."

Thirty minutes later she pulled up in front of an aluminum sided two story. In McCordsville. In Don's territory.

Her heart sank. It didn't look bad from the outside. Maybe it would be terrible inside. Maybe they would be asking too much. Then she would have no problem walking away. If not...

She sighed. If not she would buy it and figure out a way to deal with Don.

Paul was waiting for her on the porch next to a stubby guy with a big gut and thinning hair an unnatural shade of black. "Mina, this is my buddy from school Mike. It's his parent's place."

Mike shoved a thick fingered hand her way. She took it, surprised at the limp grasp and soft wrist. She didn't shake hands like a girl and most men met her grip for grip, usually giving her an approving grin. Not this guy. He shook hands like a wet noodle and smiled like a salesman with oceanfront property. This should be lots of fun.

Mike went in first followed by Paul with her bringing up the rear. The smell of fried food and moth balls smacked her in the face before she even crossed the threshold. Piles of... stuff lined every wall in what she guessed was the living room. A narrow path of exposed orange shag mashed into felt from years of traffic, led the threesome through what should be a dining room and into the kitchen.

All were packed floor to ceiling with various stacks of papers, clothes, and boxes.

RUN

"When do you guess they'll be moved?" She eyeballed the basement door. If this is what they had going on up here, who knew what the basement was like.

Paul followed her gaze. He opened the door and led the way down the wood stairs into the cool dank air. Normally basements creeped Mina out a little, but at least down here she wasn't worried about being smothered to death by a toppling pile of crap. Just the spiders.

"Oh they got out a couple months ago," Mike called from the top of the stairs. "They just left a little trash. Shouldn't take much to clean the place up and turn it around."

"Holy shit Paul." Mina whispered when she was sure they were out of earshot. "Granny chic? This is an episode of *Hoarders*."

"Yeah. It's changed a bit since I was here last." He made his way around the dark basement, pulling cords on dead bulbs. "Same Crayola carpet though."

"I didn't even notice it had carpet." She edged around the furnace standing next to the only functioning light, inspecting the stickers. "This is new. Basement seems dry." She tipped her head back. "I don't know about all that up there though. If he was gonna get it all out so we could really see what we were working with that would be one thing, but that doesn't sound like his plan."

Paul clicked on a flashlight he pulled out of his back pocket. That's why Mina liked him. He was always prepared.

He ran the beam around the basement, revealing copious amounts of boxes piled up in every available corner. "Yeah, I caught that too. Let me talk to him. See if he has a realistic number in mind or if he's willing to clear the shit out and let us get a good look."

She took a deep breath, blowing it back out. "All right. That's a good place to start. If I have to deal with all the crap and not knowing what's behind it, the price better be real damn good." Especially since Don would also be part of this deal. "I mean really good."

She pulled her phone out of her pocket as they headed back up the stairs into the kitchen where Mike was waiting, that same slimy smile on his face. "I've got to run. I'm meeting a friend for lunch."

"Are ya now?" Paul cocked a thick eyebrow at her.

"Yes and her name is Nancy." Both men stared at her. One track freakin' minds. "Not that kind of friend."

The men acted like they didn't hear her. "Nancy Richards?" Mike pulled a comb from his back pocket and ran it through his freakishly black hair. Sliding it back in, he looked over his shoulder and sucked in his gut, standing up straight. "She meeting you here?"

Oh God. Not another one. Maybe she should have Nancy negotiate this deal instead of Paul. She'd probably get a hell of a deal then. "No. She is not."

"Oh." He deflated a little bit. "Where you goin'?" He tried to look casual but just ended up looking creepy and sort of bug eyed.

"I'm not even sure yet." She fibbed, pretty sure Nancy would thank her. "We always decide at the last minute."

"Maybe you could put in a good word for me."

"You're married Mike." Paul's voice growled deep and almost threatening in a way she had never heard before.

Mike didn't seem to notice. "Minor road block." He gave Mina a seedy smile that she wanted to slap right off his face. From the way her contractor was clenching and unclenching his fists at his side, it seemed like she might not get the opportunity. Grabbing his elbow, she began leading Paul to the front door.

"Thank you for showing us the house." She stepped behind one very angry man and pushed him ahead of her as she called over her shoulder, "Paul's got another appointment he has to go to, but we'll be in touch after we make a decision."

"Okay. Might want to hurry, I got lots of interest in this place."

Yeah. Sure he did.

She herded Paul quickly across the front yard trying to put as much space as possible between the two men. "What the hell was that about?"

"Sorry." He took off his ball cap only to put it right back on. "Sometimes Mike is just kind of a dick."

"Yeah. No. Don is a dick every time we see him and you have never gotten like that."

Paul shifted on his feet looking at Mina like he couldn't decide what to say. "Nancy's just been through a lot and doesn't need a guy like that giving her a hard time."

"You know Nancy?" It never really occurred to her, but it made sense. They were about the same age and both grew up here.

"We all went to school together." Paul seemed very uncomfortable with their conversation as he crossed and uncrossed his arms and avoided her eyes. "You met her son?"

Mina wanted to shake him. Why in the hell did he think she would just let this Nancy thing drop? She sighed. Because she would. "Thomas? No."

Paul seemed to relax a little. Nancy was clearly a touchy subject for him. One they would definitely be revisiting later.

"He's a good kid. Took over the family farm with his cousin after Nancy's dad died. Works his ass off running that place and helping his mom."

"Farm?" She knew Nancy had a decent garden, but that was all they had really talked about. Mostly they chatted about their own businesses and unfortunate commonalities in their past relationships. That alone could keep a conversation going for years.

"Oh yeah. Good sized too, just outside of town. Runs between Union and Chamberlain." He paused squinting his eyes at Mina. "You all right? Got a weird look on your face."

"I'm fine. Just have a lot on my mind." That was an understatement. "I gotta go."

"Oh, yeah. Have a good lunch. I'll call ya."

"All right." Mina got in her van and waved as she pulled away, trying to smile even though she felt like crying. When she was a few streets over, she pulled over and leaned her head back against her seat.

She had been lusting after her friend's son.

Not just lusting. She had been imagining her farmer... Nancy's son, as more than just someone to warm up her bed. Meeting him that day at the market, if you could call almost falling at his feet meeting, changed her fantasies of him.

She had replayed that day over and over in her mind. Seeing him face to face, the warmth in his eyes, the way he smiled at her, the soft deepness of his voice, made her once strictly physical imaginings turn much sweeter. She'd started to think maybe if they met again, there could be something there.

Unfortunately now when they did see each other again, and there was no way they wouldn't, she would be his mom's friend. Not something most men would consider a plus.

Tears nipped at the corners of her eyes.

"Oh my God, this is so stupid!" She swiped at her lids, trying to keep her make-up from being ruined. Even though the only times they'd actually been face to face were short and clumsy and more than a little awkward, Mina hadn't been able to shake the thought of his laughter as he tried to wrestle Daphne off him or the way his strong hands caught her as she fell against him. Even his spicy, woodsy scent that clung to her clothes long after she got home that night was burned into her memory.

What in the hell was wrong with her? What normal person got this upset over some guy they didn't actually know?

Crazy girls.

She wasn't a crazy girl. Was she? Was she so starved for companionship that she'd mentally created what felt like a real relationship with a man she didn't know?

Apparently she was.

And now it was over. It had to be. She was Nancy's friend. Real friend, in real life and that was more important than an imaginary emotional attachment.

It still kind of sucked.

Now that she knew, it was easy to see the features mother and son shared. Same tall, strong build. Same straight, narrow nose. Same small space between their front teeth. She spent the past month imagining running her tongue along that gap. Now that she knew it was genetically gifted by one of her best friends, the thought seemed more than a little wrong.

It would figure the only man in this town who caught her interest was most definitely, strictly off limits. Now she was back at square one. Single and lonely, with no prospects in sight.

"What in the hell am I gonna do?"

She was going to go have lunch with her friend and pretend like someone didn't just pee in her cheerios. Then she would go on and do her best to be a good friend and forget about the man she'd been dreaming of for months.

SEVEN

THE SOUND OF a screen door slamming echoed off the barn walls.

"Shit." He'd avoided this for as long as humanly possible, but the tractors had to have their gas tanks drained so it didn't turn to sludge over the winter.

Footsteps crunched through the gravel driveway, getting louder as they closed in on the barn. Thomas stood, wiping his hands on the rag he had stowed in his back pocket, and braced himself for the tornado coming through the door any second.

He'd been avoiding her for more than two weeks. Partly to protect her, partly to protect himself. There was just too much going on that he didn't want to be grilled about.

An unexpectedly calm Nancy opened the sliding door and stepped into the barn. "Hey."

He wasn't sure how to handle this. He was prepared for a fight. A knock down drag out one at that.

"Good morning." Better to keep it simple and feel her out.

"What have you been up to?" She meandered his way. "Haven't heard much out of you."

"Uh. Just had to get everything off the fields, help Rich finish up on his end." He'd been busting his ass trying to do the work of two men. Luckily he was able to get all Rich's paperwork finished up and billing done.

"Anything you want to tell me about that? About Rich?" She stared at him waiting as he decided what to say.

"Nope." No reason to tell her about anything that had gone on the past month. It would only upset her.

Rich seemed fine now anyway. Better than ever actually. Almost like he had a new lease on life. He even got Beth to come home. They were sleeping in separate rooms, but she seemed willing to give him another chance and he was making the most of it, taking her out and spending time with the girls. With the bulk of the work on the farm over for the season, he would have plenty of time to smooth things out. Try to fix the damage he'd done. Again.

"I figured as much. You two always were thick as thieves." She eyed him for a minute. "Maybe you can use your free time this winter finding me a new daughter-in-law."

Thomas turned back to the tractor. Ever since that night at the market he had been trying to wrap his mind around the fact that his runner and his mother's friend were actually one and the same. One beautiful dark haired specimen with eyes the color of amber and a smile that hit him like a punch in the gut.

"Maybe." He fiddled with the gas cap, trying to avoid his mother's stare. "Got a lotta work I want to get done on the house."

"I know someone who could help you."

He turned back and cocked his eyebrow at her.

"My friend renovates houses. She's between projects and could maybe help you out."

Another friend? Apparently his mom was more social than he realized. "What friend is this?"

"Mina. I told you ab--"

He stopped her right in her tracks and repeated the excuse he'd given himself every time he imagined seeing her again. "Yeah. I'm not so sure I want to get tangled up with a woman with an ex like hers."

It was out before he realized the entirety of what he said. In his own mind, it could be a valid reason for him to steer clear of her. He'd been so wrapped up in supplying himself with an excuse that he hadn't considered what it would mean to his mother.

"That's how it is, is it? You're gonna hold what some piece of shit did against her?" Nancy's eyes began to shimmer with years of unshed tears. "I thought you would be a man who would understand what happened to her. How it can happen." Her lips trembled. "Maybe show her it isn't always that way."

She spun on her heel and headed for the door stopping to turn and look at him as she reached it. "You don't deserve her." And she left, gravel flying under her feet.

Thomas leaned back against the tractor. "Shit." He just royally fucked up.

Nancy had been alone for years. Now he knew why. She assumed any man would judge her for her past, and he'd just basically told her they did. Even worse, he made her think he did. And it wasn't even true.

He tried to make it true, telling himself over and over Mina was a bad idea. It wasn't working. He didn't care about her ex. If anything it made him want to be close to her more. Make sure no one hurt her ever again. No, she wasn't the problem. He was.

His mom was right. He couldn't be with Mina because he didn't deserve her.

She deserved a man who knew how to be the kind of husband a woman needed. If there was one thing he learned from his first marriage, it was he obviously didn't know how to be that kind of man.

If he was, Mary wouldn't have changed her mind. About their plans. About their marriage. About him.

His own marriage went belly up and to this day he still wasn't sure why. He'd been blindsided when Mary left. Everything seemed fine, better than fine. One day they were making plans for a family and it seemed like the next she was packing up her stuff and giving him some half-assed excuse about different priorities. Even looking back he couldn't see signs of her unhappiness. How would he know if it happened again?

He wouldn't.

Not until he was sitting alone in a big house eating off paper plates because his ex-wife took all the dishes.

He thought his life with Mary would give him the chance to be what he never had. He wanted a family. He wanted to be a good father and an even better husband and prove to himself and everyone else the apple couldn't have fallen farther from the tree.

He bought them a house, a big brick two-story near the farm for them to fill with kids and spend their lives together. It was solid and strong, just like he thought they were.

He found out too soon, or not soon enough depending on how you looked at it, the house was much more capable of standing the test of time than they were. Two years into their marriage, Mary took a new job and quickly decided a family wasn't anything she wanted in her near future. And neither was he.

She decided what she wanted, was in her boss's pants.

He picked up a bucket at his feet and chucked it across the barn, the thud as it hit the hardboard wall making him feel oddly satisfied.

He was still just as angry as the day he found out. Maybe more.

When Mary left, everything he'd always wanted, a wife, kids, the chance to be happy, walked out the door with her leaving him alone in his misery. He wanted to try again, but he'd failed miserably the first time. There was no reason the next would be any different. It was unfair to test his luck on a woman who'd been through so much already.

He crossed the barn and picked up the bucket. A large crack ran the length of the plastic side. He set it on a shelf in the work area then sat on the floor, his back against the wall.

He needed to talk to his mom.

He hadn't been fair to her either. She deserved the truth and avoiding it had only made him hurt her. He stood up and started across the barn. A car door slammed and by the time he slid the heavy wood door open, she was pulling onto the road shrinking as the distance between them grew.

"Shit."

He thought about calling her, but decided against it. She deserved his apology in person. Maybe she would be back soon.

He decided to finish the tractors while he waited. Leaving the door open so he could catch her as soon as she got home, he went to the corner where he kept his gas cans. All full. Good thing he kept a few extras in the loft.

He started up the ladder trying to remember where he put the hoses he used for siphoning. As his dirty boot hit the second to top rung he felt it give out under his weight. Searing pain ripped up the side of his leg where the jagged edge of the broken rung tore into flesh as he slid between the rails. He grabbed wildly for the top rung hoping to at least slow his fall, but his hands met only air. The ten feet between the betraying rung and the hard floor of the barn seemed to take an eternity. His mom was gone. There was no one to help him. His cell was in his truck parked in the driveway. He was in trouble.

His slashed leg hit first, the sickening sound of splintering bones filling his ears in the milliseconds before the rest of him landed. The force of the impact forced the air to explode from his lungs and flung his head back against the cement. His last thoughts as darkness descended like a million spiders crawling in to smother out the light were the words he carelessly threw at his mother. They might be his last.

EIGHT

AS FAST AS he hit, the barn floor beneath him evaporated, replaced by... nothing. Above him. Beside him. Below him. Nothing. No tractors. No broken ladder looming above. No hard, cold concrete under his back. He was surrounded by complete emptiness.

There was no sound. No birds chirping. No cars driving past. Not even the sound of his own breathing.

Confusion clouded his mind. How did he end up here? He should remember, but it was a struggle to even tell where here was. He looked around hoping to find a shred to cling to, something to offer a clue of what was going on. Was he dead? Could this be it, the great hereafter was limited to an eternity of consuming emptiness?

He didn't feel dead. He didn't really feel alive either.

There must be some explanation. Maybe he was lost. Lost where? Panic contorted his gut as a sick feeling washed over him. His skin clammed and drops of cool perspiration collected across his skin.

He wasn't lost. You had to be somewhere to be lost. He was nowhere.

The air around him became heavy, almost suffocating making it difficult to catch his breath even as it came faster and faster. His body began to spin. He flailed his arms trying to find anything he could grasp to stop this spiral into certain oblivion. He spun faster and faster, dizziness stealing what little grip he'd managed on the situation. His eyes darted wildly, searching for something, anything to cling to.

A pinpoint of light appeared in the distance. What seemed like the distance anyway. With no point of reference, it was hard to tell. Thomas watched closely as the small dot grew incrementally larger. He tried to reach for it, but his arm felt so heavy, like this world of nothingness suddenly had an unbeatable gravitational pull. He focused all his strength, slowly lifting his arm only to feel it being drug back down by that unseen force.

Abruptly, the light began growing quickly. Faster and faster, becoming unbearably bright, forcing his eyes to close against the intensity as it came barreling toward him.

As light came crashing all around him he was overtaken by unbearable pain. Pain in his head jumbled his thoughts. Pain shooting up his thigh. The agony forcing a low groan to climb up his throat as it tried to squeeze the air from his lungs.

"Shhhhhhhhhh. I'm so sorry I have to do this." A soft voice whispered gently from above him. He tried to open his eyes against the light, see where the voice came from, but an immediate, crushing pressure around his leg just below the joint forced them tightly shut as he screamed in agony.

The already unbearable pain quadrupled and the spinning began again. Bile surged up his throat, burning as it climbed, the sickeningly bitter taste threatening to fill his mouth before retreating.

"So sorry. I'm so sorry." The soft voice was back. Soothing him. "You have to breathe Thomas. I know it hurts." Soft warm hands stroked his face, smoothed his hair. "It will be okay. The ambulance will be here soon." It was a woman's voice.

He tried to raise his arm again. Reach for the voice, the hands that were touching him so gently.

"No." the voice whispered as he felt his arm carefully pressed back at his side. "Be still. Just breathe."

He tried to open his eyes. He needed to see her, but the light was so blindingly bright. He squeezed them shut again.

"Please Thomas," she pleaded. "Please be still." The soft hands swept across his brow and paused on his cheek.

One more time. He had to see her. He fought against the pain the light brought, gritting his teeth as his vision focused through the small slit he managed. He could make out a form leaning over him.

Rays of light streaking from somewhere in the distance angled around her shoulders like the wings of an angel. He tried to make out more, but the stabs of light caused pain to sink deep into his skull as the threat of darkness began creeping in around the edges of his vision. Just a few more seconds. He just wanted to see her face, this angel desperately trying to save him. His angel.

The blackness eased in and cold prickled his skin as she began to blur and fade.

No! He fought back, straining against the draw of unconsciousness, trying to see her, just for a second, but he was too weak, too tired. The darkness came quickly crawling back in, consuming all but the same small point of light. A small point of light that held two golden eyes.

Blackness overtook him. For how long, he didn't know. He hadn't even fully realized it happened until he found himself suddenly and violently thrust back into the blinding light. The pain came screaming back, overwhelming him. Hands were on him, but they weren't gentle and calming like before. They were rough and forceful, moving him, squeezing him, bringing more pain.

A cool, sharp path made its way quickly up one leg, then the other. Cool air bit at his bared flesh raising goose bumps that made his skin ache as tremors he couldn't control wracked his body and made his teeth chatter. The sharp sting of a needle pierced his arm. An eyelid was forced open before a piercing light swung back and forth across his vision. He tried to turn away but his head wouldn't budge no matter the direction he tried. He swiped blindly at the light assaulting his eyes.

"I need you to relax." The man's voice was so loud he could feel it reverberate in his skull. "We are trying to help you. You've been in an accident."

Who was this man? Where had she gone? He needed her.

"Wh-s-sh?" His voice sounded slurred and messy. He swallowed, trying to regain control over his words. He tried again. "Where... is... she?" He managed to rasp out.

"She's in the waiting room." A soft voice assured him. He slowly opened his eyes, giving them time to adjust to the light, hoping to keep the pounding in his head to a minimum. A pretty woman stood by his side and gently patted his shoulder. "You'll see your mom soon, but first we have to fix you up." He lifted his arm, trying to tell her that wasn't who he meant, but she was already turned away. His mom was waiting. Only his mom. She was gone, or never was.

The woman turned back to him and smiled. "Time to rest." As soon as the words left her mouth, he began to feel very heavy.

Within seconds, everything around him fell away replaced by a soft cloudiness.

A peaceful quiet settled over him, a welcome change from the pain and chaos he just experienced. His muscles slowly relaxed as he floated into this warm, tranquil existence, breathing deep and steady as he tried to make sense of what just happened, but he struggled to put thoughts together. The synapses of his brain simply wouldn't connect.

What was he trying to recall? It felt important. He wanted to remember, but he couldn't recollect... anything. There was only here, now. He drifted along in the misty abyss as it soaked into him, relaxing deep into his very core. His body felt light and heavy at the same time. He floated on air, but couldn't move a muscle if he wanted. He simply was here at the mercy of the fog, unable to do anything except exist.

Out of the denseness came a quiet, feathery sound. The clouds began to swirl and shift, changing color and shape. He watched, transfixed as they slowly gathered, becoming more and more solid.

"Tho-mas." The sound again. So soft he could barely hear.

The swirling cloudy mass dissipated, slowly revealing the source of the sound. It was her. She stepped close to him, her body unaffected by whatever was holding his hostage.

"Thomas."

His name was barely a whisper across her lips. Her long dark hair softly caressed her shoulders as it shimmered in a light that seemed to radiate from her. She bent over him, the chestnut strands spilling over his cheeks like a thousand dandelion seeds caught in the wind. He tried to raise his hand, he wanted to feel them slide through his fingers, but he was paralyzed. His body wouldn't, couldn't obey.

She leaned closer, so close he could count the copper flecks scattered within the golden irises of her eyes. He felt her breath warm and sweet on his face as her lips slowly, tenderly brushed his.

Then she was gone.

He was alone.

Was he?

A mechanical beeping slowly became louder bringing with it an awareness of his surroundings. He took a deep breath. The cool air smelled of antiseptics and bleach aggravating his throat. His body was covered by a blanket that felt soft and worn under his fingers. Quiet murmurs of faraway conversations joined the steady beeping.

He fought open heavy lids, blinking slowly as his vision cleared. A dimmed fluorescent light above his head cast shadows across the hospital room. Heavy curtains were drawn across a window. No light edged its way in between the panels of heavy blue fabric. Nancy was curled in a chair in the corner, softly snoring.

Dull pain radiated from his head and left leg. An IV stand loomed beside him, holding a bag of clear fluid. He watched hazily as drop by drop fell silently into a thin clear tube.

Something happened. What, he wasn't sure. He should wake his mother. Make her tell him, but he was so very tired. He blinked hard, trying to force himself to wake all the way up. Each time he blinked the urge to keep his lids closed became stronger. Soon, the fight to keep his eyes open became overwhelming. He relented, letting sleep take over.

He is on the farm. The sun is warm on his face and neck. A quiet breeze ruffles his hair and pushes the green fields around at its mercy. He walks along the break between rows, taking long strides, sure of his destination. He can see the road. She is there, not running but walking slowly, her hair loose in waves that swirl about her head in the soft wind, catching on her lips before she gently tugs them away with delicate fingers. The gauzy white dress she wears alternately clings and billows around her form revealing soft curves and peeks of long graceful legs.

He walks faster. His fingers ache with a need to hold her, stroke the smooth skin of her arm, press her body against his. He starts to run. Faster and faster, but the distance between them remains unchanged. His breath comes in heaves, one barely clearing his lungs before another shoves it's way in. Desperation makes him push harder, but no matter how fast he puts one foot in front of the other, he remains fixed in place.

Exhaustion overtakes him and he drops to his knees, hanging his head, defeated. As the burning in his lungs and legs subsides, he looks to the road, resigned to watch as she passes him by.

Her gold eyes lock onto his as a soft smile eases its way onto her lips. She steps off the asphalt and slowly makes her way across the field, coming closer and closer, her eyes never leaving his. He's frozen, hypnotized by the sight of her. Before he can blink, she is standing before him, her dress billowing around them. Slowly, she sinks to her knees.

He's waited so long to touch her, feel her skin, her hair, yet he hesitates, afraid touching her will again break the spell holding her here with him.

"I'm so sorry I hurt you." Regret fills her beautiful eyes and furrows her brow. Tears well along her lashes and threaten to spill onto the smooth skin of her cheeks. The sight of her pain steals the air from his lungs. Without thinking he reaches for her. As soon as he feels the softness of her skin under his palms, his stomach drops. He freezes. What has he done? He refuses to even blink, not wanting to lose even a millisecond of seeing her. He holds his breath waiting for the inevitable, but it does not come.

She places her hands over his where they remain gently cupping her face. Warm tears dampen his skin. "So sorry," she repeats. "It was all I could do to save you."

Hazy memories slide through his mind, just beyond his grasp. Whatever happened, he was sure she would never intend to bring him pain. He pulls her to him, brushing his lips across her forehead, tangling his hands in her hair. Her soft sobs are like salt in a wound. He tucks her under his chin, wrapping her in his arms, pressing her soft body against his. "Shhhh. I'm fine." He strokes her hair, rocking them gently as her tears soak into his shirt and the fabric clings to his skin.

"Please be okay," she whispers into his chest. "You have to be okay."

NINE

BEEP... BEEP... BEEP... Beep... Beep... Beep...

"I swear to God." Mina rubbed her eyes trying to ease the throbbing behind them that was keeping time with the endless beeping of the heart monitor across the room. The noise was wearing on her already fried nerves.

The last two days left her drained, physically, mentally and emotionally, wandering through the day in a fog created by an adrenaline hangover, fear and guilt.

And exhaustion. Can't forget the exhaustion.

Maybe the beeping was a good thing. The irritation it was inflicting might be the only reason she was still upright and currently the only conscious person in the room. That and this God-awful chair. She shifted against the rock hard cushion as she attempted to find a comfortable position.

On the other hand, sitting here in the dimly lit hospital room with just the never-ending beep, beep, beep to keep her company was about to make her lose what was left of her sanity.

She spent the past fifteen minutes sitting silently, staring at the floor and picking at her demolished cuticles, listening to that incessant noise and reminding herself she should be grateful to hear it.

That sound meant Thomas was alive.

Right now she needed to keep that at the front of her mind. She had to find some way to come to terms with what had happened... and what hadn't. Her mind needed peace and maybe seeing that he really was alive and breathing would bring that peace.

Unfortunately, she hadn't yet been able to drag her eyes from the floor and look at him where he lay unmoving on the bed. When she got up this morning she was sure seeing him would make her feel better. Now, the thought of it terrified her.

Facing him, even unconscious, had her already twisted gut trying to strangle itself. Would he remember what happened?

She groaned inwardly at herself and leaned forward in the ridiculously uncomfortable chair, resting her forehead on her knees. Please God don't let him remember. If he did what would she say? *'Yeah sorry, I got a little handsy while you were trying to die. My bad.'*

The sight of him suffering hit her in a way she never would have imagined. All she was trying to do was comfort him. Before she realized what she was doing, her hands were all over him. On his face, in his hair, touching him in ways usually reserved for someone you know on a much more intimate level. Not your friend's son who you have been secretly lusting after for months. Especially not if he's lying on a cold barn floor bleeding to death.

She sat up straight and leaned her head back on the chair. What was wrong with her?

Fantasizing about Thomas when he was some random farmer was fine, but after finding out Nancy was his mother it should have stopped.

But it didn't.

When he almost died and was lying in a hospital, it absolutely should have stopped.

It still didn't.

Now she was here, weirdly sitting alone in the corner of his hospital room staring at the ceiling. What if he woke up? Oh God, what if he woke up? Her stomach hit the floor. She needed to get out of here. Launching out of her seat, she was halfway across the room when she heard a noise and froze.

Shit.

He was awake.

She slowly turned, her mind racing trying to come up with any explanation for her awkward presence in his room. But he wasn't awake.

His eyes were closed, his face screwed into an odd expression. Pain? She watched the nurse shoot a hit of morphine into his IV line when she got there so he shouldn't be feeling too much of anything. His eyebrows were drawn low making two vertical lines in the space between. His jaw was clenched tight, a tiny vein easily visible through the skin at his temple bulging from the pressure. He looked angry, but not quite.

He began to struggle, trying to move his legs, fighting against the blankets and tubes that restricted his movements. She watched, frozen as he became more desperate in his actions, struggling against the bandages protecting his mangled thigh. Shit. He was going to hurt himself.

Before she could stop herself, she was across the room, beside him, her hand in his.

"Shhhh. It's okay."

She cupped his cheek, the scruff on his face that almost qualified as a beard softly scratching her palm. All at once he stopped moving, stopped breathing.

Panic filled her belly and she felt sick. He was supposed to be fine. They assured Nancy he would be okay.

She needed help. Now. Her mouth was open to scream, just as that damn beeping registered.

Beep, beep, beep, beep.

A few minutes ago, the noise made her want to pull out her hair. Now it was the sweetest sound she could hope to hear. She lowered herself into a bedside chair and blew out a long sigh of relief.

The sound of Thomas letting out a matching breath almost made her laugh. The kind of giddy, adrenaline fueled laugh that only comes out of a person just this side of crazy.

She sat, holding his hand in hers, the fear of him waking from earlier forgotten as she tried to get some sort of a grasp on her wildly out of control emotions. The past two days, she'd been all over the map. Scared, relieved, embarrassed, guilty. Add to that trying to live normally for her kids and being a strong friend for Nancy and she was just about tapped out.

A low ache formed in her throat. Damn it. She was going to cry.

Tears welled in her eyes, blurring her vision before they broke free, running down her cheeks, one quickly streaming behind another. Soft sobs, wracked her body as she leaned forward, resting her head on the blanket, too exhausted to hold herself up.

She hadn't slept since the accident. Every time she tried, it played like a movie on continuous loop, forcing her to relive every second. To remember every detail. As if she would ever forget the sight of him lying there, bleeding everywhere. The sound of him screaming in agony... because of her.

"I'm so sorry," she managed to whisper between sobs. "I had to. It was all I could do to save you."

She thought coming here to see him alive would help, but it hadn't. Seeing him lying here, broken, was just making it worse. He almost died. If she left her house a few seconds later, or ran just a little slower she would have found him dead.

The thought brought on a new round of sobs and tears that only subsided when her nose was so stuffy it was hard to breathe. She sat up, hoping the change in position would discourage the swelling in her nose.

Wiping the last tears from her hot cheeks, she glanced down and noticed a large wet circle smack dab in the middle of the blanket covering Thomas' chest. Great. Now she could add crying on her best friend's son while he was unconscious to the list of crazy she had going. At this rate, she'd be able to fill a book before the week was over.

She sighed, wiping the last tears off her face. Against her will, her eyes made the short trip from his damp chest to his face.

She expected him to be pale and weak looking but the man on the bed in front of her was anything but. Even after almost bleeding out, a pretty substantial blow to the head and quite a few hours in the operating room, he was still ridiculously handsome. Stubble so long it was almost soft covered his jaw line, a few red hairs standing out against the dark blonde majority. Remembering the feel of it under her hand just a few minutes ago made her want to run her fingers over it again which she most certainly would not be doing. Not right now anyway.

"Damn it."

There was something about him. Every freaking time she thought of him, immediately her brain wandered off into the land of illicit thinking. She needed to get out of here before she did something really stupid. *Like kiss him.*

"Jesus Christ Mina. Get it together."

And now she was talking to herself. While she lusted after her friend's son. Sitting alone in his room watching him sleep. This just kept getting better and better.

She stood up, allowing herself one last, a little too lingering look. Damn he was handsome.

Without thinking, she gently brushed a few wavy strands of sandy hair that managed to escape the bandages covering his head off his face. "Please be okay."

* * * *

"Holy shit." *Did I drink last night?* Must have. That was the only thing that would explain the intense pounding in his head. Hopefully it was worth it, but considering he couldn't remember anything, it might be one of those epic nights you only know about because someone is only too happy to remind you.

Sleeping it off sounded like the best idea, but he had shit to do. As terrible as it sounded, he was going to have to open his eyes and let in the light. If it didn't split his already throbbing head in half, he'd get his shit together and confront the day.

He went to rub his temples, hoping to ease the transition a little bit. His fingertips bumped into a thick layer of gauze. "What the-?"

"Tommy, stop." His mother's hands were on his shoulders, gently pressing him to the bed as he tried to sit up.

"What in God's name are you doing here?" Couldn't a guy sleep in just once without his mother ruining it? As he squirmed around in the bed, he felt the covers shifting... everywhere. Grabbing at the blanket he tried to spare himself the added humiliation of his mother finding him not only extremely hung over, but naked.

Nancy leaned over him, her face pale and tired looking as she tried for a small smile. He looked past her shoulder expecting to see the un-curtained window of his bedroom but all he saw was a flat white wall. "Where the hell am I?"

Nancy drew a deep breath, and paused, clearly in no hurry to answer his question.

Between the pain in his head and a deep ache he was beginning to notice in his leg, his patience was lacking. "What the hell is going on?"

Nancy's eyes searched his face. "You don't remember?"

"Remember what? What is going on? I'm not in my own bed, I have a splitting headache, I feel like I had the shit beat out of me and all this talking is starting to make me feel real sick, so if you could hurry it up. I either need to barf or go back to sleep."

"You've been asleep for days Tommy."

His already aggravated stomach churned. He swallowed hard trying to push the rising pressure back where it belonged. How could he have been asleep for days? Even if he was, it still wasn't enough, because all he wanted to do right now was close his eyes and sleep some more, and he planned on it, but not until he got some answers from his mother.

"Please. For the love of God, tell me what happened. My head is killing me and I just want to know what the hell is going on."

"You fell."

That's it? You fell?

This was going to be like pulling fucking teeth. He was tired. He was in pain and as much as he wanted to know more, he didn't have the energy or really even the inclination to lay here and coax more out of her.

Closing his eyes, he decided it would wait until later. "Whatever. I'm going back to sleep. Maybe you'll feel like telling me later."

"Maybe you'll wake up in a better mood."

Smart Ass. He smiled as he drifted easily back into sleep, hoping his mother would be right.

Thomas was awakened by the sound of someone rustling around him. He opened his eyes, finding a pretty young woman in pale green scrubs standing beside his bed, her attention focused on a bag of clear fluid she was working to hook up to an IV stand he could only assume belonged to him. He watched quietly, not wanting to startle her and risk ending up in worse shape than he already was.

She finished fiddling with the bag and looped it onto the stand. She glanced down at him, doing a double take, clearly surprised to find him awake. She smiled warmly. "Good morning. Have a nice nap?"

"From what I hear, it was a little more than a nap." His voice sounded raspy and his throat was painfully dry. "Could I have a drink?"

"You can. How is your stomach feeling? Your mother said you were feeling nauseated when you woke up before."

"Better, maybe." He rubbed a hand over his stomach, feeling it rumble ever so slightly under the pressure. "Can I sit up?"

"Let me get a few pillows to help prop your head up if you need it. You will get tired pretty quickly so don't be surprised." She crossed the room and gathered a few pillows from the chair beside the window. "Want me to open the curtains since you're awake?"

"That's fine." He tried to sit up on his own, struggling to get his arms under his body. Almost immediately, his head began to throb at the change in position.

One hand went to his head in reaction to the pain. He had forgotten about the bandages he'd discovered earlier. He felt around gingerly for the edges as he attempted to identify the point of injury.

The nurse swung the heavy drapes open. Soft morning light streamed gently across the room only making the throbbing in his head slightly worse. She turned back to him, arms full of pillows and watched him for a minute. "How's it feel?"

"It hurts to move."

"Still want to sit up?" She deposited the pillows in the chair beside the bed and waited, hands on hips, for him to answer.

"Yeah, I think so." He tried to heave himself up again, a little more carefully this time, hoping to keep the throbbing in his head to a minimum. The dizziness brought on by that little bit of exertion surprised him.

"You're probably going to be pretty weak." She pushed and held a button on the side of the bed. "Might want to let the bed do the work or you'll be ready to lay back down as soon as we get you situated." A mechanical whir sounded as the bed inclined, slowly raising him to a 45 degree angle. "I'd start there for now. Once you have something in your stomach, we'll try to get you moving a little." She propped the pillows around him. "Good?"

He nodded. She was right. He wanted to lie back down and rest. He wasn't tired. He was exhausted. His whole body hurt.

A deep pulsating throb he imagined would be pretty unbearable without the help of whatever was being shot into the tube feeding into the vein in his left hand radiated from the back of his head. He noticed a sharper type of soreness bothering his thigh. Taking advantage of his new position he cautiously lifted the blanket draped over his lower half.

He blew out a breath. "That does not look good." His left leg was wrapped in thick bandages from just below the knee up to the joint of his hip.

"It looks a heck of a lot better than it did when you came in here." She gave him an appraising look. "You do too. Not that it would take much."

"That bad huh?" He dropped the blanket back onto his lap and rested his head back against the pillows interested to hear what she had to say. He was more than ready to find out exactly what landed him here.

"You almost bled out." Said like the medical professional she was. No beating around the bush, no avoidance. Looks like his mom wouldn't have to explain after all.

"Almost only counts in horseshoes and hand grenades."

"Yeah, well that was not your only problem."

"I figured that." He fingered the bandages covering his skull. "Do you know what happened? How I ended up here?"

Her eyebrow rose. "Your mother didn't tell you?"

"She said I fell. I assume that was a pretty condensed version and I'd like to know exactly what happened."

"Apparently you were climbing a ladder to the loft of your barn when a wooden rung split under your foot. The side of the rung still anchored to the ladder ripped up the inside of your leg and made quite a mess. You hit the floor pretty hard, breaking the same leg and hitting your head, giving yourself a pretty nasty laceration and concussion."

Thomas sat silently, stunned. He expected her explanation to jog his memory, help him remember what happened, but nothing she said sounded even remotely plausible. That ladder had been around for years. His grandfather climbed up and down it as far back as he could remember and Jim had at least fifty pounds on him. Never once in all those years had the ladder been anything but solid.

"If that woman hadn't been there and done what she did, you would have been a goner."

"What woman? My mom?"

"No. I think it was just some random woman out on a jog. Talk about fate. You never know how—" She kept talking, but her voice faded into the background as realization swept over him. It was no random runner that saved him.

He realized his nurse was quiet and looking at him expectantly.

"Sorry, what?"

She smiled at him. "It's okay. It can be a little hard to keep a train of thought after a head injury."

He had a train of thought all right and it was running full steam ahead. It was Mina who saved him. What had she seen? Was she okay?

He needed to talk to his mom.

"Thomas."

"Sorry. Again." He did his best to focus on the nurse, trying to force everything else aside and actually listen to what she was saying this time.

"Juice. Would you like juice?"

"That would be great. Thanks." His stomach rumbled again. "And crackers maybe?" It had been who knows how long since he ate and crackers seemed like the best place to start. If they sat well, maybe he could move onto a big juicy burger.

His stomach lurched at the thought. Maybe not.

"I'll work on it. My name's Sara. If you need anything else push the little button on the side of your bed. I just came on so you're stuck with me all day." She gave him a wink, turned on her heel and was gone, leaving him to digest the information.

His leg was broken, maybe worse. At least he could tell it was still there.

His head hurt like hell, but he was awake and coherent. Hopefully the time he was missing would fill in over the next few days.

His injuries should have been more concerning, but he wasn't all that worried about it. What he was really worried about right now was Mina. If his guess was right, she was the one who found him... and saved his life.

TEN

"AWAKE AND UPRIGHT? That's a definite improvement from the last time I saw you." Nancy blew into the quiet of the hospital room like a tornado, large bags swinging from each forearm and a large vase of flowers in her hands.

"Flowers?" He watched as she centered the arrangement on the table in front of the window, spinning it until the side she liked most faced the room.

"They're not for you, they're for me. I hate this place and if I have to be here, I at least want something pretty to look at."

"I'll try not to be offended by that."

"Well have you seen yourself? You look like crap." She dropped the bags to the floor and slid her arms out of her jacket. "Not that it's surprising." She laid the jacket over a chair and pointed her finger at him. "You almost died you know. Did they tell you that? Say what you want about Mina and her history, but that girl saved your life Tommy."

He hoped to ease into this conversation, but his mother clearly had other ideas. It looked like she'd had a good night's sleep and a healthy dose of caffeine since he saw her last and she was ready to handle him head on.

Luckily nurse Sara hooked him up with juice and crackers which seemed to be helping settle his stomach and fuel his brain back into the land of productivity. Once he was fully awake and had a little something in his stomach, it hadn't taken long for his memory to begin filling back in. He still couldn't remember falling off the ladder, but he did remember the conversation that had his mother so fired up this morning. He knew they needed to talk about what he said, but he was hoping she'd take it a little easy on him, considering.

"Yeah, I heard that."

"Good. Hopefully it made you feel awful about what you said about her."

So much for his hopes of her going easy on him.

"You know shit happens Thomas. You can't control what the people around you do." She flopped down in the chair smashing the coat she so carefully draped across the back. "All you can control is how you deal with it and I'm afraid I've not been a great example for you over the years." Nancy sighed as she leaned back in the chair and looked squarely at him.

"I was relieved when your father died." She waited, looking at him expectantly.

His brain was functioning enough to realize he needed to keep his mouth shut and let his mother get this out. In the years since his father's death, they never discussed what happened. They simply moved forward, ignoring the past and the hurt it caused them both.

"He brought me so much pain, so much embarrassment, so much shame over the years. I could just never imagine leaving, but the idea of staying made me sick. I didn't want to admit I failed, but you growing up with him as an example of how to be a man..."

Nancy was no longer looking at him. Her gaze was fixed across the room as she absently spun a strand of hair between her fingers, in another world remembering a time in her life she would happily forget.

"I decided you and I were leaving. I told him and he just went crazy. Screaming, throwing furniture."

"He threatened to kill me. Said he would cut me into pieces and feed me to the hogs." A single tear rolled down her cheek.

"Mom. You don't have to-"

"He left that night, already drunk. I should have called the police, but I didn't want to risk making him any angrier. I hurried to pack whatever I could and was loading up the car when the sheriff came to tell me about the accident. I knew I should be upset, but I wasn't."

"I remember the way he was. I doubt you were the only one not mourning the loss."

Nancy sighed. "His parents certainly did, blaming me until the day they died. They never saw him for what he was. He was always their perfect prodigal son. I was always the woman who tied him down and limited the greatness they were sure he would achieve."

"They blamed you?" He was shocked. It was ridiculous.

"Is that why we never saw them?" After his dad died, he rarely saw his grandparents. He always assumed it was too hard on them to be reminded of their dead son.

"Oh, I saw them. All around town, it seemed anywhere I went, there they were, glaring at me. They even called a couple of times to tell me I was the one who should have died."

"What?" Thomas leaned forward in the bed, forgetting his current state, rage making him ignore the pain caused by the sudden movement. "How could they say that? Who in the hell did they think they were?"

"Kind of explains how your father turned out the way he did." She waved her hand at him in a shooing motion. "Lay back, you're getting all upset over something that happened years ago. Plus they're dead, but that's the whole point of my telling you this, Tommy. You can't control what other people do. I let what other people did dictate the way I lived my life. I let your dad and his actions make me feel embarrassed and ashamed. I let his parents make me feel guilty. I let people I hated control my life. Hell, I even let it keep happening after they died."

This conversation was not going the way he thought.

He thought Nancy would rip into him about what he said to her in the barn, not to mention the weeks of avoiding her before that. Maybe tell him he was an ass. He would apologize until he was blue in the face, tell her how wrong he was and hopefully get away without really scratching the surface of their issues. Instead, this was getting really deep, really fast.

What was bringing all this on? They had successfully avoided any talk of his father for over twenty years and now suddenly she was an open book.

"Have you been seeing a therapist?" That would explain this emotional purging. Hopefully she wasn't expecting the same from him.

Nancy laughed. A happy, light laugh that went completely against the tone of the conversation they were waist deep in.

"My son almost died. I've had two days to sit around and think on that."

She fiddled with the flowers she'd set on the table. "Where would I be if you died?" She didn't wait for him to answer. "Sad and alone, that's where. I have no one to lean on. I have relied on you to be my support and that's not fair." Abandoning the flower arrangement, she crossed the room and perched on the side of his bed.

"I'm sorry. I'm sorry I made you think one failed relationship meant never to give another one a chance. I'm sorry I showed you other people's opinions should dictate your own. I'm sorry you feel like you have to take care of me and I promise to work my way through this."

"Is this your way of telling me you've met a man?"

"No and don't try to distract me with humor."

Thomas wasn't sure what else to say. His mother had some kind of revelation while he was out and it appeared she expected him to follow her into the land of self-discovery. "I'm not sure what you want me to say."

"You don't need to say anything. I just want you to think about what I'm telling you. Whether you want to admit it or not, you have some serious issues that were spawned from my serious issues. I don't want to be alone forever Tommy, but even more, I don't want you to be alone. You are a good man and you were a good husband. You need to realize what Mary did is not a reflection of you. Only her." Nancy reached for his hand, holding it between hers as she looked at him seriously.

"And she was a bitch."

Thomas busted out laughing. Maybe he would like this new and improved version of his mother. Probably not until his head hurt less though.

He pressed the hand Nancy wasn't holding to the side of his head trying to calm the pounding that came with each laugh. "Oh God, don't make me laugh like that. Didn't you hear I have a pretty nasty head injury?"

Nancy released his hand and marched back across the room, digging through the two large shopping bags she brought. "I brought some things I thought might make your stay here a little more enjoyable." She pulled out a small zippered bag and dumped the contents onto the bed beside his uninjured leg.

Shaving cream, his razor, body wash and deodorant littered the blanket. "I brought a few of your v-neck t-shirts too. Hopefully they will fit over that." She motioned to his head and the thick layer of bandages. "Maybe we can talk the nurse into helping get you a little cleaned up."

∗ ∗ ∗ ∗

Mina pulled into the parking garage at the hospital and was pretty sure she was going to throw up. She was a grown freakin' woman for God's sake, not some teenage girl. She had to get herself together.

Ever since her discussion with Nancy, she had been in an escalating state of panic. The butterflies that started when Nancy told her Thomas wanted to ask her about what happened had mutated into a flock of starlings arguing over a single worm. Angry starlings.

She parked her van and jumped out immediately. If she thought about what she was doing for any length of time, chances were good she would pull right back out.

The soft soles of her ballet flats made her walk across the garage a silent one. A cool breeze swept through the open walls, chilling the exposed skin of her ankles where they peeked out from the hem of her skinny jeans.

It had taken her way too long to get dressed. She spent a stupid amount of time obsessing over the outfit, especially since it was supposed to look like she hadn't spent any time figuring out what to wear. The floor of her closet was covered with rejects all waiting to be hung back up when she got home.

Forcing one foot to move in front of the other, she crossed the enclosed bridge joining the garage to the hospital and made her way to the bank of elevators. As she waited for the silver doors to open, she wiped her damp palms down the sides of her jeans.

The cool air outside had kept the nervous perspiration at bay. After just a minute in the warmth of the hospital, she was already starting to sweat.

She could feel a flush creeping into her cheeks as she shrugged out of the soft leather jacket she threw on as she ran out the door, mostly for the ride home when her nerves would crash and she would be freezing. Thank goodness she had the forethought to wear a gauzy white tunic over a tank. Maybe it wasn't such a bad thing she spent so much time deciding what to put on. "Much better."

"Were ya hot honey?"

Mina started at the sound of a voice behind her. She'd been so wrapped up in where she was headed, she hadn't even noticed the small old woman at the back of the elevator when she jumped on.

"I was. I'm better now." She smiled at the little lady decked out in a lavender suit, camel colored shoes with a matching purse. A pill hat with purple flowers sat cockeyed on her head.

The woman smiled back, deepening the wrinkles beside her eyes. "I remember when I went through the change."

"The change?"

She looked around to see if any of the zero other people in the elevator were listening before she whispered, "Menopause dear."

Mina nearly laughed, but the seriousness on the woman's face stopped her.

"It was terrible. All the sweating. I just hated to wear anything. Of course I did anyway. My dear Wilbur would have given me an awful time, and that's the last thing you feel like with the menopause. But those men though. They never have that problem. Always eager, right until the day they die."

"Oh."

The elevator dinged as it stopped and the doors began to open. "Oh. This is my floor." She stepped out and sidled up to an equally old man with hair growing around the hearing aids in his ears. He wrapped a grey sport jacket clad arm around her shoulders and gave her a squeeze as he planted a kiss on her unnaturally pink wrinkled cheek. She gave Mina a wink.

"Remember what I told ya dear."

As the elevator doors quietly slid closed, Mina tried to decide which part of the last five minutes disturbed her more. The idea of her elevator mate getting busy or the fact that the woman thought she was old enough to be in menopause.

Definitely menopause.

Offensive as it was, she was thankful their little conversation had distracted her for a few minutes. It gave the sweat that was beginning to prickle on her forehead and upper lip time to dry.

Too soon, the bell sounded again signaling her arrival at Thomas' floor. She stepped onto the tile floor happy to discover this area was significantly cooler than the lobby. Walking past the nurse's station, she swallowed hard when the door to his room came into view. As she got close, a young nurse came quickly out, nearly colliding with Mina.

"Oh! I'm so sorry." She paused, giving Mina a smile. "Are you headed in to see Thomas?"

Mina felt aggravated as a little flush came back to her cheek. Why in the hell should she be embarrassed about this girl knowing she was here to see him? "I am."

"You wouldn't happen to be the woman who found him would you?"

She nodded. That was kind of an odd and irrelevant question. Why was this girl being so nosy? What business was it of hers anyway?

Then it hit her.

This girl, baby really since she looked to be all of twenty-one, had her eye on Thomas. Talk about an unprofessional little-

"You deserve a pat on the back. Most people could never have thought on their feet so fast. You probably saved his life." She adjusted the tray she was balancing on one hand. "Are you in the medical field?"

"No."

"Well you might have missed your calling. Most people freak out over stuff like that." She patted Mina's shoulder. "Good job." She looked back into the room. "Thomas! You have a visitor."

She smiled at Mina as she started to walk away. "It was nice meeting you."

Mina smiled back. "Thanks. You too."

She watched, feeling like a jerk as the girl made her way down the hall waving at fellow nurses. Why would it even matter if the nurse did like Thomas? They weren't in any sort of relationship and never would be. Actually he probably had no clue who she even was. What in the world was it about him that made her so damn out of her mind?

She turned her attention to the open door in front of her. Should she knock? Should she go in?

"Mina? You can come in."

Holy shit. He was expecting her.

She made her way past a darkened bathroom just inside the door and into the openness of the room. The smell of flowers reached her almost immediately.

A large, beautiful vase sat on a table in front of the window. The jealousy of a few seconds ago came roaring back. It was an expensive arrangement. Someone liked him. A lot.

Thomas was sitting up in bed, watching her.

"I'm glad you came." His voice was deep and smooth, wrapping around her, almost making her forget about the flower sender. Almost.

"Nan- um your mom, said you wanted to talk to me about… about what happened."

"Did she now?" He smiled wide, revealing that gap she was so fascinated by. "Then I suppose I do." He motioned to a chair close to the bed. "You want to sit down?"

She glanced sideways at the chairs by the window, next to those damn flowers. Sitting so close to him was probably a really bad idea, especially considering she decided she would stop lusting after him first thing tomorrow morning, but she really didn't have an option.

"Sure."

She slid into the chair, immediately remembering how awful they were to sit in. She looked up and found him watching her. *Please don't blush, please don't blush.*

Holy cow he was close. Almost as close as the day she spent a few wonderful seconds in his arms. Sort of.

He looked different than yesterday, and not just awake different. He was freshly shaved, the whiskers she could still feel on her palm if she tried hard enough, gone. His hospital gown was replaced by a soft looking, dusty blue deep v-neck t-shirt that matched his eyes perfectly.

"I believe I owe you a huge thank you." That voice again. He spoke not necessarily softly, but gently. He drew his words out almost in a drawl, without the twang. The voice definitely matched the man.

"I don't know about that." She shrugged. "Anybody would have done what I did."

"What exactly did you do?"

She swallowed, trying to moisten her dry throat. This wasn't really a story she was eager to tell. "I was jogging by and the door to the barn was open."

He was watching her intently as she spoke making it difficult to maintain her train of thought. "Luckily I um, had forgotten my ear buds. As I came up on the barn I heard a weird noise. I could see through the door as you fell." She paused, dreading the next part of the story.

"You saw me fall?"

She nodded, chewing on her bottom lip.

"What did you do?" His voice was soft and gentle, almost as if he knew how hard this had been for her to handle.

"I ran into the barn to make sure you were okay." She gulped trying to keep the emotion out of her voice. "You…" She took a deep breath trying to keep it together.

He reached for her, engulfing her hand in his. She suddenly forgot what they were talking about. His hand was warm and calloused, but not rough. His palm pressed against the back of her hand as he rubbed his thumb across her knuckles. "I'm sorry. I'm so sorry you had to deal with this."

"It's okay. Believe it or not, I've dealt with worse."

He chuckled, a dimple she hadn't noticed creasing at the side of his lips. "So I've heard."

Oh no. Damn it Nancy. Mina shifted in her seat, suddenly feeling very uncomfortable. What did he know? Everything?

"Your mom told you what happened with my ex-husband." It didn't matter. It shouldn't anyway. She didn't try to hide what happened. It just maybe would have been nice if Nancy had given her a heads up.

"She did." He squeezed her hand. "You are one tough girl."

"Just so we're clear, I don't make a habit of handling things that way." She gave him a smile to let him know she wasn't upset. "Now I carry a stun gun."

ELEVEN

THOMAS' CELL PHONE buzzed from the table beside the recliner, slowly vibrating its way across the glass top. His mom was calling for the fourth time this morning. She was hell bent on him going to physical therapy and it wasn't going to happen. Not today, not ever.

The doctors didn't seem to hold out much hope for him to ever be normal again. They pretty much said it would either get better or it wouldn't. Considering his leg hurt just as much today as it did the day he woke up, maybe even more, he figured this was the life he was left with.

The phone buzzed one last time. That made four calls and four voicemails.

He flipped the lever on the side of his chair, holding his breath and clenching his teeth as the movement ignited a stabbing pain deep in his leg. He reached for his walker, wincing as he tried to pull himself up, keeping as much weight as he could on his arms.

He stood for a minute, waiting for the nausea that accompanied the pain to subside. Then he slowly began to shuffle along, supporting himself on his arms and good leg. One front leg of the walker caught on the edge of the couch, knocking him off balance causing him to twist his injured leg.

"Goddamn it." He struggled to yank the walker free, hurling it across the living room when it came loose. It clamored across the floor, knocking over the TV tray beside his chair and spilling the full bottle of beer he just opened. "Piece of shit."

"I thought she was exaggerating, but that doesn't seem to be the case."

Thomas looked up. "Calling in reinforcements is she?"

Rich looked around the darkened house. "Looks like she could have called sooner." He crossed the room and stopped next to Thomas. "Need help back to the chair?"

"I gotta piss."

Rich righted the walker, placing it in front of Thomas. "I hope that's something you can handle on your own."

"I got it."

He came back from the bathroom to find the blinds open, bright light reflecting off the snow covering the ground. Rich was on the floor with a towel, wiping up a puddle of beer. "This is cold."

"It was fresh."

Rich stopped mid swipe to look up at him. "It's nine in the morning."

"Why does it matter what time it is?"

"I guess it doesn't." Rich stood, standing the TV tray back on its legs. "You know you can't drink with pain pills, right?"

"Not takin' any." Thomas headed for his chair. He needed to sit back down and get his leg up.

"What? Didn't they give you a prescription?"

"They don't help. Didn't fill it."

"Holy cow man. You fuckin' mangled your leg." Rich shook his head, the line between his eyebrows drawn tight. "You gotta get those pills and start taking them."

"I don't want to take any fucking pills."

"So you're just gonna sit here and be miserable?"

"Seems like."

"That's fucked up. What about that girl? The one who saved you. Your mom is hard up that you two are gonna get together."

"That's her problem." Thomas angled himself back into the recliner and snapped it back into position. He swiped is arm across his forehead at the sweat brought on by pain and exertion.

Fate really fucked him on this one. Just when he thought maybe he could get past what happened with Mary, finally move on, his whole world came crashing back down again. He was a fucking invalid. It was all he could do to make it to the bathroom and back and the last thing he needed to be reminded of was Mina.

She hardly left his mind since the night she came to see him at the hospital. The night he held her hand as she explained what happened in the barn that morning. How she found him bleeding out. The way he screamed when she cinched his belt around his injured leg trying to stop the bleeding. She told him about trying to keep him awake, afraid if he closed his eyes, he wouldn't wake back up.

He watched as she apologized for hurting him, pain and regret etched into her beautiful face. All he wanted to do that night was hold her. Wipe away the tears she was crying because of him. Run his hands softly through her hair as he told her how grateful he was. How amazingly strong he thought she was.

But he couldn't. Not then. That night though, he decided one day very soon he would.

His mother was right.

No one would understand what she had been through like he could. No one else could appreciate the strength required to not only survive, but thrive after the life you once had falls apart. He could be the man she would finally be able to lean on. The man she would look to for support, and acceptance and love.

The next day, he woke up from his little fantasy land.

The doctors gave him the facts about his injuries and recovery. Actually, what they gave him was a bunch of *maybe's* and *potentially's* and *possibly's* and more bullshit answers.

Would he walk on his own again? Potentially.

How long till the pain went away? Could be six months, could be two years, could be never.

Would he be able to work again? It depends.

What about his memory? The brain is complicated.

His future was a crap shoot. Nobody knew, most wouldn't even guess. He was a cripple. No use to himself and definitely not to anyone else. Mina deserved a man who could give her everything, not some lame fucking duck she had to take care of.

"If you don't get your shit together you're gonna have a problem." Rich went to the kitchen and came back with a clean rag to wipe the worn wood floor clean of any stickiness.

"She's going to drive you crazy until you give up and do it just to get her to go home." He swiped the floor clean and stood back up.

"Why don't you give me your prescription and I'll go get it filled for you. I'll bring you back some lunch and maybe it will improve your disposition."

"I don't want the goddamned pills." The pills couldn't fix what was really wrong.

Rich sighed. "Whatever man."

He expected Rich to leave, but he continued to stand in the middle of the living room, blocking the television, folding and unfolding the rag in his hand.

"We have something else to talk about."

Thomas' head hurt. His leg hurt. He was tired and aggravated and he just wanted to be left alone. He was regretting not answering Nancy's calls. She would have been easier to deal with at this point.

"SureFarm is looking to expand. They want to make an offer on the farm."

What was he talking about? The farm wasn't for sale. Had never been for sale. "What, you want to sell the farm now?"

"They've been asking for the past year. Maybe running the farm is just too much for us. With my... setback, and you now having some things going on, maybe it's a sign we just need to move on."

Thomas rubbed his head trying to ease his headache. Maybe it would make sense. "They say how much they'd pay?"

"Three point five."

"Mom's place?"

"We'd keep." Rich stared at him like he expected an answer right now.

He wouldn't be getting one. This wasn't a simple cut and dry situation. The farm had been in their family for years. The boys grew up there. Just like their mothers did.

Thomas flicked on the TV and reached for a swig of beer.

"You knocked it on the floor in your little temper tantrum."

"Kiss my ass."

"Hell, somebody needs to. Might put you in a better mood." Rich headed to the kitchen, turning as he reached the doorway. "You gonna think on it?"

"Yup."

He nodded. "I'll call you in the next couple days, see what you decide."

"Yup."

Thomas could hear him cursing under his breath as he made his way through the kitchen and out the door. Something about being a son of a bitch pain in the ass. He didn't feel too bad considering he'd probably said the same thing about Rich a time or two.

His thumb pressed the button on the remote, changing channels every second, not really seeing what was on any of them.

If he wasn't going to get better, he had to sell the farm. Financially it didn't make sense to keep it if all their money was eaten up paying for labor. But he didn't want to sell the farm.

He wanted to get better. He wanted to be back out in the fields this spring putting everything in the ground. He wanted everything to go back to normal. And he wanted Mina. He wanted to show her how very much he appreciated what she did for him. He wanted to do everything for her every day and everything to her every night.

You know what they say. Shit in one hand and wish in the other and see which one fills up first. He shifted in the chair, trying to find a comfortable position, but only succeeded in aggravating his already painful leg.

Maybe he should have let Rich get those pills.

* * * *

"I swear to God Tommy. I am just about over your shit."

A pillow flung at him from across the room hit him square in the face just as he was opening his eyes from a restless sleep. "What the hell mom?"

"You heard me. You're supposed to be a grown man aren't you?"

Nancy stood at the foot of the recliner hands on hips, eyebrows halfway up her forehead, glaring at him.

"Aren't you?"

"Yes I'm a goddamned grown man and I can sit here on my ass and rot if I freakin' want." He tossed the pillow back on the couch where Nancy'd found it.

"How do you figure? The way you're acting, you can't do anything. That means somebody's gotta bring you food and take out the trash and all but wipe your ass while you rot. And let me tell you, it certainly is not going to be me."

"I guess I'll starve instead. It'll be faster"

Nancy grabbed another pillow off the couch and chucked it at him. This one, he saw coming and deflected with his forearm.

"You're a pain in the ass you know?" She huffed her way into the kitchen. Much to his dismay, the noises coming from that direction were not the sound of her slamming the door and stomping off in a fit, but running water and dishes clinking. The soft rustling of plastic bags was a good sign he wouldn't be starving to death. Not today anyway.

Ten minutes later Nancy returned, plopping down a turkey sandwich and chips on his tray. She crossed her arms and glared at him.

"Right now I'm working under the assumption your being an ass 'cause you're hungry. Get some food on your stomach and then you can take your pills and hopefully your outlook will improve."

"I don't have any pills."

"Yes you do."

"No. I don't"

Nancy pulled a bottle out of her jeans pocket. "You do now."

"I don't want them. They don't help."

"You didn't even give them a chance."

Thomas eyed the sandwich, his stomach rumbling. He grabbed one half and bit off a third. He hadn't realized how hungry he was.

"This is good." A chunk of tomato landed on his lap as he shoved another bite in.

"Why are you doing this?"

He swallowed the mouthful. "I'm not doing anything."

Nancy flopped down on the couch. "That's the problem Tommy. You are sitting here, doing nothing but feel sorry for yourself and for the life of me, I can't figure out why."

He looked up from his plate. "What the hell do you mean, you don't know why? My head looks like fuckin' Frankenstein. My leg's mangled to hell. What am I supposed to do?"

Nancy stared at him silently, eyes wide.

"That's right. Nothing. And that's exactly what I intend to do."

Nancy clamped her mouth shut. Her lips thinned into a straight line as she stared at him. "Everything was lining up for you Thomas, and you're just going to walk away?"

"No. I'm not." He took another bite of sandwich. "I can't walk."

"That's your choice."

"How in the hell do you figure any of this is my choice?"

"It's the same damn thing as when I said you can't control what other people do. You can't control what happens, but you sure as hell can control how you react and right now I'm pretty freakin' ashamed and definitely questioning my abilities as a mother."

"I can't handle a goddamn guilt trip right now. You were in the damn room when they said I won't really ever get better."

Nancy's eyebrows shot up. "That's what you heard? They aren't psychic Tommy. Some people do the work and get better, some people," she stared right at him, "don't. If you don't want to put in the work it will take to get better, then you aren't the man I tried to raise you to be. The man I raised was never afraid of working for something he wanted." She leaned back on the couch and crossed her arms.

Two seconds later, she sat back up straight. "Speaking of that, what the hell about Mina? She asks how you are doing every damn day. I imagine after that hospital visit, she thought you might call her. She's a good girl Thomas and she'd be a good woman for you, but after what she's been through already, she doesn't deserve your shenanigans."

Why did everyone have to keep bringing her up? Every waking moment he wasn't being harassed by one of his family members, he spent thinking of her. Replaying every second he'd spent with her. Remembering the softness of her skin as he held her hand in his. The strands of gold that ran through her coffee colored hair and perfectly matched the flecks that glistened in her amber colored eyes.

"You're right. She deserves someone who can give her everything. That's why I'm leaving her alone." Even though it was the last thing he wanted to do.

* * * *

Mina's middle finger broke through the tip of the latex glove for the ten millionth time today.

"These things are shit Paul." She stripped the ruined glove off, shoving it in the black heavy duty garbage bag propped against her leg.

After about the fifth time of hunting down the box for a fresh glove, she thought to stash a handful in each back pocket. Pulling one free, she snapped it on her hand and grabbed another armload of random crap off the pile looming in front of her and crammed it in the bag.

Paul came lumbering in from the kitchen, a full bag dangling from each hand. "Sorry, they didn't have a lot of options in your size."

He kept moving past her through the living room and out the front door. A heavy thud sounded as each bag hit the bottom of the dumpster parked in the driveway. He swung the front door back open, a swift gust of cold air sneaking in with him. "I'll check someplace else tonight, see what I can find. Have you tried wearing two at a time?"

She snorted. "Of course I'm wearing two at a time." She held up both her hands as evidence. "Why would I only glove one hand smart ass?"

Paul bit his lip trying to hide a smile. "Two gloves on *each* hand. Like double bagging your cans at the grocery store."

"Damn it Paul." Mina snagged two more gloves out of her pocket and wrestled them on. What in the hell was wrong with her lately? This was something she should have thought of after the first couple blow-outs. "Looks like you are officially the brains of this operation today."

"What do you mean, *today*? I'm always the brains here." He gave her a pat on the back. "You need to cut yourself some slack honey. You have been through a lot in the past few weeks. It's gonna take some time to get back in the swing."

She didn't have some time. She had shit to do. She had two kids to take care of plus they were already behind schedule on Mike's parents' house. She closed on it the day before Thomas' accident and should have started right away. It had to be emptied out before she could even come up with a concrete plan and here they were, almost two weeks later just now starting project hoarder.

"That doesn't really work for me. I was hoping to get this place done before Christmas."

"You know what they say..."

"Yeah, well." She held up two handfuls from the pile. "Right now both my hands are full of shit."

Paul chuckled as he shook his head. "Everything here is full of shit." He scanned the living room Mina spent all morning and half a box of gloves on. "You're makin' headway though."

"Well, I'm hoping to get at least this room empty today."

"Want me to help you?"

Mina rolled her eyes. "Hell no. You promised if I bought this place you'd handle the kitchen and there is no way I'm going to come help you, so you do your room, and I'll do mine."

Mina could hear him laughing all the way to the kitchen. She grabbed another pile of papers and shoved them in, topping off the bag. She tied it off and hauled it outside, swinging it into the dumpster. She paused on the porch, enjoying the fresh air in spite of the cold.

She had looked forward to starting the house, hoping it would be a nice distraction. Instead, spending hours each day doing nothing but bagging trash was giving her ample time to think. More like obsess actually.

She just couldn't figure out what happened.

The night in the hospital Thomas was so concerned for her, even though he was the one in the hospital covered in bandages. The way he held her hand felt so intimate, so natural.

Mina left him feeling nothing short of terrified. She spent so much time building him up in her mind and never imagined the real man would be anything like the one who resided in her head. And he wasn't.

His eyes were bluer. His hands bigger and a little rougher. His voice was deeper but softer. And the way he looked at her was like no man had ever looked at her before. It made her stomach flip and the rest of her ache.

But that was it.

Apparently she was the only one who felt the earth move because she hadn't heard a peep from him. Not that she was expecting a declaration of undying love, she was just hoping for a phone call. Maybe dinner. Maybe finding out what those big hands could do.

Her nipples tightened underneath her sweatshirt. She took one more deep breath of chilly air, hoping to convince herself the reaction was because of the cold and not the idea of labor calloused hands rolling them between rough fingertips.

"Shit." She picked up a loose paper and wadded it up before tossing it into the dumpster.

Obviously she needed to work on reading people. First she missed the obvious fact that her ex-husband was a sociopath and now she had clearly over-estimated Thomas' interest in her.

As she stood shivering in the cold, wondering how she would get Thomas out of her mind, a white city pickup pulled up in front of the house.

"Son of a..." She swung open the front door and stomped in. "Paul!"

TWELVE

MINA SAT ON the cruddy carpet she found hiding under twenty giant garbage bagfuls of what probably started as an acre of trees. She had hoped to fly under Don's radar until the last possible second. Lucky her, he shows up on day one just to say hi and see if she needed anything.

"Annnnyyyythiiinnng." When he winked she thought she might puke.

It took over an hour to get rid of him, as he insisted on walking through the whole house and asking a million questions, none of which she had an answer to. "What are your plans for this room? What about that room?" She could hardly see the walls, let alone the floors. She had no freaking idea what she was going to do.

Luckily the place wasn't that big and he ran out of things to question her about. Then he continued to hang around for fifteen long painful minutes before his phone rang and duty drug him away, but not before promising to come back soon and see how she was doing.

Goody.

Mina closed her eyes and thumped the back of her head against the wall. "What did I do to deserve this?"

The hinges on the front screen door squeaked as it swung open. *Oh god. He's back.*

"Well seeing this makes me feel a little better."

Shit shit shit damn. Mina jumped up from the floor. "Oh God, Nancy. I'm so sorry."

"Oh, honey." She looked around the room. "Don't even worry about it. Looks like you got your hands full."

Her stomach growled. Damn it. Why didn't it do that an hour ago to remind her of their lunch date? "Don showed up."

Nancy's brow furrowed. "For what? Make sure you're picking up trash correctly?" She snorted. "He's just trying to figure out how to get a permit pulled to get in your pants."

Just the thought of Don in her pants gave her the willies. "So not funny."

Nancy laughed. "It's hilarious actually. And you'll let it slide since you forgot me."

"I can't believe I did that. I don't know what's been with me lately."

"It's really no big deal. I wanted to see your new project anyway and figured you were here, so I got it to go." For the first time, Mina noticed Nancy had two white plastic bags slung over her wrists.

She stepped forward to help with the bags. "Do you know how much I love you?"

"I'm hoping it's a lot because I have a favor to ask."

Just then, Paul came through the doorway connecting the living room to the dining room, headed out the front door with an armful of garbage bags. He saw Nancy and stopped dead in his tracks, frozen.

Nancy gave him a small almost shy looking smile. "Hi Paul."

Paul stood silently, staring at Nancy.

Nancy held up the bag left on her arm. "I brought Mina lunch and thought you might be here with her, so I asked Joe to give me something for you too."

"Oh."

Nancy flashed Paul a much bigger smile as she pulled a large foam box from the bag and held it out to him. "I didn't ask what it was, he just said it was your favorite."

He took the box. "Thank you. What do I owe you?"

"Oh, gosh. No. It's my treat. A thank you for protecting my friend from the big bad building inspector." She flashed that smile again.

"Um. Well, thank you." He turned to Mina, an odd look on his face. "I, um. I gotta go, I have an appointment I forgot about. I'll see you tomorrow." He paused on his way out the door and looked back at Nancy. "Thanks again." The door swung closed behind him and Mina looked at Nancy.

"What in the hell just happened?"

Nancy was already on the floor peeking into the remaining box she pulled from her bag. "What are you talking about?"

"Pretty sure you know what I'm talking about."

Nancy ignored her, taking a big bite of her sandwich. "Oh man, this tuna is on point today. You better eat yours before it gets all soggy."

"Yeah, this is just making it worse. What is with you and Paul?"

Nancy plunked her sandwich back in the box and finally looked up at Mina. "It's complicated."

After the way Paul reacted to Mike and now seeing them face to face, she imagined complicated didn't begin to scratch the surface. "Yea, I kinda got that. Complicated how?"

"Just... we have a history, I guess."

"A history."

"Yes."

Nancy was just as eager to talk about Paul as he had been about her. Something was up. Something interesting. Mina hoped her friend would be more forthcoming than her contractor, but obviously that wasn't the case. She sighed. It would have been nice to think about someone else's relationship issues for a change.

Plopping down beside Nancy, she opened her tray and inhaled half her sandwich before she remembered. "What's the favor?"

Nancy popped the last bite of her sandwich in her mouth and shoved her box back in the bag. "He's making me crazy."

"Who? Paul?" Maybe Nancy wanted to talk about him after all.

"Thomas. I need you to go talk to him."

Yeah, that wasn't going to happen.

"I'm not following. I need to talk to him, why?" She had talked to him. Then never heard from him again. Obviously he wasn't that interested in what she had to say.

Nancy stood and pulled a black bag from the roll. "Are you just chucking everything?"

"Yeah." Mina yanked a pair of gloves from her pocket and tossed them to her. "Why is it I need to talk to him?"

Nancy started loading the bag. "The day after you went to see him, he had a long talk with the doctors and somehow he has decided they told him he would never be... hell, I don't really know what he thinks, but he's acting like his life is over, like he's never going to get any better than he is now."

She started shoving trash in the bag faster. "He won't take any pain pills. He barely moves and he's being... he's just being a huge pain in the ass." She already had a bag filled. Tying it off, she stomped out the door before throwing it as hard as she could. The black bag bounced off the back wall of the dumpster before hitting the steel bottom with a thud.

"Wow that felt good. I'm think I'm gonna do another one." She pulled another bag off the roll and started stuffing.

"He is freaking miserable and he's making me miserable. I've tried to talk to him, his cousin's tried talking to him and he's just refusing to listen."

Mina shoved her empty lunch box into the bag Nancy was filling at warp speed. Maybe she should just keep Nancy pissed until the house was empty. Pissed Nancy was productive. "What makes you think I can help?"

Nancy head was down, her arms flying. "He knows what you went through. Maybe you can give him some perspective."

"That's like apples and oranges. I don't see how my experience would be relevant. There aren't many similarities there." That and the fact that seeing Thomas again would be the equivalent of poking a stick into her own eye.

"I just was thinking he might listen to someone who's been through something terrible too."

"You've been through something terrible."

"I don't count. I'm his mother. I know nothing." Nancy finished filling the bag she was working on and tied it off.

"Just think about it. I was going to bring him dinner tonight, but maybe you could go instead. I'll take the kids out for dinner or something."

"Tonight?"

"He needs to start on physical therapy now or he will get worse and I can't handle him now, I can only imagine if he got worse." Nancy walked to Mina and grabbed her hands. "Please think about it. I think you would be really good for him." She paused. "Talking to you I mean."

Nancy was one heck of a mother. Only a mother could lay on a guilt trip like this.

They both knew she couldn't say no. If Nancy only knew what she was really asking her to do. *Could you please go over to my unbelievably beautiful son's house and make him feel better?*

Mina could think of more than a few ways to make him feel much better and she was sure none of them were what Nancy had in mind.

She blew out a breath. "I'll go." She had to. Nancy had successfully made her feel like there was simply no other option. Well played.

Nancy grabbed her into a tight hug. "Thank you so much. I'll come get the kiddos and bring you his dinner at five."

"Okay." Mina felt like barfing, but she was positive the tuna sandwich she just finished tasted much better going down than it would coming back up.

Nancy let her go smiling brightly. "I gotta go. I'll see you at five." She grabbed her filled bag and gave Mina wave as she headed out the door, throwing the trash in the dumpster as she left.

Well, shit.

Mina looked at her watch. It was 2:00. She could work another hour before the kids were done with school. Her eyes traveled from her wrist down to her hands.

Or she could go get a manicure so at least her nails would be pretty when she died of a panic attack.

She grabbed her purse off the floor and locked up the house before jumping in her van and heading for the nail salon.

Her mind was reeling as she drove through town. What was really going on with Thomas? He seemed okay when she saw him in the hospital. Why was he so upset now?

Nancy said he thought he would never get better, but from what she said after their meeting with the doctors, he would have to go through physical therapy and give it some time, but he would be okay. Maybe he knew something his mother didn't.

If he told her, she wouldn't be able to keep it a secret from Nancy. Then she would be caught in the middle with no good way out.

Mina pulled into a spot right in front of the shop and shut the van off. What in the heck had she agreed to? She took a minute to lean her head back, close her eyes and take a few deep breaths.

This was going to be hard, and not just because it could put her in an awkward position.

As much as she wanted to say this meant nothing, that seeing him would be no big deal, it wouldn't be the truth. This could end with him feeling better, and her feeling worse, longing even more for something that would never be.

This was getting out of control.

She yanked her keys out of the ignition and grabbed her purse. Whatever happened tonight, she would be fine. Conjuring up scenarios in her mind was only going to get her more wound up and she needed to calm the fuck down.

Way down.

* * * *

Thomas opened his eyes. Even with the blinds shut, he could tell by the shadows in the room it was already dark outside. The satellite company's screen saver floated across the television. He'd been asleep at least the two hours it took the box to shut off from inactivity.

The pain in his leg woke him up. That and a bladder full of filtered beer. He needed to head for the bathroom, but moving around was going to make the pain worse. Stalling, he clicked the remote, searching for something interesting. He settled on the news and stared at the screen as the talking heads recounted the happenings of the day.

More snow was coming to replace the layer that just melted. A new Italian restaurant was opening. Interest rates were down, more people were buying houses. Life was going on.

He looked around the dark living room littered with empty beer bottles and dirty dishes. This wasn't fucking fair. He was a good fucking person. He looked back at the TV as a mug shot flashed across the screen. Some guy got arrested for robbing an old lady.

That's the guy who should be like this. He deserved this shit, not someone who took care of his mom and carried old ladies groceries to their car.

"Goddammit." He swiped his arm across the tray beside his chair, sending three empty beer bottles crashing into the wall before shattering on the floor.

He leaned his head back against the chair and rubbed his eyes.

Sitting here day in and day out was making him lose his mind. *You might as well get used to it.* He rubbed his hands across his face, two weeks of unkempt beard making his skin itch. He scratched his cheek through hair just long enough to be soft.

This sucked. His life sucked.

Deciding he'd put off the inevitable long enough, he reached for his walker and drug it in front of the recliner. Pulling the lever, he slowly and carefully adjusted his injured leg as the chair dropped his feet to the floor.

He heard tires crunching in the driveway and a car door slam. He hit the menu button on the television and squinted at the screen. It was after six.

It had to be his mother. Lovely.

Hopefully she was feeling a little less combative than the last time he saw her. He stood slowly, bearing most of his weight with his arms, trying to keep pressure off his leg.

The kitchen door opened and shut quietly. She probably though he was asleep.

"It's fine. I'm up."

He heard the sound of bags softly hitting the table and footsteps slowly making their way across the kitchen. What was she up to?

"Mom. Did you hear me?"

A woman appeared in the doorway and it wasn't his mom.

Shit.

THIRTEEN

NEVER BEFORE IN his life had he contemplated killing someone. Not until this moment, standing in his living room, if you could call relying on a walker to keep yourself upright standing, staring at this woman who was not his mother.

It was a good thing it wasn't his mother, because right now he thought he might kill her.

"Hi."

Her voice was just as soft and sweet as he remembered. He wondered if it was always so soft and sweet or if a man did just the right things, she would be loud and demanding.

"Hi."

For a second they just stood, staring at each other. He had no idea what to say to her. Should he apologize for not calling her? Did she even care? Maybe she didn't leave their last meeting with the same feelings he did. Maybe she was only here out of pity.

"What are you doing here?"

"I... brought you dinner." She pointed over her shoulder into his kitchen.

"Where is my mother?"

Mina took a few steps closer, each one bringing her further into the dim light the TV cast across the room. He knew he shouldn't, but he couldn't stop himself from appreciating how absolutely beautiful she was.

Her long hair was slung over one shoulder in a thick braid. A few strands escaped their confines and lay in soft waves around her face. A thick grey sweater hid her most feminine assets, but it didn't matter. The flimsy shirt she wore to the hospital did much less to camouflage her figure and he remembered every curve. He'd had weeks to think about it, burn it in his memory since that would be the only place he would ever have it.

"She's with my kids. Having dinner."

"She throw you under the bus?"

"Yes she did."

Thomas laughed. For the first time in weeks, he laughed. If this poor woman only knew what his mother was really up to.

"Are you hungry? I can bring you in a plate."

"No. I mean yes. I am hungry, but no you don't need to bring me a plate. I'll come to the kitchen." His bladder reminded him of the reason he was standing in the first place.

"First I have to use the bathroom." He glanced down the hall. The bathroom seemed like it was miles away. He glanced back at Mina. She didn't head into the kitchen like he'd hoped. It appeared she was staying put and he would have to make it there with her watching.

"Do you need help?"

No way was he going to let her help him. It was bad enough she was here to see him like this. "No thanks. I'm good. I'll be in in a few minutes."

She smiled and by the grace of God, headed into the kitchen. He turned and shuffled as fast as he could down the hall, praying with every step she didn't come back out to check on him. Then she would see just what a pitiful sight he made hobbling along with his walker like a decrepit old man.

He made it into the bathroom and shut and locked the door behind him. After using the bathroom he checked himself out in the mirror. He looked awful. His beard was scruffy and unkempt, made even more obvious by the lack of hair on his head.

He sniffed under his arm. He smelled awful. He grabbed a stick of deodorant off the counter and popped the lid off rubbing it under his arms. He took another whiff.

That wasn't going to cut it. He had to take a shower. He flipped on the faucet before struggling out of his clothes and under the stream of warm water, trying his best to hurry.

Five minutes later, he was dried off and wondering what to put on. He picked up the clothes he had on and decided between the odor and the stains, that was not an option. He was going to have to get down the hall and grab something fresh to wear.

He opened the door a crack and peeked out. Mina was nowhere in sight, but he could hear noises coming from the kitchen. He softly closed the door back and wrapped his towel tightly around his waist. As he reached for the walker he paused. That thing was loud. She would hear him a mile away. He had to go without.

He peeked out the door again and once he was sure the coast was clear, he gimped his way down the hall, one hand on the wall as he half hopped trying to keep his balance without putting too much weight on his bad leg.

The door was in sight as he felt the tuck of the towel around his waist begin to loosen. He grabbed at it with his free hand just as it came loose, dropping and baring his naked ass as he finished the last few feet to the laundry room. He stepped in, quickly shutting the door behind him before turning on the light. Damn he was tired.

He leaned against the wall as he dug through the dryer, searching for something he could get over his leg easily, but wouldn't be too terrible looking. He pulled out a pair of cotton jogging pants and a t-shirt and wrestled them on. Both were a little wrinkly from being left in the dryer, but at least they were clean. He quickly stuffed his feet into a pair of thick socks then headed back out to the kitchen. He considered grabbing his walker as he passed the bathroom, but decided against it. Damn thing was a pain in the ass anyway.

He quietly made his way through the living room and into the dining room. From there he could watch as she made her way around his kitchen putting away the dishes she found in the dishwasher.

He should stop her, but watching as she stacked cups and organized silverware, he was struck by how much he missed this. He loved having someone to come home to. Someone to take care of. Someone to take care of him.

He loved being married. Maybe that was why he had been so unable to see the flaws in the one he was in. The past two years he'd been so focused on being mad at Mary and embarrassed by what happened that he forgot how much he loved being a husband. How much he loved having a wife. Watching Mina now, he couldn't help but wonder if she would be different.

She turned, smiling as she saw him. "Hey. Feel better?"

His shower had not gone unnoticed. Being a mother he should have known she would have ears like a bat.

"I do. Sorry I took so long. I figured since you went to all the trouble to bring me dinner, the least I could do was make myself presentable." He made his way into the kitchen, slowly lowering himself into a chair. He was exhausted and his leg was starting to throb.

"Does it help if you prop it up?" She angled a chair beside him.

He pulled his leg onto the chair with his hands. "It does. Thank you."

"Your mom sent a..." Mina lifted a corner of aluminum foil off a baking dish. "Casserole?"

Thomas reached out and pulled the foil the rest of the way off. "That appears to be tuna noodle casserole."

"Do you like tuna noodle casserole?"

"No."

Mina laughed as she pulled two plates from the cabinet. "She *is* mad at you."

"Is that why you're here?"

"Are you insinuating I'm your punishment?" She grabbed two forks and the roll of paper towels, setting them on the table as she gave him a grin.

"Maybe I'm not the only one being punished." He smiled back at her. "Do *you* like tuna noodle casserole?"

"I do, but my kids hate it so I never make it."

He dropped a scoop of steaming noodles onto the plate in front of Mina. "Looks like today's your lucky day then."

* * * *

Mina eyed Thomas as he slid a small spoonful of casserole on his plate. She didn't know what to make of the man sitting across the table from her.

It was obvious he was rattled when she showed up instead of Nancy and to be honest, so was she. After how good he looked at the hospital, she wasn't prepared for him to look so... different.

The golden waves she spent more than a few nights imagining running her fingers through were gone, probably a casualty of his head injury. A full, unkempt beard hid most of his face. What she could see was pale and noticeably thinner, like the rest of him appeared to be.

All she could do was stand and stare, stunned. Her heart aching for him. For a second during the awkward silence, Mina thought he was going to ask her to leave. Instead he showered and changed clothes, returning without help from his walker. Now here he was teasing her and smiling in spite of the pain he was obviously in.

Mina jumped up. "I almost forgot. Your mom said to be sure you had these with dinner so they didn't upset your stomach." She grabbed the prescription bottle off the counter and popped the lid, fishing out two pills. She held them out.

Thomas stared at her outstretched hand. Slowly he reached out and gently took the pills from her, his fingertips softly brushing across her palm. Her knees went weak. Even in his current state, he was one heck of a good looking man. There was just something about him that did things to her and boy did she want him to do things to her.

Reaching back, she grabbed the chair and quickly sat down before she fell down and really made an ass out of herself. She smiled hoping he hadn't noticed.

He grinned back, putting that hot as hell gap on full display. If she hadn't gotten worried about how long he was taking in the bathroom and gone to check on him, she might consider it the sexiest thing about him.

He tossed both pills in his mouth and washed them down with a sip of water. "Thank you."

She nodded. "Are you still in a lot of pain?"

He looked at her for a minute, probably to decide whether or not to lie. "Yes."

"Is the physical therapy helping?" She already knew the answer, but he didn't have to know that.

"I um..." He looked down at his plate as he shoved food from one side to the other. "I haven't gone."

"Oh." She took a bite. Nancy made a pretty darn good tuna casserole. She watched him as she chewed. He didn't look up, just kept relocating noodles.

"Why?"

"I don't think it will help."

"You don't?"

"No."

Mina was beginning to see why he might be driving Nancy a little crazy. It seemed like if Thomas didn't want to talk about something, he made it very difficult and hoped you'd lose interest. Unfortunately for him, Mina could stare at him all night and the longer this conversation took, the more she was able to indulge herself. "Why is that?"

His eyes were still glued to the plate in front of him as if tuna noodle casserole was the most interesting thing he'd seen. "My leg was shredded. They couldn't save part of the muscle. You can't fix what's not there."

Up until now, Mina assumed he was wallowing in self-pity but the look on his face, the set of his jaw was not pitiful. This man was angry. He was about to get angrier.

"Your mom talks about you a lot." She paused trying to gauge his reaction so far. He finally looked at her and she almost lost her nerve, but he needed to hear this and she might be the only person with balls big enough to say it to him.

"I never got the feeling from her that you were a man who let someone else tell you what your limits were."

He stared at her silently, the muscle in his jaw twitching. She held her breath, waiting.

"And what do you think now?" His voice was low and rumbly in his throat. His clear blue eyes turning dark like a storm as it smothers the sky.

Holy f-ing hell he was sexy when he was mad.

"I think I was right which is why this is all so confusing. Why did you give up before you even started? You run this whole farm so I know you're not lazy. You survived an injury that would kill most people, so I know you're not weak."

"So what am I?"

"Scared."

She scooped herself some more casserole and waited for the shit to hit the fan. The idea of coming over here had not thrilled her, but mid-way through her manicure this afternoon she realized a few things.

First. Nancy needed her. That was reason enough to do whatever she could to help Thomas.

Second. Nancy might be right. She may be one of the few people Thomas would listen to. If he really did know what she had been through with her ex, he would realize she had a little experience moving forward after something awful. Maybe not the same kind of something awful, but equally terrible.

Number three. The idea of Thomas suffering seriously bothered her. Like, a lot. Way more than it should, which also bothered her, but she could worry about that later.

Right now, what he needed was to hear the cold hard truth. He wasn't going to like it and might not like her afterwards, but it had to be done and if it helped pull him out of his funk, it would be worth it.

She had more than enough time to finish her food while Thomas sat in silence. Finally, as she was standing to begin clearing the table he spoke.

"What is it you think I'm scared of?"

Not the reply she was expecting. She anticipated yelling, denials or maybe just being asked to leave.

"The unknown."

He continued to look at her, making her feel the need to explain. "You might get better with physical therapy. You might not. I don't know and neither do you. I do know you will not get better sitting here alone all day being angry."

She took the plates from the table, scraping Thomas' untouched dinner into the trash. "Bad things happen. Terrible things. But they only ruin your life if you allow them to. At the end of the day, you decide what will happen." She stood at the sink and twisted on the hot water, squirting in dish liquid as it filled.

She turned, expecting an argument and prepared to defend her opinion, but he was no longer sitting at the table. He was right in front of her, so close she could feel the heat from his body and smell the clean freshness of the soap from his shower. The storm was still raging in his eyes as they bored into her, dark and threatening. She gripped the counter behind her, determined to stand her ground. "So what are you going to do?"

The question barely had time to escape her lips before Thomas closed the small distance left between them. Before she realized what was happening, his mouth was on hers, his hands cupping her face as his fingers tangled in her hair.

She couldn't breathe. Oh my God what was happening?

He eased closer, pressing more of his weight against her as his lips continued to tease hers. He was so warm. His fingertips began to slowly massage her scalp as his heat began to soak into her. She felt dizzy. The only thing keeping her upright was being trapped between him and the counter.

He pulled his lips from hers and tilted her face up towards his. "Maybe you can come back tomorrow and we can talk about this some more."

FOURTEEN

MINA ALTERNATED HOLDING the wheel with one hand while wiping the other down the leg of her jeans. Her palms were sweating. She was sweating.

She grabbed the neck of her shirt, flapping the fabric against her chest trying to get the air moving. It was thirty degrees out and she had the car vents on full blast trying to keep her perspiration under control. This was ridiculous. She was a grown woman, not a teenager in heat.

She was more nervous to see him now than she was when she went to the hospital. Of course that was before he'd kissed her. Twice.

It was also before she began to suspect Nancy had been setting her up this whole time.

After that first kiss, Thomas asked her to come back the next day, and she happily agreed, a little make-out drunk, temporarily forgetting her children. Something that would definitely land her at the top of the list for mother of the year.

The next morning, Nancy was calling by eight, going on and on about what a wonderful time she and the kids had together and asking for them again. It wasn't until this morning when Nancy showed up at the hoarder house wanting to take the kids to a movie tonight, that she became suspicious. Less than ten minutes after she left, Mina's phone rang, a low sexy voice asking if she would like to have dinner with him again.

They were tag teaming her. And they were good at it. But she couldn't help but worry. What if this didn't go anywhere? Where would that leave their friendship? Worse yet, what if it did? Would their relationship be the same if Nancy was her mother-in-law? Didn't Nancy say she could only imagine Thomas with an amazing woman? That was a pretty high standard to live up to.

She reached down and kicked the blower up a notch, angling the vent at her face. She felt sick. This could be a terrible idea. Unfortunately being with him didn't *feel* like a terrible idea. Actually it felt like the best idea she'd had... ever.

She knew she should say no each time he asked to see her again, but she couldn't. Literally. She couldn't. Her mouth was agreeing on its own, completely ignoring the hesitation in her brain.

She jammed her finger on the button in the door, the frigid air blowing her hair around as the window slid down.

Taking a deep breath of the chilly air filling the van, she tried to clear her mind and calm the heck down. As ready as she thought she was to start dating, she never imagined there would be so many complications right out of the gate.

A few more minutes of slow breathing had her calm enough she thought it was safe to roll the window up. She glanced at herself in the review mirror. Shit. Her hair was all over the place. She raked her hands through the tangled mass, trying to get it at least a little under control. All that time spent curling it and now it was everywhere. At least the cool air kept the sweating to a minimum and her make-up was still intact.

She took one last deep breath as Thomas' house came in to view. And so did he. Standing in his driveway, leaning back against the tailgate of his truck in loose fitting jeans and a tan fisherman's knit sweater, his hands tucked into the pockets of a rich brown leather jacket. A knit cap covered his newly bare head, protecting it against the cold winter air.

Her stomach flipped at the sight of him and she thought she might start sweating again. He was one hell of a good looking man. Maybe the complications weren't as big of a deal as she was making them. They certainly didn't seem as problematic when she was with him.

As she pulled up in front of him, he flashed her a smile, the whiteness of his teeth standing out against the dark strawberry blonde of his beard. Man she was glad he hadn't shaved it off. It made him seem more rugged.

She rolled down the window as he came around the passenger side of the van leaning on the cane she brought him at their last dinner date.

"Need a ride?"

* * * *

"I believe I do." He popped open the door and carefully angled himself into the seat beside her, trying to avoid bending his leg, but failing.

"You can push that seat back if it will help. The switches are on the side."

"I might take you up on that." The seat slowly moved back, giving him room to stretch out. "Much better."

He pulled the door closed, ready to soak up the warmth of the car. Inside the van was just as cold, maybe somehow even colder, than outside the van. "Is your heat out?"

Her already pink cheeks flushed a little more. "No. I have been busy today, running around, and I was a little warm." She reached up, turning the dial on the dash to the red zone. Warm air began blowing through the vents. "Sorry."

He held his hands up, the feeling slowly coming back into the tips of his fingers. He hadn't wanted her to come in after him and risk her trying to help him down the stairs, hoping to preserve any shred of masculinity he had left. It hadn't taken as long as he anticipated to negotiate the steps and uneven driveway, thanks to the cane she brought him, so he was there propped against his truck, freezing for over a half hour. Seeing the surprise on her face was worth every icy second.

"Where are we going?"

He pulled the seatbelt across his lap and clicked it into place. He made reservations for them at a new little Italian place in town his buddy just opened. "Head into town." It was time for him to take her on a proper date. Show her how much he appreciated everything she had done for him. Maybe get to show her off a little too, and she was looking pretty fucking worthy of that right now. "I like your hair."

She was backing out of his driveway and his comment must have thrown her a little bit because she missed the edge of the pavement as the van swung onto the road.

"Oh, thank you." Her hand immediately went to her head, smoothing down the strands.

"It's bigger. More..." What was a good word for it? Wild? She might not like that. He wracked his brain trying to remember any shampoo commercial he could. "Tousled."

Judging by her reaction, that was an acceptable description. She grinned and glanced at him sideways as she drove down the quickly darkening country road. Initially he hated that she would have to drive anywhere they went. Now after realizing it afforded him the ability to watch her, basically undetected, he decided it might not be as bad as he thought.

She looked amazing. Cold, but amazing.

Hopefully she had a coat stashed in the back of the car because the pale pink shirt she was wearing could double as a negligee. The panels of open lace at the shoulders and the see through fabric that made up the rest of the garment would not do anything to keep her warm.

It did however, give him an almost un-obscured view of her upper body including her perfect breasts taunting him from their temporary home, tucked inside a tank top. A tank top that didn't appear ready or able to put up a fight to defend their honor. That was a war he would most certainly win. Maybe tonight.

He shifted in his seat trying to take the pressure off his quickly expanding dick without jarring his leg. It suddenly felt very hot in the van. He glanced over finding she had the heater blasting. He cursed himself for complaining about the cold.

"Which way do I head?"

He looked up and discovered they were almost at the edge of town. He'd spent the whole ride staring at her, planning the demise of her wardrobe and imagining the way her breasts would fit in his hands.

"Left. We're going to a new place in town."

Her eyes got big. "Campioni's?"

"That would be it."

"They have been packed every night since they opened." She glanced at him, her eyes traveling down to his leg. "They don't take reservations."

She was worried about him. She didn't think he could even handle the wait at a restaurant. Jesus. Obviously his mother, God bless her, was very open with Mina about his behavior after his accident. That's what he got for being such a whiny pussy. That just meant he was going to have to spend some time showing her how capable of a man he actually was.

"Sometimes they do." He gave her a smile. "It helps if you know the guy who owns the place."

She smiled back, obviously relieved. "I've heard their food is amazing."

"I'm sure it's much better than if I cooked which was plan B."

"Well thank God for plan A then." They both laughed as she turned onto Magnolia Street, the glowing lights of Campioni's coming in to view. As predicted the place was packed, the parking lot overflowing. "Want me to drop you off at the door?"

Christ. He might have to spend a lot of time proving he was an able bodied man. Actually the idea didn't bother him as much as he thought it would.

* * * *

Mina flopped her napkin over her food hoping to deter any more 'one last bites'. She was sure she couldn't physically fit any more food into her body, but she was also sure of that five bites ago. "That was amazing."

It was by far the best Italian food she'd ever tasted. She would have to bring the kids here for dinner one night. Spaghetti was Charlie's favorite.

"So you're ready to talk again?" Thomas' eyes twinkled in the soft lighting of the restaurant, the same pale blue as the tablecloths and the morning sky painted on the ceiling.

"I didn't hear you trying to start any conversations farmer Tom." She shoved her plate further away, hoping to escape the delicious smell beckoning her to take just one more taste.

Their waiter suddenly appeared. "Can I box that up for you?"

"That would be great." She grabbed her napkin off the plate as he picked it up, turning to Thomas.

"Any room for dessert?"

"To go. A cream cake and a tiramisu."

"Excellent choices. I'll be right back."

Ten minutes later, they were slowly meandering through the parking lot. Mina had the bag of food looped over one arm, the other was linked through Thomas'.

He refused to be dropped off or picked up at the door, insisting he was more than able to make the walk. In the summer, she wouldn't have minded, but it was freakin' cold and with a belly full of carbohydrates, all she wanted to do was curl up on the couch under a blanket and go into a food coma, not take a leisurely stroll through the parking lot simply to prove a point.

They were finally back at the van, getting settled when her phone rang. She started the van with one hand as she grabbed it from her purse.

Nancy must be wondering what time she would be there to get the kids. "Hey."

"Mom, can we stay the night? Miss Nancy is helping us bake cookies and then she says we can make popcorn and watch another movie and have a slumber party."

She turned to look at Thomas in the passenger seat. He was sitting quietly, staring out the window. "Can I talk to Miss Nancy?"

"Hey honey. How was dinner?"

"It was really good. What is this about a slumber party?"

"We were just having so much fun, and I thought you might enjoy a night to yourself."

Sure she did.

"Well, they don't have any pajamas, or toothbrushes or clothes for tomorrow."

"Oh honey, it will be fine. I'm sure I have some stuff lying around here we can make do with. Is it okay?"

Mina sighed. Her kids didn't have any grandparents close by, they probably did eat up getting to spend time with Nancy. "It's okay. But I'll be by to get them first thing in the morning."

"It doesn't have to be too early. Sleep in. Relax. Whenever you get here is fine." Did Nancy know about the third date thing? The idea of her friend thinking she would be having sex with her son tonight was more than a little mortifying. That she seemed happy to facilitate it was downright disturbing.

"I'll be there first thing in the morning."

"Bye honey."

Mina disconnected her phone and dropped it back in her purse, zipping it back up as she looked at Thomas.

"Who was that?"

Like he didn't know.

"That was your mother."

Now she wasn't sure what to do. She imagined this as being dinner, a little kissing goodnight and off to grab the kids before snuggling into her big, comfy bed. Alone. "She wants to keep the kids tonight."

"Oh. She really likes kids."

Uh-huh. Right. That's why.

Mina pulled out of the parking lot, her mind racing. Should she just take him home? She glanced sideways at him and caught him leaned back in his seat, arm resting on the door, looking at her, the smallest of smiles on his lips. He was definitely in on this. Fine then.

"Would you like to stop by my house before I take you home? Maybe we can watch a movie?"

"And have dessert."

Holy shit. Did that mean what she thought it meant? No, no, no, no. No sex with Thomas tonight.

"I ordered the cream cake for me." Her pulse slowed. She forgot they actually had dessert in the back seat. He really did mean dessert. "I might be able to be persuaded to give you a bite though."

Or maybe not.

FIFTEEN

MINA COULD BARELY hear what sounded like the Fine Young Cannibals. She shifted, trying to determine where the sound was coming from, but a heavy weight on her left side kept her pinned. She squinted her eyes open and the cloud of confusion vanished instantly.

A very large, very warm and surprisingly heavy Thomas was propped up against the back of the couch, one arm draped around her waist, his leg propped up on a pillow. She was flat on her back, a blanket crocheted by her mother tucked around her. The index screen of Shaun of the Dead glowed on the television across the room.

What time was it? The room was still dark, so it was before dawn. She rubbed her tongue across her teeth. Gross. Her mouth tasted like old garlic and espresso. She needed to get to the bathroom.

Slowly, carefully she slid away from the very handsome man sleeping on her couch. Years of sneaking away from sleeping children served her well and he didn't budge.

She crept up the stairs through her bedroom and into the bathroom. Flicking on the light, she inspected herself in the mirror. Holy hell, she looked like crap. Her hair was matted from too much window air and a night sleeping on the chenille couch. Eyeliner was smudged out the corner of one eye, almost reaching her temple. She needed a shower... and mouthwash.

Ten minutes later, she felt like a new woman. Her face was scrubbed clean, her hair was washed, conditioned, and combed already waving into its preferred state of chaos. She brushed her teeth and quickly swished around a little Listerine hoping to kill any lingering Italian evidence. After throwing on a comfy top over a pair of grey leggings, she snuck back down the stairs her fingers crossed he would still be asleep. He was, but a new bedmate had taken her place next to him.

"Daphne! Get down."

Her whisper yell only made the shaggy dog flop her head up as she gave Mina sad puppy dog eyes. "No. Don't give me that look. You know you're not supposed to be up there. Get down." She pointed her finger at the floor for inflection.

Daphne blew a raspberry through her lips and slowly rolled her way off the couch deciding if she couldn't be on the couch she might as well go outside. Sauntering over to the door, she whimpered at Mina.

"No."

She whimpered louder.

Mina glanced at Thomas, still sleeping soundly on the couch. "Fine." She disabled the alarm and slid the door open, trying to keep the noise to a minimum. Sliding the door closed behind Daphne, she turned back to look at the couch hoping the commotion hadn't woken him.

A dark shadowy figure loomed over her. She jumped back against the door, her hand on her chest. "You scared the shit out of me!" That man moved awful quiet considering he had a bum leg.

"I see that."

The outside flood light she switched on for Daphne cast a soft glow through the sliding door at her back barely illuminating Thomas' face.

Her heart was pounding, but she wasn't sure if it was from surprise or just being this close to him. "I'm sorry I fell asleep last night." And she was. All that anticipation and she'd passed out fifteen minutes into the movie. They didn't even get the chance to have dessert.

"So am I." He stepped closer, seeming far taller that he had before, forcing her to tip her head back to see his face. He continued closer still, until his body was barely touching hers, his shirt brushing the tips of her breasts through the thin knit of her sweater. In her haste to get back downstairs, she had forgotten to put on a bra. An oversight she was kicking herself for.

One more small step and he was pressed against her, the cool glass of the door chilling her back as his hands gripped her hips before sliding back to cup her bottom. Her lungs seized as she watched the pale blue of his eyes darken as he gazed down at her. Before she could catch her breath, his lips were on hers, not soft and sweet like the kisses he'd given her before, but hot and demanding.

His hands gripped her backside firmly and she began to slowly slide upwards against the glass until they were face to face. She wrapped her arms around his shoulders and opened her mouth eager to taste him. His tongue immediately found hers, the flavor of mint barely discernable.

He pulled her higher, tucking her legs around his waist, then pressed harder against her using his weight to keep her in place, freeing up his hands.

One arm slid around her waist, pulling her against him. She gasped as he slowly drug his hips forward, rubbing his erection against her.

He broke their kiss to trail his way to her neck. She took the opportunity to try to catch her breath. Holy shit she was panting.

Don't hyperventilate.

She tried to force her breathing to slow, but the feel of Thomas' hot mouth nipping at the sensitive skin just behind her earlobe was making it impossible. Add to that the slow rhythmic pressure he started with his groin and she might be finished before they even started.

His mouth moved back to hers as his free hand traveled up her ribcage. His palm cupped her breast as his thumb slowly brushed back and forth across her hardening nipple, all while his hips continued that slow, maddening friction.

Oh God. She was going to come.

Thomas suddenly stopped. She heard a frustrated whimper and realized it came from her. Luckily she wasn't the only one making that noise and Thomas was paying attention to the other guilty party.

His arm tightened around her waist as he pulled her away from the door, sliding it open with the other hand to let Daphne back in. He slid the door back closed and his lips were immediately back on hers.

She was waiting to feel the press of the door at her back, but instead he turned, carrying her across the room. She soon felt herself falling backwards. Pulling her lips from his she tightened her arms around his neck in panic.

"Relax angel. I won't drop you." His mouth was on her neck, moving down to run his tongue along her collar bone as she landed softly on the couch, his weight on top of her. She tightened her legs around his waist, trying unsuccessfully to encourage him to begin moving against her again.

She needed his mouth. She unlinked her arms from around his neck, sliding her hands across the width of his shoulders, the muscles taunt as he supported his weight above her. Continuing around, she ran her fingertips across his pecs and up the sides of his neck, finally reaching his face.

His beard was soft against her hands. She dug in her fingers feeling his warm skin beneath. She pinched her fingers together, trapping the hairs between. "Come here."

Gently, she used her grip to pull him back into a kiss immediately plunging her tongue into his mouth, his subtle taste of mint teasing her palate. He growled into her mouth, pressing his weight against her giving her the contact she craved.

His reaction to her boldness egged her on. Releasing his beard, she clutched at his shirt dragging it up his body. She could only get it half way up his torso, the weight of his body against hers keeping it trapped. Frustrated, she tugged it back down, settling to slide her hands under the uncooperative fabric and up his sides.

His body was substantially wider than hers, leaving her quite a bit of unobstructed area to explore. Her thumbs brushed against the edges of his abdominal muscles as her fingers felt their way up his back. As she felt the tickle of chest hair, she moved both her hands to his front.

Her palm rubbed against one flat male nipple, feeling it tighten under her touch. She slowly ran back across, teasing the hard bead with her fingers. Thomas sucked in his breath and wrestled her hands free, gripping both wrists with one hand and pinning them above her head.

"You've got to stop angel." His voice was hoarse in her ear. "I can't."

Knowing what she was doing to him made her feel unbelievably sexy. She wanted more. Tightening her legs around him, she raised her hips rubbing her swollen mound against him.

"Jesus Christ." His free hand gripped her hip, his fingers digging into her flesh, as he shoved her away from him, pinning her to the couch. "Not a very good listener, are you?"

She loved seeing him this way. Knowing it was because of her.

Shaking her head slowly, she felt a smile creep across her lips. Lying here underneath this big man as he held her pinned down, able to do anything he wanted to her, she should have felt intimidated and nervous. But she didn't. She felt powerful and in control. And ridiculously turned on.

He leaned towards her, his good leg between her knees. She closed her eyes waiting to feel his lips against hers. Instead, she gasped as heat enclosed the peak of her breast through her shirt. The wetness of his mouth quickly soaked through the thin fabric, as he swirled his tongue around her hardening nipple. He sucked it into his mouth, tugging gently.

He suddenly released, her breast gently bouncing. Cool air moved across the wet fabric as he blew softly until her nipple was so tight it was almost painful.

"Please." Her voice was barely a whimper. She tried to rub her legs together to find some relief from his teasing, but his thigh blocked her, hard and immovable.

He chuckled into her chest as he rubbed his face across her sensitized bud. "What's wrong angel?" He moved across, gently grazing his teeth across the fabric covering her other nipple. "Don't want to be beat at your own game?"

Part of her wanted to kill him. Part of her wanted to screw him first. All of her wanted release.

She writhed under him, straining against the hand keeping her arms above her head, but he held fast as he continued to tease her with his mouth. Suddenly, he released her hip and used the fingertips of his now free hand to gently pinch and pluck her chilled nipple. He pulled her other breast into his mouth, wetting and warming it as his tongue rubbed back and forth. The different sensations were almost enough to send her blissfully over the edge. Almost.

He slowly trailed his way up her neck pausing to suck her earlobe between his teeth, letting it slide gently between them as he released it on his way to once again taste her mouth.

His lips fused with hers, harder this time distracting her until all at once the sensation of his thumb slowly circling focused all her attention on one small bundle of nerves. She whimpered as he lowered his head to her breasts, moving from one to the other as he sucked, stroked and gently nipped, continuing his slow stroking across her clit, the thin fabric between them barely buffering the sensation.

"Oh God, please don't stop." He gently pinched her sensitive flesh. She moaned, her hips bucking involuntarily.

"It's time for you to come angel."

On command, her body exploded. Her back arching as she ground herself into his hand. He released her hands and she clung to him, fingers digging into the muscle of his shoulders, riding the waves of her climax unable to focus on anything outside of how wonderful he was making her feel.

As the puzzle pieces of her living room began to put themselves back together around her, music played faintly in the background. Thomas brushed his lips across her forehead, at her temple and down the line of her jaw.

Regaining her composure, she tucked her face in the crook of his neck, suddenly feeling a little shy and self-conscious. *Did you really just get off without even taking off your clothes?*

What began as mere embarrassment bloomed into full on mortification. What the hell just happened? How did an innocent little make-out session turn into that? Her face burned.

She needed to go regroup. She tried to think of a way to escape and get behind a closed door where she could kick herself. But then she heard the sound of Thomas' voice, soft and gentle in her ear. He was whispering, his words stopping her in her tracks.

"You don't know how long I've wanted to be able to touch you." He nuzzled her neck as his hands gently tangled in her hair, softly rubbing the strands between his fingers. "I never thought it would happen."

The feeling was mutual. Only it still hadn't happened for her.

With his confession, all thoughts of embarrassment disappeared. He didn't know how long *she* had been waiting to touch *him*. She decided the wait was over. Her heart pounded in her chest, the anticipation of exploring him bringing her to the brink of a heart attack.

Sliding her hands down the length of his back, every muscle tensed under her touch. Since the first night she brought him dinner and caught a glimpse of his perfect ass sneaking down the hallway, she fantasized about what it would feel like in her hands while she pulled him into her. She was going to find out.

Slipping her hands into the pockets of his jeans, she pushed her hips up as she pulled him down, feeling the full length of his impressive member on her belly. She felt her cheeks flush again, but this time not in embarrassment.

Thomas groaned into her hair as she continued rubbing her body up and down, using her grip on his backside as leverage. Almost as soon as she started, he pulled away from her. "God you're a terrible listener."

She was about to show him just how bad she was, when the sound of someone pounding on her door made them both jump. Thomas glanced at the door, then back at her. "Expecting someone?"

She craned her neck to look out the sliding door. It was still dark. It couldn't even be 5:30 yet. Looking back at Thomas she shook her head.

Pushing himself off the couch, he headed toward the door, his limp more pronounced than normal. "Stay there." He glanced down at her damp shirt. "You might want to wrap up in the blanket just in case."

She looked down. Her shirt was beginning to dry, but her nipples were still hard and obvious through the fabric. Grabbing the blanket off the couch and swinging it around her shoulders, she crept behind Thomas as he made his way in the dark.

The heavy pounding came again, making her stomach tense up. She could come up with very few people who would come pounding on her door like that, none of them good.

"Tommy! Please." More pounding. "Mina! Oh my God, please be here."

Nancy?

The voice registered and Thomas yanked the door open, his sobbing mother falling into his arms.

"Mom what in the hell is going on?"

Mina stood in the entry, eyes wide as she tried to process what was happening. Thomas looked at her, confusion covering his face as his mother sagged in his arms, holding onto him for dear life.

Mina's mind was racing. What was happening? Suddenly her stomach dropped and she felt sick. "Where are my kids?"

Her face went cold. Oh my God. Oh my God. She headed for the front door praying to find them on the porch, instead she ran head on into two uniformed police officers. "Where are my kids?"

"They are fine. Still asleep at Nancy's. One of our officers is with them."

"What the fuck is going on?" She flinched as she realized what she said, but right now she wasn't too focused on her word choices.

"Were you at Thomas' house any last night?" Cop number one was medium height and obviously never missed a meal.

"Just to pick him up before dinner. We came here after." She turned back to look at Thomas. Cop number two had gone inside to help him with Nancy. The two men were half helping, half carrying her into the living room.

"She's okay." Cop number one smiled gently at her. "Just relieved."

What? Mina gave him a confused look.

"Thomas' house burned down." He watched her, waiting for her reaction. Nice or not, he still had to do his job.

"What?" That didn't make any sense. How could his house burn down?

"It didn't just burn down. There was an explosion that started it."

An explosion. In Thomas' house. She tightened the blanket around her shoulders as her mind began working up a never ending series of 'what ifs'. He could have been there. He would be dead now. *They* could have been there. They would be...

A tear ran down her cheek. Heavy hands landed on her shoulders, turning her into a wide, solid chest. Thomas wrapped his arms around her as she buried her face against him.

"Everything's okay angel. I promise." He kissed the top of her head gently as she tried to wrap her mind around what had happened.

His house was gone and if she had made one decision differently he would be gone with it. She bit her lip trying to control the tears, but the idea of never seeing him again was more than she could handle. Thomas stroked her hair, holding her tightly as he let her cry against him. After a few minutes tucked into Thomas' warm embrace, she didn't have the energy to cry any more. She was exhausted.

"Let's get her inside so she can warm up and we can talk."

"Thanks Jer." Thomas carefully led her into the house, stopping at the bottom of the stairs. "Do you want to go get on some warmer clothes?"

She did. She needed a few minutes alone. She looked up into his eyes and felt a lump in her throat. All she could do was nod.

Thomas cupped her cheek, his thumb stroking her skin as he leaned down to gently brush his lips over hers. "Everything will be okay. I promise." She nodded again and managed a weak smile. Turning to head up the stairs, she almost made it to her bathroom before she found the energy to cry some more.

SIXTEEN

"TOMMY HONEY, I'M so sorry." His mother picked her way around the yellow crime tape surrounding what was left of his house. The fire inspector was planning to come by later today, until then, no one was allowed near it.

Not that they could get too close anyway. Even with all the water they used in attempt to douse the flames and the bitter chill in the air, the charred pile of debris continued smoking.

The cold was however, making his leg ache. Made worse by the extra pain he was in from trying to impress Mina this morning. What he wouldn't give for one of those pills he'd avoided having to take. Too bad they were probably charcoal. He'd have to add a refill to his list of shit to get when he went into town this morning.

"It's alright. Just gonna be a pain in the ass."

A huge one. His head was beginning to hurt right along with his leg as he thought of everything he was going to have to do to straighten this out.

Rich slapped him on the back. "I'm here for ya, if there's anything I can do." He looked over what was left of the house. "They know what started it?"

He came out to meet them this morning to check out the damage the fire did to the house. Damage ended up not being the right word for what was done to his house. Gut, incinerate, destroy. Those were much more applicable.

"Not yet. Said they might not be able to tell exactly what happened."

Rich nodded slowly. "You had insurance, right?"

"Yeah. Their man is coming out in the morning. Then I guess they come up with a number for me. There's still a mortgage, so they have to be in on everything too." He rubbed his temples with one hand and moved the pharmacy to the top of his mental list.

"Your lady friend going to help you put it back together?" Rich gave him a knowing look.

"How'd you hear about that?"

"Everybody who knows your mother knows about it, so basically everyone knows."

"Great."

Rich gave him a confused look. "What's the big deal? You like her right?"

"Yeah." Hell yeah he liked her.

Standing here in front of the burned out shell of his house, all he wanted to think about was their time together this morning. Either he was still in shock, or it just didn't really matter. All that really mattered was Mina was okay.

He shivered, shoving the thought of her being in the house when it happened out of his mind. He couldn't even let himself consider that as a possibility. Him, yeah. Life would go on for everyone, but Mina had kids who needed her. The thought of her kids being without a mother or a father bothered him. It bothered him a lot.

"Then who cares who knows?"

He did. He didn't like the pressure that went with everyone knowing your business and he certainly didn't want Mina to feel it. She had enough on her plate with raising kids alone and running a business. He didn't want their relationship to be one more thing for her to worry about. He wanted something to be easy in her life for once. He would do his best to make sure of it.

Rich forked a hand through his disheveled hair as he glanced at Nancy where she stood on the far end of the house scanning the debris.

His cousin looked like shit this morning with bags under his eyes and wrinkled clothes under his unzipped Carhart coat. Made sense considering Nancy probably started blowing up his phone before dawn too. Hopefully that was all it was.

"You thought any on that offer?"

He had. "I just can't imagine selling the farm."

"You've got a lot on your plate man. First your leg, now you gotta rebuild a whole damn house. Just sell it. You'd have enough money to live on for years."

Thomas watched his mother as she neared the finish of her lap around the remains of his house. Selling the farm would break her heart. "I don't think it's a good idea."

Rich followed his gaze. "Don't be stupid man. We may never get another offer like this. She'd get over it." He zipped his coat up against the cold and shoved his hands in the pockets. "I'll hold them off a little more. Start on your house. Spend time with Mina. Selling will start sounding like a better and better idea."

Thomas was over this conversation. He had too many other, more pressing things to deal with, like making sure Mina had recovered from the shock of this morning. If not, maybe he could find a way to help her feel better.

He nodded his head to placate his cousin. Eventually he'd have to tell him he had no intention of selling, but he was guessing that conversation wouldn't end well and right now he didn't have the energy to deal with it.

"Good. I gotta go. Call me later." Rich jogged across the frozen grass, giving Nancy a peck on the cheek before climbing into his souped-up truck, the engine roaring as he took off down the road, a fog of exhaust streaming behind him.

Nancy stepped to his side, having completed her inspection of the site, and wrapped her arm around his waist. "You know, he answers his phone when I call."

He would never, ever live that down. On her death bed, his mother was going to bring up the night she thought he was dead because he didn't answer his phone.

"If I left the ringer up during dinner, you would have yelled at me for being rude."

"That doesn't sound like me at all." At least she'd regained her sense of humor.

"Let's go. I can't look at this anymore." She left him to get in the drivers' side of her Camry. He limped to the back seat and scooched himself in, stretching his leg across the seat. "Would your truck be easier for you to ride in? Maybe Mina can bring us back to get it tonight."

"Can't. Keys were in the house."

"Why were your keys in the house?"

He motioned to his horizontal leg. "I wasn't driving."

"Was the spare in there too?"

He hadn't thought of that. He shook his head. "I'll call Rich, see if he can bring them over to Mina's later tonight."

"I need to stop at the store while we're out. I told her I'd bring dessert." She glanced up at him in the rear view mirror. "You're going to love her kids."

He wasn't too worried about that. With the mother they had, he was sure they were great kids.

He was worried what they would think of him. They didn't have the greatest experience with men, and they were both old enough to understand what was going on. He knew he wouldn't have been too warm and fuzzy toward a man his mother had brought around when he was a kid, maybe even now. Maybe that was another excuse she used to avoid dating.

Luckily his mother was pretty set on seeing him and Mina together. Hopefully she worked her magic on the kids and they would cut him some slack.

* * * *

Mina looked at her watch. It would figure the one time she really wanted Don to show up he would be late.

She grabbed another corner of carpet and pulled it free of the tack strips holding it in place. There were other things she'd really rather be doing, but until Don graced her with his presence, she was stuck. She pulled the utility knife from her back pocket and cut a section free so she could roll it up and chuck it into the dumpster. This may not be her favorite job, but at least the house was quiet and she had time to mentally try to work her way through the emotions of this morning.

She had gone from one extreme to the other. One minute she was experiencing pure bliss, the next she was smacked in the face by the cold hard reality of chance.

If not for chance, she could be dead. Thomas could be dead. How do you come to terms with not being in control of your own fate? Especially if, for years, the thing that kept propelling you forward was reminding yourself that you were what controlled your life. No one else, and nothing they did could control you unless you allowed it.

This morning was a reminder that wasn't true. It left her feeling out of control and that was a place she hated to be. With one exception apparently.

She obviously didn't mind when Thomas took control. Maybe even liked it. She trusted him. More than she should at this point which should scare her. It didn't. Maybe it was because of her friendship with Nancy, but she doubted it.

205

There was something about him, a quiet strength that made her feel safe. Something in his eyes, something she had not seen in any man's eyes when they looked at her before, made her feel like he was really looking at her. Not her tits, not her mouth, not her ass. Her. I mean, of course he appreciated all those other things.

Clearly.

But only because they were hers.

She felt the same way. The aftermath of his injury left him very different from the strong, capable shaggy haired farmer she lusted after for months. Yet somehow, she found him even more attractive than before.

Without the distraction of his hair, she was able to appreciate the way his eyes betrayed him, showing every emotion. His beard took away the boyish charm he held before, shoving him into rugged man territory. If there was one thing she needed it was a man and Thomas had proven himself to be quite a man.

Her pulse spiked at the thought. He was almost more man than she could handle this morning. Ugh. This morning.

He'd called to tell her the house was a total loss. He'd been through so much in the past few weeks, now this. It was ridiculous. How much could one person handle?

Oddly, he hadn't seemed that upset about it this morning. If anything, she was the one who struggled the most. Well, besides his mother, but that only made sense.

He'd been calm, comforting both she and Nancy while they fell apart. Hopefully he was still feeling the same way.

She dropped her utility knife to the floor and walked to the front window. Where in the world was Don? She needed to get this meeting with him over so she could go home and get ready for tonight. Thomas was going to be meeting Maddie and Charlie for the first time and she was a little apprehensive.

In the time since she left her husband, she had been out with exactly zero men. Her kids had never known her to be with anyone but their dad and that hadn't exactly ended well for any of them. She just wasn't sure how they would react to the idea of another man in their life.

She wouldn't necessarily have to tell them she and Thomas were dating. The kids knew she and Nancy were friends. They also knew Nancy's son's house burned down this morning. It would only make sense he came over with her, right?

Maybe they weren't even actually dating. What constituted "dating" now? At what point were you considered together? When did you decide to only see each other?

She suddenly felt sick.

The possibility of Thomas taking another woman out made her want to throw up. The potential he could be doing more than that with another woman made her want to scream. Once again, having time to think was proving to be a bad thing.

She checked her watch. Don was forty minutes late at this point. "Damn it."

"Rough day?"

Mina swung toward the door, her heart pounding. Don stood inside the frame, blocking out the late afternoon light. Better late than never.

"A little I guess. You just startled me."

He didn't budge from the door. "Oh." His voice was flat and unapologetic.

"I was wondering where you were. I thought we might have to reschedule."

"I had other things going on."

Why was he being so short with her? Normally she had to pry him away from her jobs. Now he couldn't be bothered to even be on time? "That's understandable."

She smiled hoping to smooth over whatever had him so hacked. "I'm glad you made it."

"Are you? Are you really glad I'm here Mina?"

She felt her smile freeze on her face. Something was wrong. Don's tone was not his normal attempt at smooth and seductive. It was hostile and angry. She felt a familiar pang of panic deep in her gut. She was alone with a man who, for some unknown reason was pissed and it seemed to be directed at her. And he was blocking her only way out. She glanced around the living room, looking for another escape route.

Don snorted. "Maybe since you're so glad to see me, you'd want to go out with me tonight? What do you think? You wanna go out with me tonight?"

What in the hell was going on?

"You know I can't go out with you." She tried to muster up all the sweetness she had. "It is a serious conflict of interest."

"You sure that's why Mina?"

She hated the way he kept saying her name, spitting it at her. The initial fear she felt was quickly being replaced by anger. Who the fuck did this guy think he was? He shows up forty five minutes late and is going to be a dick on top of it. What in the hell was he trying to accuse her of anyway? It was time to get this situation under control.

"I guess I'm not really sure what you're trying to say, Don." Two can play at this game. If he thought he was going to come in here and scare her into a date he was wrong. Really fucking wrong.

She watched as his ears began to turn red at the tips, the heat spreading down over his cheeks, his eyes burning into her. The vein in the side of his forehead was so pronounced she could almost time his heartbeat.

If he stroked out right here, she was just gonna let him die. There would be no mouth to mouth for him today. She might call 911. Eventually. Forty five minutes later.

Finally, he ripped the top couple of sheets off his pad and wadded them up. "Maybe I'll just give you a little time to think about it then." He spun around, knocking the screen door open with enough force to break the catch. He stomped down the steps and tossed the wadded up inspection forms into the dumpster.

Mina watched from the porch, arms crossed, as he managed to peel out in the city truck, the smell of burnt rubber traveling quickly in the cold air. She knew he would see her in his rearview and considered flipping him off. She didn't want him to get off on the idea he left her cowering.

She groaned as she went back inside. This project was already behind schedule. Now she had to report him and they'd have to figure out how to get this damn house inspected by someone else. It was going to set them back even more. Until then, she couldn't do much of anything, leaving her stuck with a lot of free time on her hands.

It only took a second for her to consider maybe this wasn't the worst thing that could have happened. New man in her life, lots of spare time. *Might not be such a bad thing after all.* Plus, she'd finally be done with Don and his bullshit.

She shoved the last lingering thoughts of the argument with Don out of her mind, he didn't deserve any more of her time. Lucky for her, she may have found someone who did.

SEVENTEEN

"HAVE YOU MET Nancy's son?" Maddie grabbed a pile of plates from the cabinet and headed into the dining room. "I bet he's hot."

Mina watched her daughter as she plunked a plate down on each placemat. "I have, and he is way, way too old for you." The last thing she needed was her daughter crushing on Thomas.

"Oh. Like how old?" The string bean of a teenager went boy crazy a few months ago. Now boys and their varied levels of hotness dominated most of her conversations.

"Old enough to be your father."

"Sick."

"Exactly."

Maddie came back in the kitchen, a thoughtful look on her face. "Does he have a son?" Her face brightened with hope.

"He does not."

She dramatically huffed and stuck her lip out. "How am I ever going to find a boyfriend around here?"

"What in the world makes you think you could even have a boyfriend? You are only thirteen!" This girl was going to be the death of her.

Mina turned back to the steaming pot of beef and vegetable stew, stirring it before cutting the heat and popping the lid on it. Nancy and Thomas should be there any minute and she really did not want to be arguing with Maddie about age appropriate relationships when they arrived.

"That's what Miss Nancy said too."

Go Miss Nancy. "That's because Miss Nancy is smart."

The doorbell rang and Maddie took off obviously still eager to check Thomas out. She flung the door open and stopped dead in her tracks.

Mina sighed and headed to the door. By the time she got there Maddie was at least past the open mouth staring stage and smiling, but was still blocking the doorway.

She stood behind her and fought not to have the same reaction to the man standing on her porch in faded jeans. An

213

almost fitted, navy long sleeved t-shirt he had pushed up over his forearms with thin pale blue stripes made his eyes look even more blue than usual. She knew from experience if she ran a finger along one of the stripes, she would feel the ridges of the muscles across his stomach. A light brown belt and its brushed silver buckle peeked out from the waistband of his jeans where he tucked the front of the shirt in.

You gotta say something.

She looked up to his face so she could invite him in, but got tongue-tied all over again. He'd trimmed is beard, cleaning up the edges so they set off the line of his jaw. His eyes were set on her, his smile bringing out the dimples that were clearly visible through his newly cropped facial hair. Her heart flipped in her chest.

"Hey." His voice was smooth and soft. The small puff of vapor accompanying it caught her attention.

"Hi." She herded Maddie away from the door to give him space to come inside. "Come in where it's warm."

He thumbed over his shoulder. "My mom asked if one of the kids could help her." He grinned. "I guess she didn't trust me not to go down and take her brownies with me."

She turned to Maddie and found her still gazing at Thomas. "Honey, why don't you go help Miss Nancy?"

"Okay." Tearing her eyes away, she skipped down the stairs.

His eyes were still on her with an intensity that gave her butterflies. He stepped close to her in the entry way. He smelled different today. Woodsy. Earthy. He must have bought new cologne to go with his new clothes. It was a good buy. Made her want to press herself against him. Then again, everything made her want to press against him.

She turned to look at Charlie. He was still glued to the video game he'd switched on a half hour ago. Maybe she had a quick second to get her hands on him before--

"Hi honey! Dinner smells great. We are starving." Nancy flung her arms around her, squeezing tight. "How are you doing?"

She hugged Nancy back, happy to see she'd recovered from this morning. "Good. A little tired. I tore out a bunch of carpet at the house."

Nancy held her at arm's length, her face serious. "You know sometimes you need to take a day for yourself. Relax and recoup."

She grabbed Nancy's coat and passed it to Maddie. "Looks like I might have plenty of time for that. Seems I've pissed Don off somehow."

Thomas' face turned serious. "Don Jenkins?"

"Yeah. I'm not sure what-"

"Hi Nancy." Charlie appeared at Nancy's side and gave her a sideways hug. "Is this your son?"

Nancy beamed at him, clearly in love with the freckle faced ten-year-old. "It is. This is Thomas." She wrapped her arm around his waist. "Thomas, this is Charlie."

"Hey." Charlie looked at Thomas sheepishly then leaned into Nancy's ear. "Does he like video games?"

Nancy smiled. "When he was your age he loved video games." She leaned down. "I bet he'd love to play with you."

Thomas gave Charlie a wink. "She's right. I was pretty good at Mario Brothers when I was a kid."

"I have Mario Cart."

"Think you can beat me?"

Charlie craned his neck and looked up at Thomas straight faced. "Yes."

Thomas laughed as he headed to the couch with Charlie. "You are probably right."

As the boys got settled in Maddie grabbed Nancy's hand, dragging her toward the stairs. "Come see my room."

Mina headed back into the kitchen. She checked on the pot of grits, stirring to make sure nothing was sticking to the bottom.

As she turned to grab the cheese from the fridge, she ran smack dab into the middle of Thomas' chest.

"How do you keep doing that?" The man should have been a ninja.

"What happened with Don?" His face was serious.

"He's just a pain in my ass." She skirted around him to grab the cheese and began dumping handfuls into the steaming grits.

Thomas stepped against her back, his hands on her hips. "What did he do?" His voice was quiet in her ear, but had an edge to it she'd never heard before.

She stirred the grits, watching the cheese melt into the creamy mass leaving swirls of gold. Leaning back into the hardness of his chest, she let herself imagine what it might be like if this was how she made dinner every night, for him.

"Mina."

His voice snapped her out of the fantasy. She didn't want to talk about Don right now. She wanted to enjoy being close to him, the cedary scent of his new cologne hopefully rubbing off on her clothes so she would be able to remember it after he left.

"What did Don do?" The edge to his voice was a little more pronounced.

Why was he so worried about this guy? Not like Don even held a candle to him.

She sighed, relenting. "Don's always seemed to have a thing for me I guess. He was irritated that I would never go out with him I guess. He was supposed to inspect the house I'm working on today and showed up forty-five minutes late pretty pissy at me and then just walked off."

She stepped away from the warmth of his body, her daydream ruined by having to think about Don. Grabbing the salad from the fridge, she turned to find Thomas leaned back against the counter looking less than happy. His knuckles were white where he gripped the counter edge and it almost looked like his eye was twitching.

"It's no big deal. Really." She shrugged. "I'll call the city tomorrow, tell them what happened and they'll have to find somebody else to come inspect my stuff."

"I don't think you should do that." He took a step closer. "Let me handle it."

She started to remind him she was grown and had handled men way worse than Don. That she could take care of this.

But then he laced his fingers gently through her hair and held her face in his warm hands. "Please."

He looked worried. He also looked determined. And gorgeous. Maybe she could let him feel like he was saving her. Just this once. He did know everyone in town. Maybe he could handle this better than she could anyway.

"Okay."

"Mom. Is it ready yet? I'm starving."

Thomas quickly stepped away as Maddie came bouncing into the kitchen. He gave Mina a wink and retreated to the couch joining Charlie where he was giving Nancy a quick tutorial on video game controllers.

"Almost honey. Why don't you get out the salad dressing and put it on the table?"

Maddie snuck a look at the couch. "He's hot for you." She mouthed as she thumbed over her shoulder at Thomas.

"I don't know what you're talking about."

"Be quiet."

Maddie came right beside her as she poured the thick stew into a serving bowl. "You don't want him to hear us."

Mina gave Maddie a serious look. "He won't because there's nothing to talk about."

"There so is. He wants to do you."

"Now you don't know what you're talking about."

"Yes huh I do and so do you. You've done it twice. There's proof."

Damn sex-ed in schools.

"And he's super-hot so you should let him."

Mina turned to face Maddie, resisting the urge to strangle her. "This conversation is over. No more. Understand?"

Maddie sighed, obviously disappointed her extensive knowledge of the birds and the bees was unappreciated by her mother. "Whatever."

There came that strangling urge again.

"Yes mother." Mina could feel the crazy eyes starting to take over her face. She did not need this tonight. Nothing was more terrifying to a man than a teenage girl, let alone a teenage girl with an attitude.

"Yes mother."

"Thank you." She shoved the bowl of grits at her. "Now put this on the table."

* * * *

Thomas leaned back in his chair, resisting the urge to rub his stomach. It turned out spunky, smart and beautiful were not the best Mina had to offer. She was one hell of a cook. If he hadn't already decided to do whatever it took to make her his, the dinner he just ate would have sealed her fate.

She smiled at him across the table as she stood to start clearing plates. "Good?"

Good did not begin to describe it. He was going to have to learn to pace himself or he would end up being five hundred pounds. "Really good. Thank you."

"Anytime."

He hoped she meant it because that was the plan. There were a few kinks to work out, but very soon every night would be like tonight. He watched as she walked into the kitchen, wishing he could find a way to get his hands on her. Make her feel like he did this morning.

His lusty thoughts were interrupted by the doorbell. It took a second for him to remember who it was.

Mina looked to the door, obviously confused. Probably a little nervous after the last time someone unexpectedly rang her doorbell.

"It's my cousin Rich dropping off the spare key to my truck. Sorry, I hope it's okay." He should have told her. He started to get up, but Nancy was faster, jumping up and heading to the door.

"I'm glad he had the spare. Better than having to get a new one made." She was at his side, grabbing his plate.

The kids had already cleared their plates and were piled on the couch watching cartoons. He slid his hand up the back of her thigh as she reached across him for Nancy's plate. She froze as he trailed his hand higher, cupping the fullness of her bottom with his palm as his fingers barely brushed between her legs. He could see her chest beginning to flush where it peeked out the neckline of her top.

He loved her reaction to his touch. He'd never been with a woman who was so responsive to him. The blush continued to her cheeks as she gave him a shy smile and moved away and back to the kitchen, leaving him empty handed.

Rich followed Nancy into the family room, keys in hand. "Hey buddy. I brought all the keys I had of yours. House spares are probably here too, won't do you much good now though, huh?"

Thomas hoisted himself up and headed across the room to take the keys from Rich. "No they won't." By the time he made it to grab the keys, Mina was beside him.

"You must be Mina." Rich grabbed her in a bear hug. Mina stiffened, probably a little shocked at Rich's immediate show of affection. "You're even prettier than Tom said."

The instant he released her, Mina stepped away from Rich, back to Thomas' side, a smile that didn't reach her eyes plastered on her face.

Rich was a bit much for some people and clearly Mina was one of them. He'd have to tell Rich to tone it down the next time he saw him.

"I'm gonna get out of here. Let you guys enjoy your evening. Call me if you need anything else Tommy boy."

"I will. Thanks again man."

Nancy walked Rich out as Mina stared after them, a thoughtful look on her face. "He's your cousin?"

"Yeah. My mom's sister had him young."

"It seems like you two are close."

"More like brothers I guess. His mom took off after my dad died. My mom and grandpa raised us both."

"What about his dad?"

"Not really sure. Aunt Carol said it was some boy she went to school with. Wouldn't tell anybody who. My guess is he was older. Probably trying to protect him."

"That would be hard on a kid."

"Probably why he's so... overenthusiastic. Always wants people to like him."

"Maybe." The thoughtful look remained on her face. "I'm going to finish cleaning up. Why don't you go sit on the couch and prop your leg up."

She hooked one finger in his and looked up at him. "I'll have the kids help me and when we're done maybe we could all watch a movie." She stroked her finger softly down the inside of his palm before turning to head into the kitchen, calling over her shoulder, "Children of mine. We have a kitchen to clean."

Both kids climbed off the couch. "Then can we have the brownies Miss Nancy brought?"

His mother smiled as she swung in behind the kids on their way to help. "Absolutely!"

He made his way to the newly empty couch and carefully situated his leg across the cushions. As he settled in, he couldn't help but think about the last time he was on this couch.

That woman was going to give him a run for his money. Her dinner table wasn't the only place he was going to have to pace himself. If this morning was any indication, it was going to take everything he had to keep from making an ass of himself when her took her to bed. He hadn't been with a woman since Mary left and the dry spell left him a little out of practice in the control department. Hopefully it would be like riding a bike.

He watched Mina over the breakfast bar as she moved around the kitchen, teasing the kids and joking with Nancy. Her kids really were great, which was a testament to the kind of mother she was. Especially one stretched so thin.

Running a business and being a mother was hard enough. But Mina was the only source of income as well as the only parent. She had no family here. Everything fell on her shoulders and whether she realized it or not, she needed help.

Charlie would be a hard-headed testosterone fueled teenager soon. He would need someone to look up to. Someone to respect. Man to man.

More concerning was Maddie. She was dangerously close to boyfriends and dating and had never seen the way a man should treat a woman. She needed to see the way a real man respects and cherishes the woman he loves or she would be a prime target for an abusive dick head.

He wanted to make sure that never happened. Mina, Maddie and Charlie had been through so much and it was time for them to have what they deserved. A man who loved them. A man who appreciated them. A man who would always be there for them and always take care of them. He was hoping to be that man.

Mina turned and caught him watching her. For a second her eyes stayed on his, and he saw something he recognized in their depths. Maybe tonight felt the same way to her as it did to him. Maybe she realized her time of being alone was over too.

EIGHTEEN

THOMAS LEANED ON his cane as he made his way up the cement steps leading to the yellow brick city building. Mina may think she could handle Don, but she had no clue what that man was capable of.

He stepped through the heavy metal doors and into the warmth of the building, pausing for a minute to let the heat soothe the instant ache brought on by the cold, and aggravated by the steps.

He made his way to the front desk, the woman attending it smiling as he approached. They had gone to school together, but right now her name escaped him. Hopefully he could get away without needing it.

"Thomas! Oh my God, how are you doing? Is your leg any better? It was so awful when I heard what happened. Good thing that lady was there to help you, huh? Oh my God and now your house. Just awful."

Terri. Her name was Terri. Better known during their school days as 'talk a lot Terri'. He was going to have to keep this moving or he would be stuck here all day and he had other, more important things to do. Like go see that lady who helped him.

"I know. Crazy." He kept walking past her desk as he spoke. "Don in his office?"

"Oh, yeah. Gotta get stuff together to get your house fixed, right?"

"Yup." Something like that.

He continued on, heading to the row of offices beside Terri's desk. Hopefully he would find Don in one of them.

"Hope everything works out." Terri hollered down the hall after him.

So did he.

He was counting on catching Don in the office in the hopes the loose cannon of a building inspector would be better behaved. Thomas was in no shape to take on someone like him right now.

Hopefully that would start to change soon, but for now it was true. As much as he hated it, his injury limited him. But that would only save Don's ass for so long.

Approaching the offices, he could hear Don's annoyed voice coming from the first door on the left.

"That place wasn't anywhere near ready for inspections of any sort." A pause. "I don't care what they said." Another pause.

He was on the phone and it sounded like he was getting his ass chewed and Thomas was afraid he knew why.

"Where are you gonna find somebody else? I'm the only city inspector you've got."

Thomas was more than a little shocked. He really thought Mina was going to let him deal with this.

"Whatever." Thomas heard the receiver of the phone crash into the base. "Fuckin' Paul."

Mina hadn't called. She'd told Paul. From what he'd heard, Paul treated her like his daughter and any man would raise hell if someone was messing with their daughter.

Thomas would have raised hell too if he hadn't seen firsthand how Don reacted to situations like this. Not too long ago, he'd spent a night in lock up for slashing the tires on a woman's car after she turned him down in the bar. That was mild compared to what Don could do to Mina. Slashed tired were a whole lot easier to deal with than a ruined business.

Thomas had to try his best to get this situation under control before things got worse. Unfortunately after the conversation he just heard, he was pretty sure it was already out of control.

He stopped at the open doorway of Don's office. The building inspector was in his chair turned away from the desk and the door staring out the window at the back of the room, tapping a pen against the arm of his office chair.

"Morning Don."

Don spun his chair around, his eyes narrowing as he saw Thomas. "You come to fight your little girlfriend's battle?" He dropped the pen he was holding onto his desk as he stood up and headed toward Thomas. "You're too late. Her other man beat you to it."

"Nothing to fight about. I just came to make sure you were doing your job."

Don stopped in the middle of the room and started laughing. "Last time I checked you weren't my fucking boss."

"You need to take a long hard look at what you're doing and decide if this little fit you're throwing is worth losing your job over."

The smile left his face. "Fuck you Thomas."

Don finished crossing the room, stopping two inches from Thomas' face. "You think you can just come in and take Mina from me?"

"She isn't yours. Never was. Never will be."

"What, cause she's yours now?" Thomas could see every vein bulging in Don's face, the extra blood flow making it get redder and redder.

"Pretty much." Whether she knew it or not was another matter he could handle later. Right now he was doing his best to keep from punching a meat head in the throes of a steroid fueled temper tantrum.

Don took a step back, giving Thomas a look up and down. "I guess I didn't realize she was into gimps."

Mother fucker.

Resisting the urge to cane this prick to death right here in the middle of the city building took every bit of strength Thomas had in him.

He could hear his blood racing through his veins, his heart thundering in his chest as he fought the rage building inside him. "Leave her alone Don."

"Or what?"

"You don't want to find out the answer to that."

Don laughed again. "Right." He grabbed the door. "I'll keep that in mind." Still laughing, he slammed the door shut.

Thomas stood on the other side of the door, breathing deep as he talked himself out of opening the door back up and beating the shit out of Don.

"Everything okay?" Terri must have heard the door slam.

"Everything is fine." He gave her a forced smile as he headed past her toward the front exit. "I'll see you later. Take care."

"Thanks. You too." She followed behind him, close on his heels. "If you need anything, you know with your house, you can call me." She was blushing all the way to her ears.

Looks like Terri had a thing for gimps too. "I will."

He kept walking to the doors, ready to get on with the better parts of his day. The cold hit him the second he stepped outside. This time he welcomed the chill hoping it would calm the anger still boiling under his skin. He knew coming here it was going to get personal. Nothing pisses a man off more than someone else having what he wanted. Especially a man who's out to prove something.

"How'd it go?" Nancy turned in her seat to face him as he got in the back seat of her car, stretching his leg out beside him.

"Like I expected."

Nancy grimaced. "That bad?"

"Mina must have told Paul and then he called the city. Don was primed and ready when I got there."

Nancy got a weird look on her face and abruptly turned back around and kicked the car into drive, pulling out of the side lot. "Paul is a good man."

"He is. He just doesn't realize how Don is."

"Donnie was such a nice boy." His mother sighed. "I wish he would get it together."

"Yeah well, he's gotta stop shooting shit into him before that will happen." Until he got over his inferiority complex, the chances of that happening were null.

Thomas was still seething ten minutes later as they walked into the medical center for his first physical therapy visit.

They'd given him the hell he deserved when he called to get this appointment. He kicked himself for not doing this sooner. By now he might be able to walk without the cane, maybe even be in less pain. Then he could have easily given Don the ass kicking he deserved.

Four minutes into his session he was eating those words.

Never. He should never have done this. The pain his tiny little slip of a physical therapist was able to inflict with one small motion was excruciating. He was sweating from exertion and discomfort, trying his best not to swear at the middle aged woman as she tried to teach him the exercises he needed to keep doing between visits to loosen his muscles.

"I would try to do this after a nice hot shower or a bath. It might make it less uncomfortable." She gave him a half smile, knowing she was causing him pain. "It's kind of a necessary evil. It will be worth it. I promise."

She sent him home with a paper showing exactly how to do the movements she showed him, just in case he forgot, and an appointment for the following week.

"You okay?" His mother looked worried at his worsened limp as they walked back to the car.

"Yup." He was better than okay actually. There was only one more stop to make in town and then he would be on his way to the only place he really wanted to be.

"It will be worth it when I can be out in the field in the spring." And when he could be every bit the man Mina deserved.

Forty long minutes later he was ringing the doorbell, feeling the last of the morning's frustration melting right off him. His last stop took way longer than he anticipated. Getting caught in the lunch rush and running into friends eager to chat and happy to see him out and about set him back. It was nice to know people cared, but he had someplace else he really, really wanted to be.

The front door flew open. Mina stood in the doorway, her long hair pulled away from her face, a streak of paint running through the loose tail as it swung across her back. A pale green sweatshirt with the neck ribbing cut out, hung loosely from one shoulder and down past her hips over black leggings, hugging her like a second skin.

She beamed at him, her eyes getting wide when she saw the lettering on the bag in his hand. "Did you bring me lunch?"

"I did. Thought maybe you could use a break." He turned and nodded to his mom. Mina craned her neck to look around him, waving as Nancy backed down the driveway.

She grabbed the bag from his hand and stepped to the side, letting him move past her. Hopefully she was ready to sit. He was in agony after his physical therapy and wanted to prop his leg up. He made it to the living room before he noticed she wasn't beside him. Turning, he found her watching him closely.

"What happened?" Her voice was quiet, her eyes full of concern.

"Sometimes I'm an ass and have to pay the price."

Her eyebrows came together as she tried to decipher his meaning.

"I went to therapy today."

Her smile returned immediately as she came toward him. "How did it go?" She set the bag of food on the coffee table, watching him as she unloaded the foam containers, the smell of garlic and tomato sauce filling the air.

"Sucked." He peeled off his coat and slung it over the back of the couch next to him. "A lot." He eased himself onto the couch and gingerly propped his leg across the seat, blowing out the air he'd been holding once he was situated.

"Looks like it." She fished around in the bag, pulling out two plastic sleeves, each containing a set of utensils. She handed him a set and then popped the lid on the box closest to her. She smiled and looked up at him. "Is this mine?"

During their dinner together at Campioni's, she'd struggled to choose between two different entrees. That night she picked one and today, he brought her the other.

"You can have whatever you want."

She was talking about the food. He was not.

As she sat cross legged on the floor, barefoot with paint in her hair he knew he would move heaven and earth to give this woman whatever she wanted, and to make sure she was his.

Mina looked up at him and their eyes locked. She held his gaze for a second before her eyes dropped to his mouth. He almost smiled. It was nice to know she was thinking the same thing he was.

She cleared her throat, obviously a little flustered.

Handing him the other container, she smiled at him sheepishly as if she knew he'd read her mind.

"Thank you." He made sure to brush his hand across hers as he took his lunch from her. He heard her breath catch as his fingertips brushed across the smooth skin on the back of her hand. The sound made him reconsider his decision to be slow with her.

The way she reacted to him made him struggle to maintain control. He could see the heat build in her eyes when he touched her. He wanted touch her now, all of her, but he wouldn't rush this. He wanted to savor every moment he spent with her, take his time.

Taking the first bite of eggplant parmesan, she moaned softly and he almost dropped his pasta.

Maybe taking it slow was overrated.

She needed to eat fast. Being this close to her and not touching was getting harder by the minute.

"You want something to drink?" Mina stood up from the floor and headed to the kitchen.

"Anything is fine." He took a bite of his lunch. He needed to get some food in his stomach too so he could take his pain meds.

The appointment this morning had roughed him up and he really didn't want to have any of his attention focused on pain today.

He heard ice clink into glass just before the soft fizzing as Mina poured something carbonated over the cubes.

"Coke okay?" She set the glass on the coffee table beside him before plopping back down on the ground and taking a pull out of her glass. "For some reason I really like carbonated stuff while I paint."

He was hoping she'd decide to be done painting for the day. He had other ideas for how she would spend the afternoon.

"Coke is good." He pointed at the bag sitting on the table beside her. "Can you grab me a pill out of the bag?" He needed to get it in his system so it could start working before he did.

She fished around in the bag, popping the lid on the bottle and sliding one into her palm before dropping it into his. He washed it down with the icy soda and dug back into his food. Even a little cold it was good. He glanced at Mina, happy to see she was shoveling in bite after bite. "Good?"

"It's great. Thank you. I was starting to get hungry." She ate one more bite, then closed the lid over her food and leaned back, letting out a sigh. "I think I'm done. Anymore and I'll just want to go to bed and take a nap."

Bed maybe. Nap definitely not.

He finished off his food, willing the pill to take the edge off the pain in his leg. Placing the empty box on the table with one hand, he rubbed the other up and down the outside of his thigh, hoping the heat from the friction would help the knotted muscles loosen.

He looked up to find Mina watching him.

"Maybe I could help." She scooted across the floor to kneel between his legs.

"Is it the muscles?" She wrapped her hand around the outside of his leg and gingerly squeezed, rubbing her thumb across the top as her fingers explored the tension up the back. "Wow." She looked up at him concern written all over her face. "They are really tight."

It was amazing how quickly his attention shifted from the ache in his leg to the ache in his pants.

He hadn't given her the opportunity to touch him like this and from the way he was feeling right now, it had been the right thing to do. If he were a better man, he would stop her now too, but apparently he wasn't that good of a man.

Her touch was gentle but firm as she carefully worked her way up his thigh, seeking out every knot and slowly working it out of his tortured leg. Her hands climbed higher, his heart beating faster as she moved dangerously close to--

"Is this helping?"

He gritted his teeth. "Yes."

He wanted to tell her how much better she made everything. How she was all he thought about, all he wanted.

But he couldn't. It was taking every bit of strength he had to control himself. To keep his hands off her, knowing if he touched her right now, chances were he wouldn't be able to stop. It was the hardest thing he'd ever done.

It was about to get worse.

NINETEEN

MINA EXPECTED THOMAS to relax a little more as the pain in his leg eased. She could feel the muscles relax under her fingers and he'd taken his pain pill almost twenty minutes ago, but he seemed to be getting more and more tense. Almost to the point she thought he was going to jump off the couch any second.

Worried she may be hurting him, but he didn't want to tell her, she looked up, expecting to find pain written all over his face. All it took was one look at his darkened eyes and she realized he was suffering, but not from pain.

She looked back down at her hands as she continued to knead and rub at the thick, tight muscles not yet ready to give up the first opportunity he'd given her to touch him.

He sat, one leg stretched out on the couch, the other on the floor, completely still while she ran her hand up and down his leg, coming very close to an area she couldn't help but be intrigued with.

All the knots she'd felt, were gone, the muscles beginning to soften and she knew she could stop, but she didn't want to. She'd waited so long to be able to touch him like this and now that she could, all she wanted was to touch him more. Hopefully he would let her.

Slowly, she leaned forward and instead of stopping, let her hands run up his body, gently grazing the bulge pressing up against the zipper of his pants. He sucked in a breath between his teeth. She kept going, up across the flat plane of his stomach, over the rise of his pecs and up to his shoulders. Bracing herself on the arm of the couch behind him, she leaned her weight forward and brushed her lips across his as she shifted her knees to straddle his hips. She leaned forward, letting her weight press against him.

Wrapping her arms around his neck she sucked his lip between her teeth, gently raking across it as she let it slide slowly back out.

"Mina, you've gotta stop." He was panting, his hands both pushing and pulling her. Even as he told her to stop, his tongue swept her mouth egging her on.

"I don't think I do." She grabbed his shirt, pulling it up to expose the skin she wanted so desperately to feel. She slid her hands up and under, palms flat against his warm skin as she kept shoving it up. The trail of sandy hair just above his waistband teased her fingers. Following it up his stomach, she shoved the shirt higher, feeling his muscles flexing under her touch. This damn shirt was coming off if she had to wrestle it off him, which didn't sound like a bad option either.

"Please." He grabbed for her hands but she dodged him and held them behind her back. He seemed relieved for the second it took her to find the insides of his legs and slowly trail her fingers toward his-

"Mina I need you to stop."

She smiled at him and raised her eyebrows. "I disagree." She continued running her fingers up his thighs until she found what she was looking for.

She ran one hand up and down his length watching as he closed his eyes and gritted his teeth. Her other hand began unbuttoning his jeans. She almost had the zipper all the way down when he gripped her hips and tried to flip her under him.

Luckily she saw it coming and dropped one leg to the floor, using it for leverage to secure her position. As she slid her hand inside the open fly of his pants he let out a frustrated groan.

She leaned forward to change the angle of her reach, slipping her hand further down and into the fly of his boxers, sighing as she was finally able to get her hands on him. She wrapped her fingers around him, able to feel the quickening of his pulse as she slowly ran her grip up and down his substantial length. She wanted more of him.

Rising up, she grabbed the waistband of his jeans and tugged down, careful to avoid hurting anything important in the process. She must have caught him by surprise because she was able to get them below his hips, freeing his very hard, very large cock. Watching his face she eased down the length of his body.

Shock and fear flashed through his eyes. For some reason he was scared to give up control. He was going to have to get over that. Right. Now.

She closed her eyes as she slowly pressed her lips against him, rubbing her tongue against his skin as she pressed forward letting him slowly fill her mouth. Thomas let out a long groan as she pushed further, taking more in, as far as she could go. She pulled back, immediately missing the feel of him. Discovering she enjoyed pleasuring him as much as she enjoyed him pleasuring her.

She barely made it halfway back down before he was gasping her name his hands cupping her head as she moved. "Angel you've gotta stop. I can't... I'm going to..."

He suddenly became harder than she thought possible, teetering on the edge. She pushed harder, wanting to send him over the brink. She wanted to taste him, feel him as he came in her mouth.

Wrapping one hand around the base of his shaft, she moved it up and down with her mouth as she took him in as deep as she could. Her other hand gently cupped and stroked his balls as they tightened up against his body.

"Jesus Christ Mina."

His whole body tensed as spurts of heat slid down her throat. She held him in her mouth, sucking gently until he was completely spent.

Sliding her lips slowly off him she felt a little awkward. The heat of the moment had passed and she didn't quite know what to do now. She didn't have to feel weird for long.

Thomas grabbed her, tugging her onto his lap and pulling her tightly against his chest. "You didn't have to do that."

"I wanted to return the favor." He earned it after yesterday morning.

He pulled back to look at her, his face serious. "Mina, nothing I ever do to or for you is a favor you have to repay." He brushed the backs of his fingers across her cheek. "I want to take care of you. Make you happy. That's all."

Tears she didn't want to cry burned the backs of her eyes. The only other man she'd been with certainly didn't want her to be happy. Hell, by the end, he'd wanted her dead. After that, she worried she would never be able to trust anyone again.

Now, here she was with a man she had only known a short time, someone she should still feel like she was getting to know, and she trusted him with every fiber of her being. He meant every word that came out of his mouth. She could see it in his eyes when he looked at her. Feel it when he touched her.

He tucked her head under his chin as he stroked his hands up her back. "Don't cry. I didn't mean to upset you." She felt his breath tickle the small hairs around her face as he rested his lips on her forehead.

The gentle way he treated her was enough to send those damn tears loose. "It's not you."

How could she explain the way he made her feel without sounding crazy and way too invested for the short time they'd known each other? "I just... I've never been with someone like you."

He stilled under her. "I know." His words were clipped, his voice quiet. His breathing was slow and steady, but his heart was pounding beneath her ear. "How did your marriage end up like it did?"

Her heart sank.

Did knowing her past make him question her? Her judgment? Maybe even her sanity?

Rolling off him, she tried to hide the tears of embarrassment and uncertainty as they trickled down her face and headed to the bathroom. She heard him behind her as he struggled up from the couch.

He grabbed the back of her shirt and tugged her back into his chest, wrapping his arms around her. "Don't run from me angel. Please." He littered kisses down the nape of her neck. "I want you to talk to me. I know it was a terrible time for you, and if you don't want to talk about it with me just yet, I understand."

He spun her in his arms and tipped her chin forcing her to look in his eyes. "But don't run from me. Tell me you're not ready." He pressed a chaste kiss into her lips.

"It's hard to talk about." It was. Even after all this time. Did she know it wasn't her fault? Of course. Should she be embarrassed? Hell no. Was she anyway? Absolutely.

"It's hard to hear about."

Her stomach twisted in knots. God only knows what he must think of her. She didn't care what anybody thought of her. Until now.

She cared what he thought. The idea that her past could come between them made her sick to her stomach. The idea her ex-husband would ruin something else for her made her want to kick him in the nuts all over again. Well, nut.

"Hearing about someone hurting you, especially someone who was supposed to protect you..." He stood quietly for a minute, the small muscle in the side of his jaw twitching. "It's difficult for me to handle."

Fresh tears sprung to her eyes. He wasn't judging her. "I just feel so…"

She sniffed into his chest, breathing in his scent, letting it soothe her fears. "I should have known. Should have realized sooner. I just… I don't know how I ended up there."

She'd never discussed the way the incident affected her. She'd relived the events more times than she could count. Cops, attorneys, juries, she'd explained what happened to them all. Telling the factual information was easy, dealing with her feelings about it proved much harder.

He crushed her to his chest. "How could you have known? People hide who they are Mina. The scariest people are the ones who are the best at it." He rubbed her back as he held her. "Come on. Let's go sit back down."

He held her hand, leading her to the couch. He sat down, tugging her onto his lap. Holding her against his chest, he gently ran his hands up and down her arms. The softness of his touch relaxed her as she melted into him.

"I was married before too."

What? A surge of jealousy ate through her body making her stomach clench. It was a ridiculous reaction, especially given she had also been married *and* had children, but the idea of Thomas proposing to someone, taking care of her, treasuring her made Mina feel a little crazy.

She tried to keep her voice casual, as casual as possible when you were considering murdering some poor woman simply for being the ex-wife of a man you were sort of dating. "I didn't know that."

She was dying to know what happened. Why they were no longer married. Should she ask? Could she ask? He had just asked her a similar question and had to chase her across the room as she fled in tears.

"Would you like to know what happened?" His voice was flat, emotionless. If she were a less experienced person, she would assume he was over what happened. But she had been through enough herself to know that tone meant something entirely opposite. He was still hurt from the end of his marriage. Maybe he wasn't over her.

"Yes."

That might be a lie. She wasn't sure she wanted to know. But she needed to know. What he had been through would color their relationship, if that was where this was heading. "If you want to talk about it."

He sighed as he continued his slow stroking, now running his fingertips softly up and down her legs. "Mary and I were married three years. We split up two years ago. She had an affair with her boss and left."

Mina was stunned. She sat up so she could look at him. "She just left? To be with him?" What in the world would possess a woman to leave a man like Thomas? Not just leave, but cheat on him and then leave.

"No. She didn't want to be with him either." He paused, taking a deep breath.

"I wanted a family. I was ready. She told me that was what she wanted too otherwise I wouldn't have married her. Somewhere along the line, I guess she just changed her mind, changed her priorities."

Mina searched his face looking for some clue of how he felt about all this. The pain in his eyes broke her heart.

It seemed like she wasn't the only one struggling with the aftershocks of an awful marriage. Discovering the person you have built a life with is essentially a complete stranger shakes you to the core. It threatens every relationship you've ever had and will ever have, making you question the motives of every person you come across. You become suspicious and if you're not careful, you will drive people away.

Is that what Thomas tried to do with her?

"Why didn't you call me after I came to see you in the hospital?" She laced her fingers with his wanting to be sure he knew she wasn't upset. "You disappeared. Went into hiding. Why?"

Thomas looked at her, his blue eyes fixed on hers. "I was scared."

"Of?"

"You."

Happiness swelled inside her. Grabbing his face she brushed her lips against his. The soft tickle of his whiskers brushed against her skin. His hands pressed into her back, forcing her body closer against his chest as he deepened the kiss.

She loved the way he tasted, the way he smelled, the way he felt under her hands. She couldn't get enough of him. She wanted to see him tomorrow, and the next day, and every day after that.

He had been through so much in his life and came out on the other end a kind, gentle, caring man. A man who deserved to have everything he'd wanted for so long. She wanted to give it to him. Show him what it could be like to have a woman who loved him and would take care of him. Someone who would appreciate everything about him. Someone like her.

TWENTY

THOMAS MADE THE now familiar trek along the sidewalk and up the stairs. He hadn't even hit the top step before Mina had the door open and was waving at Nancy as she drove away.

He had been to see her every day this week, and other than the day of his physical therapy appointment, had spent each day helping her finish little projects on her own house while she waited to be able to get back to work at the other house. Waking up every morning knowing he would be spending the day with her was almost as good as waking up next to her would be. He wanted so much to fall asleep with her in his arms and feel her against him through the night. He just had to figure out how to get there.

If she didn't have kids, he would probably have already found his way into her bed, but this was new territory for him and he just didn't know what would be the best way for them.

Did they need to be married or at the very least be engaged before he stayed? Being away from her was getting harder and harder by the day.

Each day after she dropped him off on her way to pick up the kids he spent the evening doing his physical therapy exercises and wishing he was with her. Fixing dinner, playing with Charlie, helping Maddie with her homework. All his life he'd wanted what filled the house in front of him and now finally, it was within his reach. And he was tired of waiting.

He cleared the top step and gathered her in his arms, one arm around her waist, the other around her shoulders as he tangled his hand in her hair and pulled her to him. He covered her mouth with his letting his tongue slide between her lips, unable to wait a second longer to have at least some part of him inside her. He could still taste the little bit of sweetness she liked in her coffee.

She snaked her hands inside his open coat and wrapped her arms around his waist, trying to pull him even closer. He hadn't even made it inside and he was already straining against the fly of his blue jeans. He pulled away from her. Her small sound of protest made it damn near impossible not to grab her again, but he had to stay focused.

It was getting more difficult not to act on his desires, but he had to lay it all out on the table because once he had her, he knew he would never want to give her up. "We need to talk about some things." He ignored the dread in her eyes he knew a comment like that would bring and grabbed her hand, almost dragging her inside.

She moved stiffly beside him then leaned against the wall, her arms crossed against her chest as he closed the door behind them.

"I talked to some people who work at the city last night."

The relief on her face was quickly replaced by confusion. 'We need to talk' usually meant one thing. From the look on her face, she thought that was where this conversation was going. If she really believed that, she wouldn't be more wrong about his intentions with her, but that conversation had to wait at least a few minutes longer.

"About Don?"

He'd told her about his conversation with Don, and as he'd guessed she did tell Paul. She basically had to, she was his primary source of work and her being at a standstill affected his income as much as it did hers.

"Yeah. Turns out he was already on probation for something that happened earlier this year. They've opened an investigation into Paul's complaint."

Her eyes widened. She clearly didn't realize the ramifications of reporting a city employee for bad behavior, especially one like Don. "Oh God."

He headed to the couch needing to sit down for this conversation. He'd tossed and turned all night after his talk with his friend at the city. As soon as he hung up the phone he'd wanted to go to her house, make sure she was okay, but he knew that would be overreacting.

Mina wasn't technically the one to report Don and it sounded like he knew that. Hopefully he was splitting all his rage at the situation between him and Paul and leaving her out of it.

"They're going to be calling. They want to talk to you, hear what happened directly from your mouth."

"Oh." Her voice was right behind his as she followed him toward the couch. He stopped, remembering how sitting on the couch tended to go.

Changing directions, he went and sat at the table. Hopefully he could make it through the conversation before being distracted by the fact he could see the hardness of her nipples as they brushed against her shirt.

Propping his cane against the chair he watched as she sat across from him and folded her hands in front of her, blocking his view of her breasts. Thank God for that.

"I guess Paul told them this wasn't the first time Don was out of line, so they're going to want to hear it all."

He watched her, trying to read her face, but it was impossible. Somehow she developed quite a poker face in the past five minutes.

"I was really hoping to never have to do anything like this again."

"Like what?"

"Go to interviews where you have to recount things you don't remember perfectly. Explain why you did the things you did, or didn't do." She stared across the room, her face drawn. "You end up feeling like they are questioning you too. Why didn't you do this, or why'd you let that go." She shook her head. "It just makes you feel like an idiot."

He reached across the table, taking her hand. "Nobody thinks you're an idiot. You handled Don the best way possible. He just wouldn't give it up. You'd probably still be okay handling it if he hadn't found out about us." He stroked his thumb across the back of her hand. "I can go with you. It will be okay. I promise."

She smiled weakly. He was regretting his decision to sit at the table. He wanted so much to hold her and kiss the look of worry off her face, but he had one more thing he needed to talk about before he could do that.

"Mina, I will take care of this. I'll take care of you." He took a deep breath. It was time to lay his cards on the table. "I want to always take care of you."

Her eyes searched his.

He went on. "I'm not just killing time here. My priorities, what I want in my life, it hasn't changed." He wanted to say more, but held back not wanting to push too hard.

Just then, a buzzing came from the coffee table where her phone lit up and vibrated, inching across the surface. "I should get that in case something's on fire." She shot him a little smile over her shoulder as she sat on the couch and grabbed her phone.

"Damn." Sighing she swiped her finger across the screen connecting the call. "Hello?"

Thomas made his way across the room to join her on the couch. He had a guess about who was calling and why. Whoever it was, she wasn't happy to hear from them and he wanted to be there to lend support however he could.

"That's fine. Tuesday is good. Okay. Thank you." She ended the call and slouched back against the couch. "They sure aren't wasting any time are they?"

He gently combed his fingers through the silky strands of her dark hair as she leaned into him, her head resting against his shoulder.

"They're taking this seriously. Don's been a thorn in their side for a while now and they need to deal with it before something else happens."

"What is his problem anyway?"

Trying to explain Don's issues to a woman was like trying to explain blue balls. Unless you had a scrotum, it sounded ridiculous. "He's just insecure."

She chuckled as she snuggled against him, swinging one leg across his lap. "I figured that out the first time I met him." She tucked her face against his neck and he could feel her warm breath against his skin. "I mean, why is he like this?"

The feel of her wrapped around him in the quiet of the empty house had his mind miles away from the conversation they were having. All he could think of was everything he had to look forward to with her. Peaceful moments like this. Crazy times with rowdy kids running through the house like maniacs. Intimate moments...

"Thomas?" Her lips brushed his neck as she said his name snapping him back to reality.

Thomas sighed. "Don was a scrawny kid. I don't know that anybody made fun of him for it. If they did, I never saw it." He wrapped his hand around the back of the thigh she had draped across him pulling her a little closer. "Anyway, he ended up getting tired of always being the skinniest kid and started lifting weights in high school."

"So he looked like he does now in high school?"

"No way. He didn't get like he is now until a few years ago. Rumor has it he uses things he shouldn't."

"Steroids."

"Probably. It would explain the bad attitude."

"And the aggression."

Thomas felt his body go rigid. What did she mean aggression? Had she not told him everything? "Did he do something to you?"

"Oh! No. I didn't mean that. I just mean everything he does is aggressive, not necessarily in a violent way."

Her voice was quiet against his shoulder. "Not that I haven't dealt with that before."

He tried to avoid thinking about what happened to Mina, but it was always lurking in the back of his mind. Someone tried to hurt her and to a certain extent succeeded. She'd come out stronger on the other end, but that didn't erase what happened. It would be with her forever.

He hadn't known Mina then, but he still felt guilty he wasn't there to protect her. He was now though. And he would make damn sure no one hurt her ever again. Especially not some meat head prick with a chip on his shoulder.

She held up her foot rotating it at the ankle. "Hopefully I still have decent aim."

* * * *

She'd expected Thomas to laugh. She was kidding. In the self-defense classes she took over the past couple of years she learned there were much more reliable ways to take a man down.

He didn't seem amused.

In fact he seemed to be more agitated. It didn't make sense. What happened with her ex was over, this thing with Don was just starting. Maybe for guys a swift kick to the balls was no joking matter regardless of the circumstances.

She leaned up to look at him. His jaw was set, his mouth a hard line. "I'm kidding. I don't plan to make a habit of kicking men in their balls."

"Some men deserve it."

Did he mean Don? Her ex certainly had.

She thought for a minute on whether or not to explain any more of what happened. He wasn't lying when he said it was hard for him to hear about her past. Any time it came up, his mood immediately shifted. She didn't want to keep bringing it up in bits and pieces so maybe putting it all out there was the way to go. "It ended up saving my ex's life. He should probably thank me but I doubt he feels the same way."

She waited for him to say something, but he just kept watching her, his eye twitching ever so slightly a murderous look on his face. Unsure what else to do, she kept talking.

"The people he'd been dealing with were coming for him. They didn't want to risk him telling anybody anything. If he'd succeeded in..." Thomas' hold on her tightened to the point it was difficult to breathe. She shifted trying to wrangle free from his grip with no luck. "If he had killed me and took off, they would have found him and killed him. Instead he ended up in the hospital, one ball lighter, but alive."

"That's unfortunate."

"That he's missing a testicle?"

"That he's alive."

She'd felt the same way for a while. Him being dead might have actually been easier on the kids and as much as she hated to say it, she probably would have been happier too. Eventually she realized it didn't matter. Dead or alive, he was out of her life which was the only place she wanted him to be.

"What about the guys he snitched on? What happened to them?"

"Some went to prison too. Some got off. Some ended up dead."

"Do they know where you are?" Thomas' eyes were fixed across the room on nothing in particular.

"Maybe. I don't think it matters. He tried to kill me. I testified against him. They know hurting me won't bother him. Might even make him happy."

"What about the kids?" His voice was tight. He was worried about her kids as much as he was worried about her. Her heart flip flopped in her chest. A man wanting her was one thing. A man who wanted her and her kids was a whole other beast.

That was her biggest fear about dating. She didn't want someone who would just tolerate the fact that she had kids. Her kids needed a man in their life. She needed to find a man who would be there for them. Someone who wanted to be a dad.

Looking at the man in front of her and his reaction to what she was telling him, her heart swelled. Knowing he cared about Maddie and Charlie made her unbelievably happy.

Thomas, on the other hand, was clearly miserable right now.

All this was new information to him. It had been terrifying when it was new to her too, but a couple years down the road it was old news. Hopefully soon he would feel the same way. Until then, she needed to ease his mind.

"Apparently even drug cartels have boundaries. I guess all the intelligence the government gathered makes them pretty positive these people don't hurt kids. Just in case, all three of us use my mom's maiden name."

He looked unimpressed by her reassurances. She gently rubbed her finger across the vertical lines that hadn't left the area between his eyebrows since this conversation started.

"Don't worry. You'll make yourself crazy."

His scowl softened the slightest bit. She trailed her fingers across his forehead in slow strokes. "We will go handle the Don situation. The kids and I will be safe and everything is going to be fine." Moving to the sides of his face, she slid the pads of her fingers down his face, his beard soft under her hands. "You promised, remember?"

Before she could say another word, he flipped her under him capturing her mouth with his. The weight of his body covered hers, his warmth and scent surrounding her, protecting her from the worries she could easily fall victim to and fought against every day. Thomas kissed his way across her cheek, down her neck his lips leaving her skin tingling in their wake.

"Please be careful." His voice was shaky, his breath ragged in her ear. Whether it was from fear or desire, she didn't care, as long as he didn't stop kissing her.

He pulled back, but kept his face so close to hers the tips of their noses almost touched. When she looked in his eyes it wasn't fear or desire she saw. It was both. "I just found you." He brushed his lips gently across hers, the soft hairs of his beard gently caressing her skin as he moved. "I don't know what I would do if anything happened to you."

She smiled up at him. "Now you know how I felt."

TWENTY-ONE

HER ADMISSION SNAPPED what was left of the self-control he'd been clinging to. He'd never considered she had been thinking of him as long as he'd been thinking of her. He'd been trying to go slow, take his time, as much to savor it as to give her emotions and attachment time to catch up with his. Knowing she was right with him the whole time made slowing down all but impossible.

He crushed his lips against hers, invading her mouth with his tongue. He needed to show her how he felt, make her his. Bring her enough pleasure to begin taking away the pain she'd endured at the hand of another man.

Kissing and nipping his way down her neck the neckline of her sweater impeded his progress. Sliding his thumbs under the hem, he lifted his weight off her just enough to push the garment up between their bodies ready to feel her skin against his.

"Lift up your arms."

She immediately complied and he ripped the shirt up over her head and tossed it over the back of the couch. Her hands came back down and grabbed at his shirt trying unsuccessfully to wrestle it off. He raised up just long enough to yank it off his body and chuck it on the floor.

He brought his mouth back to hers, nipping at her lips as he ran his hands up and down her newly exposed flesh. Her skin was smooth and satiny over muscles tight from running and hard work. He kissed over her chin and down her throat, stopping to run his tongue across the protrusion of her collar bone.

He nuzzled between her breasts letting the soft vanilla scent of her skin soothe his nerves, frayed from a long night worrying. He took a deep breath. He needed to slow down.

Right now he was letting his dick run the show and that wasn't how he wanted his first time with her to be. If he wasn't careful he would be inside her the second he had all her clothes off. While there was a time for that kind of sex, this wasn't one of those times. This was the time she would remember forever and he wanted it to be a good memory, not a fast one.

"Let's go up to your bed."

Hopefully the walk to her room would give him time to regroup and get himself and his desire under control. He slowly stood, careful not to lean on her too heavily as he got up off of her. Standing beside the couch he held his hand out. Her gaze traveled up his body lingering on his bare chest before moving up to meet his. Slowly she raised her hand and slid it into his. Just the feel of her palm against his had him stifling a groan. He was going to be in big trouble.

He pulled her gently up from the couch and against him, her breasts straining against the confines of a black lace bra as she pressed against him. He cupped the swell of one with his palm as he ran his thumb across the soft flesh spilling out the top. With a tug of his finger, he freed the full mound from its constraints. He rolled the pale pink tip between his fingers, watching it tighten at his touch. He gently pinched before rolling it again.

Mina was clinging to him, her fingers digging into the muscles of his shoulders. Soft moans whispered between her lips, testing his control. He dipped his head, pulling the tightened bud deep into his mouth, gently nipping before releasing her.

She pulled away from him and took a few steps backward. Slowly, she unfastened her jeans and skimmed them over her hips, wiggling side to side as she shimmied them down. She bent over and drug them slowly down the length of her legs, leaving them to pool at her feet.

She stood up, her eyes locked on his. He struggled to keep his eyes on hers as long as he could, but curiosity quickly won and he let his eyes run down her body.

He knew no words that could adequately describe the way she looked standing before him clad only in a black lace bra, matching panties and a smile, not a trace of embarrassment on her face. She stepped out of her pants with one leg, then used the other to kick them across the room.

He was speechless. Knowing she had a great body hiding under her clothes was one thing, seeing it in front of him just waiting to be touched and licked was another. He wanted to reach for her, feel her tight body under his hands, but he couldn't tear his eyes away.

She took a step back. Then another. She turned and finished the walk to the stairs, giving him the chance to enjoy the way the cut of her tiny panties let the curve of her bottom peek from beneath the edge of the delicate fabric.

As she gracefully made her way up the steps, she unfastened her bra, letting it slide over her shoulders and down her arms before letting drop to the stairs. She reached the landing and looked back over her shoulder. "Coming?"

He swallowed hard. He definitely would be, and the more of her body he saw, the sooner he knew it would happen. He was going to have to pull out everything he had in his bag of tricks to make sure she did first.

He headed for the stairs and slowly began climbing. The longer he took to get there, the more time his body had to calm back down. He hit the second to last step just in time to see her stop at an open doorway arms crossed, her hands cupping her bare breasts in an attempt at modesty, the nipple he had in his mouth no more than two minutes ago, peeking out at him from between her fingers. He licked his lips remembering the feel of it as it puckered under his tongue.

As she disappeared into the room, he picked up the pace. It didn't matter how much time he took, he was screwed. He'd be lucky if he didn't shoot off in his pants in the hall.

He'd never been with a woman like Mina before. Someone so responsive to his touch. Someone so clearly comfortable with herself. In his experience, women preferred to hide under the covers. With the light off. Not stand in front of him in next to nothing, all but inviting him to look at her body. Not that she didn't have the right to be proud of what God and her mama gave her. They certainly did right by her.

He stopped just before reaching the doorway she'd disappeared through a few seconds ago and took one last deep breath, not sure he was prepared for what would meet him on the other side.

He took the last step and stood in the doorway to Mina's room. The biggest bed he'd ever seen dominated the room. Eastwardly facing windows flanked each side of the four postered monster, letting the mid-morning light flood the room. Mina stood beside it, the top of the mattress reaching high on her hip.

"That's big."

Her eyes lowered seductively, pausing on his crotch. A sexy smile spread across her face. "I could probably say the same thing to you."

He grinned back at her, nothing like a little praise to puff up a man's chest. Keeping his eyes on her, he popped the button on his jeans. Sliding down the zipper, he hooked his thumbs in the waist and pushed everything down, boxers included. Mina wasn't the only one proud of what they had.

He stepped his injured leg out, then used the other leg to lift the pile up so he could grab them. He sent out silent thanks to his physical therapist his leg was finally strong enough to support his weight. He tossed his pants to the bed making sure the contents of his back pocket would be within easy reach when the time came.

She stood silently, her eyes roaming his body, pausing briefly on the sixteen inch angry scar etched up the inside of his leg. A shadow of sadness moved through her eyes like the only cloud in a clear sky as it passed the sun. It disappeared as quickly as it came, replaced by a hunger he knew he could satisfy.

She dropped her arms to her sides, uncovering her breasts for him to appreciate. "Come here." Her voice was smooth and soft.

He crossed the room in less than a second, grabbing her by the waist and setting her on the bed as his lips found hers. She spread her legs, hooking one around him and drawing him closer until his throbbing shaft rested against her belly. He wrapped his arms around her, tangling his hands in her hair as he assaulted her mouth with his.

He leaned against her, easing her down to the bed. As she laid back, he wrapped one arm around her waist forcing her back to arch making her breasts easily accessible for his hungry mouth. He held her like that, the top of her head resting gently on the mattress, breasts high in the air while he took his time tasting every bit of them.

Her moans filled the bedroom as she held his head against her, every move she made causing the soft skin of her stomach to rub against the sensitive head of his dick. The feel of her against him made his head spin and his balls ache. He moved his hips as he suckled at her nipples, making small thrusts against her. He felt his balls tighten against is body as the need to come began to override his brain.

He needed to stop what he was doing or he risked spilling all over those pretty black panties she was still wearing. He pulled his arm from around her, lowering her gently to the bed. Her hands grabbed for him as he stepped just out of reach, taking the lacy black panties with him.

She let out a frustrated whimper as she wrapped her legs around him, trying to pull him back to her. "Please Thomas." Her voice was hoarse, barely a whisper.

He dropped to his knees beside the bed and slung her legs over his shoulders, wrapping his arms around her legs pinning them against his body and splaying his fingers across her stomach. He ran his tongue up and down her labia before gently sucking each one into his mouth, his teeth raking across the hot flesh as he released it. He lapped against her slit, hungrily drinking in her wetness.

He ran his tongue slowly up the crease, feeling her jerk under him as he found her clit. Using his thumbs he gently spread the swollen folds exposing the sensitive nub hiding beneath. He took her in his mouth, gently running his tongue over her most sensitive spot.

She began to moan and buck beneath him. He tightened his grip on her legs and used his hands to pin her firmly to the bed before he began a slow rhythmic attack, his only goal feeling her come against his mouth.

Within seconds her legs clamped around his neck and she began to quiver against him. "Stop. Please stop."

He had no intention of stopping. He wanted her to scream as she came hard, because of him. He continued his assault on her, keeping one hand firmly on her belly as he leaned forward, giving the other room to slide a finger deep inside her.

"Oh God stop! Thomas please stop." She rolled her head from side to side as she tried to wiggle away from him. "Please." Her voice was desperate, pleading. "I want to come with you inside me."

His body was strung tight with the need for release and her plea was more than he could handle. He crawled over her on the bed and drug her with him until they were in the center of the pillowy mattress, her legs locked around him.

He grabbed at his jeans, finding the protection he stashed in the back pocket. Using his teeth, he ripped open the packet. He sucked the rosy tip of one breast deeply into his mouth as he rolled the condom down his rigid length.

She arched her back, pushing deeper into his mouth as she grabbed at his shoulders trying to pull him closer. "Hurry."

The instant he was finished, he plunged inside her, groaning against her breast. She gasped as he filled her, pushing her hips against him until he was completely sheathed within her. He held completely still, adjusting to the feel of her around him trying to focus on not coming immediately.

Just as he was beginning to think he could handle it, she began to clench the muscles of her already tight channel, pulsing against him. All thought left him replaced by the need to bury himself inside her over and over, each time moving faster, deeper and harder than the time before. She met him thrust for thrust her hands on his backside pulling him into her.

"Don't stop." She moaned against his neck. "Feels so good. Oh God. I'm... I'm..." He felt her body tense then spasm around him, her movements erratic as she came hard, sinking her teeth into his shoulder.

Her climax sent him over the edge to his own. With one last thrust, he erupted, the room around him spinning out of control. He clung to her as wave after wave of heat poured out of him. He collapsed, completely spent and completely satisfied nuzzling against her as he tried to catch his breath.

She trailed her fingertips up and down his back, her legs still wrapped tightly around his waist. He breathed deeply, loving the scent of their lovemaking clinging to her skin. He didn't want to leave this moment, but certain things had to be handled. He reluctantly pulled away from her, careful to contain the mess he made.

"Bathrooms there." She nodded to the door on the other side of the bed then reached up to tug down the duvet covering the bed, sliding underneath.

He walked in and flipped on the light not prepared for the beauty of the bathroom before him. Marble tile covered the floor and up the walls. A large jetted tub lined one wall with a glass walled shower in the corner adjacent to it. It was a stark contrast to the rest of the house which was nice, but nothing like this.

He headed for the door across from the shower, happy to see he guessed correctly. After wrapping it in toilet paper, he chucked it in the trash can and headed back to the bedroom eager to have her in his arms again.

Crossing the room, he slid under the covers, pulling her tightly against him. She was soft and warm, her body molding into his. She looked up at him, blinking slowly. "Can we take a nap?"

He chuckled and kissed her head inhaling the soft floral scent of her shampoo. "We can do anything you want angel."

She snuggled into him, her breathing slow and steady against his chest. In less than five minutes she was asleep. He wanted to enjoy the feel of her next to him, tucked into bed, but after spending more time awake than asleep the night before and the post coital serotonin release, he felt himself drifting off. As he slipped into a deep peaceful sleep his last conscious thought was wondering how he would tell the woman in his arms he loved her.

* * * *

"Angel."

"Mmmm." Mina's limbs felt heavy, her whole body completely relaxed. Warmth radiated into her back. Instinctively, she wiggled up against it, snuggling deeper into the heat.

"If you keep wiggling like that we aren't going to get anything done today."

She felt his hard length pressing against her backside, the memory of their recent lovemaking bringing her fully out of her slumber. Smiling, she wiggled her hips, letting her bottom move back and forth across him. She heard him suck in a breath and curse. His reaction only encouraged her to keep the movement up. Within seconds he was fumbling beside her, grabbing for his clothes. Maybe he really did have things he wanted to do today.

Disappointed, she sighed as she flipped the covers back ready to climb out of her warm cocoon and get dressed. She scooted across the bed, yelping in surprise as Thomas' strong arm snaked around her waist, pulling her back against the warmth of his body. Releasing her, he hooked his hand under her knee, bending the leg up toward her side, the position allowing him to slide the length of his already hard shaft along her slit. He moved his hips slowly forth, rubbing back and forth.

"Did you change your mind?" His voice was deep against her ear.

She was having a hard time concentrating on anything besides the feel of him against her. His hand released her leg, letting it fall back, her thighs meeting, the pressure pulling him tighter against her as he continued to thrust slowly, sliding back and forth barely hitting her swollen clit with each pass.

"I want you again angel." His voice was husky, his breath hot on her neck.

She remembered him rifling through his clothes and realized what he was looking for. "What's stopping you?"

He growled against her ear, entering her with one smooth thrust. He slid his hand down to cup her, his calloused fingertips parting her to slip against her sensitive nub, keeping time with his thrusts. He quickly built up speed, pumping in and out of her as his fingers rubbed against her.

"I need you to come angel." He pushed harder, his hips smacking against her bottom with every stroke. "Come with me."

With one final thrust he plunged deep within her, the sound of him calling her name ringing through the empty house. Less than a second behind him, she ground against his fingers as wave after wave of pleasure coursed through her body.

It had been so long since she'd been satisfied by a man. You could argue she had never been completely satisfied especially considering most of the time her ex was only concerned about himself leaving her to finish by herself in the bathroom.

It didn't appear that would ever be the case with the man pressed against her now. Thomas seemed to take great pleasure in her pleasure. So much so, she almost had to fight him for the opportunity to bring him pleasure. They would have to work on that.

She sucked in a breath as Thomas pulled his hand away, her nerve endings over sensitized. He rested his hand on her hip as he slowly withdrew from her body. He kissed along her neck, his tongue leaving a trail of dampness that quickly cooled making goose bumps raise all over her body.

"We need to get moving." He kissed her shoulder and across her back as he slid from under the covers. "For real this time." He headed back to the bathroom. "I was hoping we could get my truck."

"You can't drive yet."

"Almost." He stood in the doorway grinning, hands on the frame above his head, gingerly bending his leg as evidence.

She laughed. He definitely had way more movement than when he started, but was still a long way from being able to perform the quick moving and bending required. "Much better, but that doesn't help us now."

"My mom said she could help too, I just have to call her when we are on our way.'

Mina looked down at herself naked, thoroughly sexed and probably more than a little tousled looking. Probably not the best look for going to see Nancy. "I'm gonna need a quick shower."

TWENTY-TWO

MINA SWUNG THE sledge hammer, the impact and resulting destruction immensely satisfying.

The city talked the retired inspector into coming back until the investigation surrounding Don was finished. She was first on his list and he made quick work of getting her set up to start demo. It was so nice to work with a reasonable human being for a change.

The timing couldn't have been better. She'd had to sacrifice her running routine when she began spending time with Thomas. There were only so many hours in a day and something had to give. It was a sacrifice she made happily but between her upcoming interview with the city and being so far behind on this project her stress level was off the charts. The opportunity to relieve some of that stress and finally get this show on the road had her swinging before the inspector was off the porch.

"You're gonna feel that tomorrow little girl." Paul stood a safe distance away watching her take the frustration of the last week out on the wall between the dining room and kitchen.

She felt it now. Her muscles twitched, growing weaker with each swing. Why'd these things have to be so damn heavy? She dropped the hammered end to the ground, propping herself up on the wooden handle as if it was a cane. "Maybe you should offer to help instead of just standing there."

Paul laughed as he walked to her, grabbing the tool out of her hand and lifting it like it weighed nothing. Damn men and their genetically superior muscle mass. "I know it feels good to beat the hell outa something, but it's not gonna do you any good if you hurt yourself and it'll only piss you off more if you tear something up we have to fix later."

He was right. The sledge hammer was only here for knocking up a little patch of concrete in the back, but when she walked in this morning, she could almost hear it calling her name. Every time she watched it sink into the drywall, crushing through the gypsum, she pictured Don's face. A couple times she imagined what Thomas' ex-wife looked like and gave her a couple whacks too. If she hadn't left him, Thomas wouldn't be with Mina right now, but she still deserved a solid punch to the face for hurting him the way she did.

Pulling her hammer up through its loop on her tool belt, she headed to the wall and began hammering herself a line. Once she had a decent sized hole, she gripped the board and started yanking, breaking off good sized chunks to stack in the wheelbarrow she had waiting. Paul propped the sledgehammer in the corner away from the wall they were taking down and came to help pull down the higher areas. At almost a foot taller than Mina, he could easily reach without needing a ladder.

"You know, I considered not calling the city and just kicking the little punk's ass." Paul threw a handful of chunks onto the stack. "Figured that might not help our case."

Mina sighed. "I'm not so sure calling did us any favors either."

She had planned on calling herself until Thomas wanted to handle it. It never occurred to her they would be this serious about it. "If they do all this and nothing really comes of it, he's going to come back even more pissed."

She had no idea how long something like this could take. For all she knew, he could be back on the job next week. If that happened, she was screwed. "We have to hustle on this just in case he comes back."

"If he comes back and messes with you, we'll just report him again." Paul made it sound like a simple undertaking.

"But how much further behind will that put us?" She grabbed a stubborn patch and pulled hard. "He's already got us over a week behind. Not to mention houses after this. We saw what it's like to stay out of his jurisdiction."

Just thinking of all the ways Don the Douche could screw up her life made her want to grab the sledgehammer again. This time hunting him down and using it the way she really wanted.

Adding to her frustration was the damn spot she'd been fighting with for what seemed like the past five minutes. Bracing her foot on the wall, she put her weight into one hard tug. Not surprisingly, it finally gave and she went tumbling backwards, landing with a hard thud against the edge of the wheelbarrow. The force of her fall tipped it over and both of them hit the floor.

"Mother fu-" The pain in her ass was no longer from only Don. She'd landed the boniest part of her ass straight on the lip of the wheelbarrow. Rolling off, she strung together every four letter word she'd ever learned. That was gonna leave a mark. A pretty interesting one at that. "Could this project be any more of-"

"A pain in your ass?" Paul stood over her, his hand held out.

"Something like that." She grabbed his outstretched hand and let him pull her up. "Thank you." She gingerly swept white drywall dust off her backside. "And thanks for not laughing."

"Didn't want to end up with a hammer to the face." He righted the wheelbarrow and began reloading the contents that were dumped on the floor. "I do fully intend on laughing about it later though." He gave her a smile and a wink as he finished picking up.

"I think I'm gonna need some Advil." She poked at her butt, wincing when she found the location of what would surely develop into a very colorful bruise over the next couple of days. "And maybe an ice pack."

"How bout you just call it a day? You've got a big day tomorrow and I can handle this. Go home. Ice your butt and have a glass of wine."

She hated to go home early on the first day now that they'd finally been able to get going. Plus she didn't know how long she'd be at the city tomorrow. However, her butt was beginning to throb and it would only get worse if she pushed through and kept working.

"All right." Taking off her tool belt, she started collecting her stuff, grabbing her purse just in time to hear her phone start ringing. Probably Thomas calling to see what time they needed to leave tomorrow morning since he was insisting on going with her.

She pulled out her phone and didn't recognize the exact number, but the area code alone was enough to make her stomach drop. Very few people from her hometown had her new number. "Hello?"

"Is this Mina Hensley?" The man's voice on the other end sounded older but at least friendly.

Maybe it was a friend of her parents. "It is. Who is this?"

"Miss Hensley, my name is Carl Schaffer, I took over Mr. Eubanks cases after his untimely passing."

Mr. Eubanks was dead? "What happened?" Her attorney was no spring chicken, but she hadn't thought him to be old either.

"Heart attack." His words were clipped and he sounded a little stressed. There was only one reason he would be calling her. She swallowed the panic rising in her throat, dread sweeping over her.

Paul was close enough to hear her conversation and crossed the room to stand in front of her, a concerned look on his face. As much as she hated to, she knew she had to ask. "Why are you calling me Mr. Schaffer?"

"I don't know how this happened. There was some sort of a mix up when I was supposed to be listed as your new lawyer and point of contact. I'm very sorry." Maybe he sounded more than a little stressed.

"What happened?" She could feel her face start to flush as her blood pressure rose. She needed him to spit it out.

"Your ex-husband was released from prison."

* * * *

Thomas sat at a high top against the wall of the dimly lit room nursing the only beer he'd be drinking. He'd been forced to take half a dose of painkillers last night to help him get to sleep. He'd overdone it helping Mina finish her projects over the weekend. He knew about halfway through he was going to pay for it, but he planned to take any opportunity to show her he was serious about taking care of her.

He checked his watch. Rich should be there any time. He'd had Nancy drop him off early so he could have some time to mentally prepare for the conversation they would be having. He'd avoided straight out telling Rich he wouldn't sell the farm for too long already. There were just other things on his mind. Prettier things. But it was time.

He was happier than he'd been in years, which was crazy considering he'd almost died, his house burnt down and there was the chance he'd be really poor for a few years if Rich made him buy his portion of the farm. None of that mattered to him.

Having Mina made everything else seem easy. He'd already gotten through almost dying and with physical therapy should be able to get to work on the farm in the spring. Rebuilding a house was no big deal either, especially with Mina by his side.

He planned on letting her make all the decisions she wanted on the project. When the time came, they could live wherever she wanted. Her house, his house or a whole new place. It didn't matter as long as she was happy. That left figuring out the farm situation and that was happening today. If Rich ever got there.

He'd finished his beer and moved on to water by the time his cousin finally showed up looking tired. He seemed to look tired all the time lately. Kids, a wife, big house and the farm. All that while trying desperately to maintain sobriety. The pressure was probably wearing him down. That's probably why he wanted to sell the farm. Lessen the load. Thomas hoped he could talk him out of it, but had a plan B just in case.

Easing up off the high chair he waved to catch Rich's attention. Nodding in acknowledgement, he paused at the bar to grab a beer before heading over. "Hey buddy. How's the leg?" He pulled out the chair across the table and sat down, leaning back to down half the bottle.

"Better every day." Thomas eyed the half empty bottle sitting on the table. He'd been a little hesitant when Rich suggested meeting at the bar, but hoped it was just out of habit instead of to feed his habit. "How's everything with you? Girls are all good?"

"Great. Good grades, Kate's playing basketball. Liza's taking art classes." Rich downed the other half of his beer and motioned for the bartender to send another.

"Beth?"

Rich shrugged. "I think she's coming around. I'm sure it'll get better soon." He looked toward the bar checking on the fate of his beer. "How's Mina? She's a pretty thing. She good in the sack?"

Thomas flinched. Rich had always been one to discuss his conquests and ask about everyone else's. Thomas always blew it off, never telling him what he wanted to know. He never liked it, but it didn't bother him the way it was bothering him now. Mina's abilities in the sack were nobody's business but his and only his from this point on. "We need to talk about the farm."

Rich laughed around the beer bottle that just arrived at the table obviously amused that Thomas didn't want to talk to him about Mina. Swallowing down a good portion of his new bottle before setting it on the table and spinning it in his palm, Rich smiled brightly. "Ready to sign the papers? Spend all your time with your lady?"

"I'm not gonna sell the farm."

Rich's smile abruptly disappeared, his gaze turning serious. "You're being stupid." He leaned back in his seat, staring darkly at Thomas.

"If you want out that's fine. I'll buy you out."

"You're gonna pay me half of what they're offering?"

"The farm isn't worth what they're offering to anyone else but them, you know that. It'll never appraise and I'll never get a loan." Rich was crazy if he thought Thomas was going to give him that much money for the place.

"Somebody's willing to pay that much. That makes it how much it's worth." His voice was getting an angry edge.

Thomas was hoping if Rich wanted out, he'd at least sell him his half for the actual value of the land, not some crazy number thrown out by a giant conglomerate. The farm needed to stay in the family and he was willing to do what it took to keep it there.

Before he could say anything more, his phone began buzzing in his pocket. He pulled it out, Mina's name displayed on the screen. He hated to do it, but he sent her to voicemail. He could explain later. Just as he slid it back in his pocket, it began to vibrate again. Again it was Mina. This time he swiped his thumb across the screen.

"Everything okay?"

All he could hear on the other end was sobbing. Fear gripped him, squeezing the air from his lungs. "Mina? What's wrong?"

He heard rustling as the sound of her cries became muffled. What was happening? He jumped from his seat and stuffed his arms in his coat. He had to get to her.

"Tom?" A deep male voice stopped him in his tracks.

"Who is this? What's going on?" He was going to kill somebody if he didn't find out what was happening.

"It's Paul. Mina's okay. Technically."

What the fuck did that mean technically? "What in the hell is going on?"

"You probably need to get here. I'll explain it to you then." Paul disconnected and Thomas fought the urge to throw his phone at a wall.

He was already halfway across the bar. He turned back to Rich. "I have to go. I'll call you later." He turned back around, not caring about the look of anger on Rich's face, moving as fast as he possibly could. He dialed is mother's number.

"I'm on my way Tommy." She sounded upset.

"What's going on?" He was covering the two blocks to the salon where Nancy was getting her hair done in record time, so focused on his destination, he didn't see the Camry pull up beside him.

"Get in!"

"What?" He held the phone to his ear trying to hear her better. A horn honked beside him.

"Dammit Thomas get in the car!" His mother had the window down, yelling at him.

He stuffed himself into the passenger side, not even caring he had to bend his leg at a painful angle. Nothing mattered except getting to Mina as fast as possible.

"Where is she?" His mother looked over her shoulder before cutting the wheel, making an illegal u-turn and speeding down the street.

"She's with Paul at the house they're working on." His mother was staring straight ahead, her hair was still damp, a few strands clinging to her abnormally pale face.

He swallowed hard. Maybe she was hurt. No. They would be on their way to the hospital then. "What's going on?"

"We'll be there in two minutes. You should wait until then."

"Why?" So many terrifying things were running through his mind right now. He just wanted to limit it to the right one.

"Because if I tell you now, you will be out of your mind until you get to her."

He rubbed his face with his hands. He felt out of his mind now. This was turning into the longest five minutes of his life. She needed him and he wasn't there and it was killing him. "I love her."

"I know." Nancy reached to squeeze his hand. "I do too."

Less than thirty seconds later, they were pulling up in front of an aluminum sided two-story. He was out the door before the car was in park.

He was past the large dumpster in the driveway and almost to the steps leading to the house before he heard her crying. Taking them two at a time, he ignored the pain screaming trough his leg in protest. He flung the door open, the sound of it banging against the porch railing barely registering.

Mina was crumpled on the floor, Paul kneeling beside her rubbing her back, murder on his face. He collapsed beside her, pulling her against him. She fisted her hands in his shirt clinging to him.

"They let him out. He's gone."

She wasn't making any sense. He looked up just as Nancy came through the door. She and Paul looked at each other for a second before both their eyes fell on Mina and Thomas on the floor.

Paul cleared his throat. "I'm going to go get the kids."

Nancy gave Thomas a sad smile before turning to Paul. "I'll go with you."

TWENTY-THREE

THOMAS HELD MINA tight against his chest, the pounding of his heart beginning to slow. She wasn't hurt. Paul and his mom were going to get Maddie and Charlie so they would be okay too.

Her words played over and over in his mind as he waited for her to calm down enough to explain. The more he thought about it, the more he was sure he knew what happened. He closed his eyes and rested his head against the wall behind him trying to stay calm. Mina needed him to be strong. She needed him to lean on right now and he wasn't going to let the building anger toward a man he didn't know stop him from being what she needed.

He cradled her head in his hand, brushing away strands of hair clinging to her tear dampened cheeks. Little hiccupy breaths replaced the tears as she began to relax in his arms. He kissed her forehead, letting his lips remain against her clammy skin.

Everything was going to be okay. He said it over and over in his mind. He had to believe it so when he promised her, he would mean it.

"They let him out." Her voice was quiet and raspy from crying. "He's been out for weeks."

Questions raced through his mind. How could they let him out? Where in the hell was he? Anger he'd been keeping at bay roared to life within him. How could they wait so long to call her? The man tried to kill her once, he could do it again. She'd taken small precautions, but a motivated psychopath would be able to find her with a couple hours of internet research.

"I guess somehow his parents shelled out a bunch of money for a new lawyer who found an issue with the investigation." She tried to take a deep breath, her larynx still spasming after the exertion of crying making it difficult. "They had to release him pending a new trial."

A new trial. She was going to have to relive everything that happened. "Where is he?"

Fresh tears began to run down her cheeks. "They don't know. He cut off his ankle monitor."

Thomas' leg was beginning to ache from the trip over and sitting on the floor in an odd position, trying to keep Mina comfortable. Cupping her head in his hands, he tilted her face up toward his. Even with puffy eyes, tear stained cheeks and a red nose, she was the most beautiful thing he'd ever seen.

No matter what happened, he would make sure she and the kids were okay. "Let's take you home. You can tell me everything on the way. Okay?"

She sniffed and nodded her head. He stood carefully, gritting his teeth through the pain it caused. Once he was up, he held out a hand to help Mina up. "Is this everything?" He grabbed her purse off a folding chair covered with drywall mud sitting in the corner.

"Yeah. I need my keys to lock up." She took the purse, fished around for a minute, finally pulling out a keychain with a smiling picture of each of her kids looped amongst the keys.

She held it in her hand for a second, staring at the pictures, her face beginning to crumple up as she chewed her lip. "How am I going to explain this to them?" Tears ran down her cheeks as she tried unsuccessfully to wipe them with her sleeve before they fell. "I promised them it was over. Everything was okay." She took a ragged breath. "Now I have to tell them it's not."

Thomas again wrapped her in his arms. There was nothing else he could do right now. He needed to get her home and comfortable and make sure his mom and Paul were able to get the kids safe. Then he had some calls to make so he could figure this out. "We need to get home. Let you relax and then we can come up with a game plan, okay?"

She wiped her nose across his shirt like a child as she nodded her head into his chest. Pulling away from him, she headed to the door, keys in hand. He stepped out behind her, scanning the neighborhood as she pulled the door shut and locked it. As she finished, she turned to him, her eyes falling to his tear and snot covered shirt. She started laughing through the tears still threatening to fall.

"Sorry." She wiped at her eyes with one hand. He took the other and led her off the porch toward her van.

"I should probably drive."

She pushed the button on her key, the lights flashing as the door locks clicked. "You sure you can?" She looked tired.

He gently took the keys from her hand as he opened the passenger door and helped her in. "I'm sure." If she needed him to run five miles right now he would do it.

She stayed quiet the whole ride, occasionally wiping her eyes with a tissue she found on the console. He'd managed to push the driver's seat back far enough to give him room to stretch out his leg and keep bending to a minimum. It wasn't comfortable and he hoped he wouldn't get yelled at tomorrow afternoon by his therapist, but Mina was in no shape to drive and he wasn't going to make her sit at that empty torn up house until his mom could come back and get them.

He pulled down her driveway and parked beside his truck. They'd brought it here in case she needed it, not expecting he would be driving anytime soon.

She was out of the car and halfway up the walk before he could make it around to her door. She obviously wasn't used to having a man around. He heard her open the door and the digital beep of the buttons as she disengaged the alarm. Thank God she already had that. It wouldn't stop someone who really wanted in, but at least they wouldn't go unnoticed.

He hobbled up the steps listening as she cooed at Daphne. Shutting the door, he locked the deadbolt and headed into the kitchen. Mina was at the back door, leaned against the frame, staring out the window, waiting for the dog to finish her business.

Thomas crossed the dining room, tossing his coat over a chair as he went. He came up behind her and slid his arms around her waist, pulling her back against him as he rested his chin on the top of her head.

"Everything's going to be okay. I promise." He turned her in his arms and brushed a soft kiss across each swollen eyelid before gently pressing his lips to hers. "You go get comfortable on the couch, I'll let her in."

"Okay." She shuffled across the room, kicking her shoes off beside the sofa.

He watched as she curled up, pulling the soft knit blanket from the back of the couch and tucking it around her. He turned his attention to Daphne as she sniffed around the yard oblivious to what was happening around her. Daphne came in just as the sound of women fighting on the television reached his ears. He made sure the door was secure before heading to the kitchen to start some tea.

Ten minutes later, Mina was relaxing on the couch, sipping some sort of spicy herbal tea he found in the cabinet and watching what appeared to be an eventful episode of Real Housewives.

While she was distracted, he grabbed his phone from his coat pocket and slipped out the front door. He'd felt like he was on fire since he got Mina's call at the bar and the chilly air felt good against his face. Scrolling through his contacts, he found the name he was looking for.

"Hey Tom. How's things goin' with the house situation?"

Jerry was one of Thomas' best friends from high school and was one of the cops who took care of his mom the night of the house fire. "House is fine, just waiting on the word from the fire inspector before the insurance company will get moving."

Right now they could take as long as they wanted. The house was at the bottom of the list of things he was worried about. He wouldn't have been staying there after today anyway. There was no way he was leaving Mina alone.

"Would you be able to look into something for me? Mina got a call today saying her ex-husband was let out of prison, sounds like on a technicality. He managed to take off his monitor and no one seems to know where he is."

"Holy shit man. That the one who tried to kill her?" He wasn't surprised Jerry knew. Word traveled fast in a small town.

"Yeah."

Maybe it was a good thing everyone in town knew. They might gossip, but people around here watched out for each other. His buddy would make sure all the cops had their eye out, it wouldn't be long before half the town was giving any strange man the evil eye.

"See if you can find out about what happened and if there are any guesses as to where he might be."

"Will do. How's Mina holding up?"

"She's scared. Worried about her kids."

"I'll make sure there's somebody at the school until we figure this out."

Jerry was a good guy and had kids of his own. Thomas was prepared to ask him to keep an eye on Maddie and Charlie, but didn't figure he'd have to and his friend didn't disappoint him.

"Thanks man. I'm gonna stay here with her and the kids. Make sure they're okay. I'll keep my cell with me. Let me know if you find anything out."

"I will buddy. If you need anything else, let me know. Give Mina my number in case she needs me."

"I really appreciate it." Thomas was going to owe him big.

He hung up and dialed his mom.

"How is she?" He could hear the kids in the background, putting his mind at ease.

"Resting. How are the kids?"

"They're good."

"Have you told them anything?"

"No."

Good. This was something they needed to hear from their mother.

"What are you guys doing?" He checked his watch. It was almost 4:00. The kids would be needing dinner soon.

"I think we're going to head to my place and do homework. Maybe order a pizza. Give Mina some time to get... situated."

He peeked through the side window of the front door. It didn't seem like she'd moved since he came outside. She was probably asleep.

"Thanks. Is Paul still with you?" It was nice of him to go with her. It made Thomas feel better than if she was alone with the kids.

"Yes." Her answer was a little abrupt sounding, but she was under a lot of stress so he tried not to worry about it.

"Well if you need anything call me. I'll text you Jerry's number in case it's an emergency."

She promised to be careful and keep a close eye on the kids before telling him to relax and she would call later.

He disconnected and headed back in the house. He was getting real tired of things screwing up his time with Mina. Hopefully Jerry would figure out what was going on and this would all be over soon.

* * * *

Mina jumped when Thomas came back in the house. She'd been able to hear his voice as he talked on the phone, but the closed door muffled his words making it impossible to understand what he was saying. After a few minutes she gave up and tried to focus on the television and must have ended up dozing off.

Thomas' footsteps were quiet as he came her way, the slight drag of his right foot barely perceptible. Her skin began to tingle in anticipation. She knew as soon as he reached her he would be touching her in some way. She loved that about him. Not just how much he touched her, but the way he touched her.

Some men pawed at you constantly, grabbing at you, usually in the boob or butt region. Thomas seemed to touch her with no other purpose than to feel her. Gently stroking her arm. Running his fingers through her hair. Lacing his fingers between hers. Every time he touched her felt natural. Every time he touched her she felt loved.

Daphne must have headed him off, hoping for some affection. She heard the rustle of her collar and the sound of happy pants as he gave in to her doggy diversion. "Is your mommy asleep?" He whispered so softly Mina could barely hear.

A couple seconds later he was at her side smiling down at her. "You're not asleep."

She shook her head. "I'm not." She smiled back at him in spite of the craziness she was currently in the middle of. Having him here with her was making it easier to get her head together.

At first she'd lost it. She was so scared, so angry she couldn't think straight and she'd just fallen apart. By the time Thomas got there she was spinning out of control, her anxiety feeding off itself creating 'what-ifs' at warp speed. But he knew what to do. He held her and let her cry herself out. He was strong when she needed it most.

"I believe you have a pretty nice tub. Maybe a bath would help?"

And he was freakin' smart.

"That is the best idea I've heard all day." She jumped off the couch and headed to the stairs. "That's not saying much though. I've had a pretty crappy day." She smiled at him and gave him a wink.

That little nap and the promise of a hot bath had her feeling much better. Thomas was right. Everything was going to be fine. She had faced this down once and she could do it again. She stopped at the bottom of the stairs and turned back to him. He seemed to be favoring his leg a little more than usual.

"Does heat help your leg or make it worse?" A hot bath could make them both feel better. She knew Thomas wouldn't expect anything more than that. He would just hold her and they could relax together.

He swallowed hard. He figured out what she was thinking right away. He stood, his feet planted to the floor. He clearly didn't know how to answer the question and it made her love him even more.

Love? Holy shit. Love.

She was very much in love with the man standing there with a look of panic he was trying to hide, on his face.

"You are allowed to say yes. I know you know it doesn't mean we will... you know." She cringed at how awkward her words sounded. Luckily Thomas seemed to find her lack of coherence amusing.

"You know I know that you know?" He grinned at her, hesitating one second longer before heading her way, the pronounced limp making her extra glad he'd agreed. "A hot soak actually sounds pretty fantastic."

She hurried up to the bathroom ahead of him, flipping on the heated floors and turning on the water to begin filling the tub, before peeling off her clothes. Thomas came in just as she was tossing the last of her clothes into the hamper.

He stopped in the doorway clearly surprised at her nakedness. She was proud of her body, imperfections included and wouldn't be one of those women who hid beneath the sheets avoiding a man's eyes.

She stepped into the tub of barely bearable water, the heat making her skin pink up immediately. "It's really hot. Is that okay or should I cool it down?"

Thomas seemed relieved once her body was obscured by the swirling water. "Hot is fine." He pulled his shirt over his head and laid it on the counter, followed by his socks. He glanced at her before turning away to take off his pants and boxers. She turned in the tub to face away from him, saving him any embarrassment. While he wouldn't be expecting sex, his penis probably had different ideas.

Scooting to one end, she made space for him to step in behind her. Slowly, carefully, he lowered himself into the steaming tub, stretching his legs up each side of her.

"How's it feel?"

"Really, really good. I've tried to soak in the tub at my mom's but it's just a regular size, so it was never really that helpful." He leaned his back against the tub and held his arms out to her. Careful not to bump against him too much, she scooted back to him and leaned against him, letting the heat of the water and the feel of his arms relax her.

"This is the only room I've really done in the house. I probably should have done the kitchen first, but..."

"I think you did the right thing."

The humidity in the air picked up his cedary scent and swirled it around her. This room had always been her sanctuary but Thomas being there took it to a whole new level. Bath time for her always brought a sense of calm to the craziness of her life. Thomas' presence added feelings of safety and protection, something she needed desperately after the call from Mr. Schaffer today.

They sat together like that until the water began to cool. Thomas held her against him, the sound of his breathing lulling her in and out of sleep. The fading light outside meant dinner time was close.

Pulling herself up, she wrapped her dripping body in a soft towel and padded into her room. She dressed quickly in soft pants and a thick sweatshirt, warmth and comfort were her top priority today.

The water in the tub sloshed as Thomas got out. She peeked in the bathroom just as he wrapped a towel at his waist, his eyes on the floor.

"Are these floors heated?"

"Yeah. Nice isn't it?"

"Not as nice as the tub. But close." He walked to the counter smoothly. She smiled, glad to see he seemed to be in less pain.

"I'm going to call and see how your mom and Paul are doing with the kids." She turned to leave.

"I want to stay here with you guys until we know where he is."

She turned back as he was pulling on his pants. He came toward her, buttoning the fly as he walked. "I'll sleep on the couch. I just don't want you on your own if anything does happen."

The serious look on his face told her 'no' wasn't an option. There was actually only one part of that statement she wanted to say no to, but she understood his reasons. Knowing Thomas was right down the hall instead of holding her in bed might turn out to be the hardest part of the next few days. Maybe she could figure out a way around that.

TWENTY-FOUR

MINA STARTED AT the sound of Thomas' voice.

"Sweetheart, it's time to get up." His voice was gentle, his hand stroking her hair. "Are you hungry?" Her stomach growled at his question in response. He chuckled softly. "I'll take that as a yes." He leaned forward and kissed her temple. I'll let you get ready and meet you downstairs."

She watched as he walked away then rolled over to check the clock. Crap. She overslept. The kids needed to get ready, she had to pack lunches and they had to be out the door.

She jumped out of bed and threw on the first clothes she found, a pair of skinny jeans and an oversized sweater. She grabbed a pair of boots and socks and headed downstairs, making it halfway before she turned around to go brush her teeth. Two minutes later she was running down the stairs.

"Maddie! Charlie! We have to hurry guys." She stopped in the living room and looked around the unusually quiet house. Thomas peeked out at her from the kitchen.

"Kids are gone." He emerged with two plates, tendrils of steam rising from piles of scrambled eggs. "Mom took them to school. You were sleeping really well so I hated to wake you up."

He set the plates on the table and went back to the kitchen, returning with two cups of coffee. "Plus it gave me an excuse to have you all to myself for a minute."

"That was really nice of her."

She sat at the table, the smell of eggs and toast making her stomach growl again. "I gave the school our history when we moved here. I know they won't let the kids leave with anyone else, but I just…"

"Don't worry about that. I made a couple calls. The kids will be safe." He nodded at her plate. "You need to eat."

She gave him a smile before biting off a piece of buttery toast. Last night Nancy brought the kids home along with a couple pizzas so Mina didn't have to cook. Unfortunately, after the stress of the day, her stomach had no interest in food of any kind. It must have recovered sometime during the night because now, she couldn't shovel it in fast enough.

"You look like you're feeling better."

She looked up from her plate and found Thomas watching her, a satisfied grin on his face.

"Much." She took a sip of the coffee. It was perfect. Creamy with a touch of sugar. She swallowed, letting the warmth seep in.

Thomas shifted in his seat, his gaze turning serious. "Are you up for today? We can reschedule."

She really didn't want to deal with the whole Don thing today. Or tomorrow. Or the next day. Or ever, really. But she learned a long time ago you can't run away from things like this. They don't go away and you only spend more time worrying. Plus this was only the beginning. It looked like she was going to have another court battle ahead of her.

"I just want to get it done and move on. It will be one less thing to worry about." She needed one less thing to worry about since they were seeming to pile up.

She watched Thomas across the table as he chewed, obviously deep in thought. His hair was getting long enough it was starting to lay down, but without the constant exposure to the sun, it was more of a very light brown than the blonde of his previous locks. Still less boyish but not quite as intimidating as when it was shaved.

"You want to stop by your mom's after we're done at the city and get some clothes to bring here? I have plenty of room in my closet."

He leaned back in his chair sipping at his black coffee, the plate in front of him empty. "That would be great." He reached across the table and put his hand over hers. "I'm sorry all this is happening."

He was sorry? Since she'd come into his life it had been one crazy thing after another and he was sorry? "I'm sorry. You shouldn't have to deal with any of this. You should be able to be home relaxing and getting your strength back for the spring. Not sleeping on a couch and running me and my kids all over."

His eyes sparkled in amusement over the rim of his coffee cup as he took a sip. "You did save my life, so I guess I owe you."

She couldn't help but smile. As soon as she was starting to work herself up into a hissy over guilt at him being involved in all this, he knocked the wind out of her little fit and brought her back down from the edge of crazy.

"That is true." She downed the last of her coffee. "If you think about it, I kinda saved your life twice since I kidnapped you the night your house burned down, so you owe me double."

He chuckled as she grabbed their empty plates and dumped them in the sink before heading upstairs. "I'm going to go make sure I'm presentable for this thing."

"I'll be right here when you're ready."

She headed into her bathroom to check out the mess she had to work with. She stood in front of the mirror and cringed at her reflection. How did she miss this when she was brushing her teeth?

She just sat across from Thomas acting all cute and funny, all the while looking like a total wreck. Her eyes were puffy and red rimmed. Her hair was a matted mess from not putting it up during their bath and not combing it after.

She needed a shower and some eye cream. She looked herself over again. And some more coffee. She started the shower and jumped in.

Ten minutes later, she was scrubbed and shaved and feeling one step closer to herself. A quick blow dry and a little bit of make-up and she was as ready as she was going to get for this thing. She headed back downstairs in search of the last thing on her list.

Thomas was on the couch watching the news. A stack of folded blankets sat on top of a pillow at the end of the couch.

"Where did your mom sleep?"

Thomas decided it would be better if Nancy stayed with them too. Mina didn't like the idea of Nancy being alone either, not knowing what was going on. If one of them got hurt because of her, she would never forgive herself.

"She slept with Maddie."

"Does she get to spend much time with Rich's kids?" If she raised Rich that would make his kids basically her grandchildren.

"Rich's wife is pretty close with her parents so I think they spend more time over there."

That was probably difficult for Nancy. She so clearly wanted to be a grandmother. Mina couldn't imagine why someone wouldn't want her to be a big part of their kids' lives.

Thomas checked his watch. "It's about time to head out, huh?"

As much as she didn't want to do this, she also didn't want to risk being late. These men hadn't done anything to deserve her being rude to them. "I'm gonna make a coffee to go. Want one?"

He shook his head. "I'm going to pass. I've already had three cups. Anymore and I'll be ready to jump out of my skin trying to sit still."

Coffee was going to have nothing to do with her inability to sit still this morning. Her hands were starting to get a little clammy and she could feel her stomach doing flip flops. Hopefully she could keep her scrambled eggs down at least until the meeting was over.

On the plus side, it was distracting her from worrying about the whereabouts of her ex, although that concern would be next in line for her attention. Hopefully, she could get all this crap straightened out and be able to give all her extra attention to the person who deserved it.

* * * *

Thomas watched as Mina poured coffee into a travel mug. She was everything he'd ever wanted and more. The fact that some unknown dickhead could come out of nowhere and take it all away had him ready to lose his mind.

He'd lain awake on the couch all night listening to every sound, hoping the son-of-a-bitch would show up so he could kill him and be done with it. Finally be able to move on with the woman he loved.

He'd waited so long for the right woman. Someone he could trust. Someone who wanted the same things he wanted. Watching the way Mina was with her children left little doubt about what was really important to her and he would bet his life he could trust her.

She met him in the entry, swinging her coat on. "I'm ready I guess." She was putting on a brave face, but he could see the worry in her eyes. He grabbed the hand not clutching a coffee cup and pulled her against him, capturing her lips in a kiss.

It felt like so long since he'd tasted her he couldn't help but sweep his tongue between her lips and drink in the sweet coffee flavor of her mouth. She pressed into him, her breath tickling the whiskers on his face. He tried to hold back, but a small groan escaped as her body softened into his.

He pulled back, using his grip on her to put some space between them. "We need to go."

She sighed. "I know." She turned and pulled the door open, grabbing for her van keys from the purse she slung over her shoulder.

"Let's take my truck." He held up his keys, jingling them in the air. "I did okay with the van yesterday and I'll have more space in the truck."

Hopefully she could just sit and focus on staying relaxed. Plus, his old truck needed to be run around a bit. It hadn't been driven much lately and he didn't want the battery to go dead in the cold.

She looked at the keys, then at him. "Sure?"

"Positive." He went out first, waiting for her to activate the alarm behind him. He opened her door, getting her loaded in before circling the front and climbing in. The ragged turn of the engine made him extra glad he decided to take the truck. He let the cold engine warm up a minute, pressing the gas occasionally to speed up the process.

Once the sound of the engine dropped to a low rumble, he rubbed his palms together for a little warmth before gripping the bitingly cold steering wheel and backing down the driveway. He coasted down the road stealing sideways glances at Mina as she stared out the window, obviously lost in thought. Probably mentally organizing everything she wanted to go over this morning.

He slid his hand across the seat between them and placed it on her leg, giving it a gentle squeeze. She turned her attention from the window and gave him a smile, placing her hand over his.

He pushed the truck a little faster, eager to get this over with and be one step closer to the happily ever after that had eluded him so long. She squeezed his hand, rubbing her thumb gently up the side of his palm before turning to look back out the window. He couldn't help but look at her profile, the morning sun shining through the window, gleaming off the soft waves of her hair.

"Thomas stop."

He must be making her uncomfortable. "I'm sorry. You're just really beautiful."

"No. I mean stop." Her voice was urgent. She let go of his hand to point out the windshield. "Stop!"

He was dangerously close to flying through a stop sign. He drove these roads every day of his life. How in the hell could he miss a stop sign?

He stomped his boot on the brakes, jerking forward as the pedal smashed to the floor with no resistance. The truck kept moving, not so much as a falter slowing them down.

Thomas scanned the road around them. He didn't have time to stop at the intersection and a car crossing in front of them would be tragic. He said a silent prayer of thanks when he saw the roads were clear.

"Thomas what's happening? Oh my God why aren't we stopping?" Mina was pressed back in the seat, her eyes wide with fear, her breath coming in short pants.

He shifted the truck into neutral and leaned forward in his seat to pull gently on the emergency brake. He had a wide open, straight stretch of country road ahead of him to get the truck under control.

"It's okay sweetheart."

Gradually he pulled the brake harder and was able to get the truck slowed down considerably.

"The brakes just went out. I needed to take it in for a once over before I got hurt and didn't." He shifted back into drive, keeping the truck at a speed he could safely control manually with the emergency brake.

"Shouldn't we pull over and call a tow truck?" Mina's knuckles were white from the grip she had on the door's arm rest.

"We will be just fine. I'm gonna drive real slow." He wanted to reach for her again. Comfort her, but he didn't dare risk not being able to use one of his hands quickly. "Once we get to the city building I'll call my buddy and have him tow it from there."

Mina's eyes darted between him and the road, still obviously not on board with his plan. He watched out of the corner of his eye as she took a few deep slow breaths and unclenched her hand from the door.

"Okay." She still sounded a little scared, but nothing like before.

He was both proud of and saddened by her ability to take control of her emotions. It spoke both of her strength and her difficult past. He doubted she learned to do it because she wanted to.

She stayed calm until they reached town. The addition of other cars and stop lights had her closing her eyes and slow breathing until they were parked safely in the city lot. He put the truck in park and turned to her, stroking her cheek.

"I meant it when I said I would always take care of you."

She opened her eyes and looked around the lot obviously relieved. "I know. It was just…"

"A little scary. I know." He slid his hand down the softness of her hair, twirling one strand around his finger. "I'm not the kind of man who would ever…" He used his index finger to turn her chin toward him so he could look in her eyes and she would see the seriousness in his. "Ever. Put you in danger." He brushed the pad of his thumb across her lips.

"I love you."

He paused, a little overwhelmed at finally telling her what he'd been feeling for what seemed like forever. "I love you more than I've ever loved anything Mina." He leaned across the truck to gently brush his lips across hers. "You saved me in more ways than you will ever know."

TWENTY-FIVE

MINA WALKED INTO the bright fluorescent lights of the city building still blinking back tears. Her day had been a roller coaster and it wasn't even noon yet.

One minute she was pretty sure she was going to die, the next Thomas was saying words she hadn't expected to hear again in her life, much less believe. Now she had to spend the next hour or two recounting every questionable thing Don has done or said since she met him.

She didn't want to be here. She wanted to be with Thomas. She wanted to go home and show him what she'd been too overcome to say in the truck.

She turned to look over her shoulder one more time before walking into the meeting room the woman at the desk pointed her towards, hoping to see him coming through the doors. She wanted to wait for him, but the little mechanical malfunction this morning ate up their spare time.

He'd promised to hurry with his calls, but he had to get the truck towed and make sure Nancy could come get them so they wouldn't have to spend any more time than necessary here.

She took a deep breath and opened the door forcing a smile onto her face. Taking a step inside, she froze, her smile disappearing immediately. One of the three men around the table jumped up, his hand outstretched.

"Good morning Miss Hensley I'm Doug and this is Stan." He gestured to the man sitting across the long table from him, who immediately stood.

She looked at Doug's outstretched hand and considered breaking one of his fingers. That probably would not help her cause right now. Instead she grabbed his hand and shook it, squeezing hard, not letting go until the look on his face signified his understanding. She was fucking pissed.

She turned to Stan, her eyebrow raised. "Apparently I was confused about the purpose of this meeting." Stan looked at Doug. Doug looked at Stan. Both men kept their mouths tightly shut. Obviously neither man had the balls to explain it to her.

She'd just opened her mouth to lay into them when a deep voice boomed behind her from the open doorway. "What the hell is he doing here?"

Don sat at the other end of the table a smug grin on his face. "Employee handbook says I can be here." He tapped the capped end of his pen against a yellow legal pad sitting on the table in front of him, smiling at Thomas.

She stood there for a minute looking from man to man to man deciding how she would handle this. Option one was to go with the overwhelming urge she felt to launch herself across the table and rip that smile off Don's face. Not the best option, but her favorite.

Option two leave and call a lawyer. She was pretty sure Don was wrong and tweedle dee and tweedle dumb were too intimidated to call him on it. "Where's the man I spoke with last week to set this up?"

Don immediately answered. "Car trouble."

Which brought her to option three. As much as she hated to, this was going to have to hang over her head a little longer.

"I'll work this out with him then." She spun on her heel and walked past Thomas, refusing to look back, knowing the smile Don would have on his face would get him a big face full of option number one.

She was halfway across the lobby before she realized Thomas hadn't moved. He was planted in the doorway and she could hear the beginnings of a heated conversation.

Don sure wanted to piss her off this morning. Turn about's fair play.

She marched her way back across the lobby reaching Thomas' side in less than five seconds. She tucked her hand in his as she curled herself against him. "Honey let's go," she purred, loud enough to be heard at the back of the room.

"We have more important things we could be doing." She smiled up at him coyly, batting her lashes and trying her best to look innocently seductive.

Thomas looked down at her, the anger in his eyes softening immediately. "Is that what you want?" His voice was soft, only meant for her. He knew what she was doing, but was ready to stay and fight if that's what needed to happen.

She nodded. "Let's get out of here. We can work it out later."

Thomas took one last look in the room, his anger from earlier absent. He grinned at Don before looking at Stan and Doug. "Tell your boss we'll be calling him to get this sorted out."

Thomas wrapped his arm around her shoulders and directed her back toward the front doors. They only made it a couple steps when they heard an ink pen hit the wall as it came out the open door, followed by the flapping of pages as the yellow legal pad joined it.

"Fuck you Thomas!" Don stood in the doorway yelling at their backs as they continued to walk away. "Laugh now, but she's gonna get tired of you." Thomas kept walking but she could see the muscles of his jaw begin to twitch. "Just like Mary did."

Holy shit balls.

Mina wrapped her arm around Thomas' waist, just in case he was considering turning around. The receptionist was standing, wide-eyed, mouth agape looking back and forth between Thomas and Don. A couple people milling around the front sitting area stopped to watch the saga unfold. Thomas never flinched he just kept his arm draped casually around her, never speeding up their pace.

They made it outside just as the tow truck was hooking up. Thomas walked up to the driver and shook his hand. "Thanks for coming to pick it up."

"No problem. I'll check it over and give you a call." He spit on the ground, the spot tinged brown from a pinch of snuff he had stuck in his bottom lip. He nodded her way. "Ma'am."

"Jeb this is Mina. Mina, Jeb."

She smiled at him. He looked to be about Thomas' age. Probably another of the many buddies he went to school with.

"Ya'll need a ride?"

Mina looked around the parking lot. There was no way Nancy was here yet and she had no desire to hang out just waiting for Don to come out. If he pushed his luck, which he would, he was going to get his ass kicked, and it wasn't Thomas he would have to worry about.

Thomas looked back at her then nodded to his buddy. "We'll come with you and wait for our ride at the shop if that's okay."

"Jump on in." He smiled, his perfectly straight teeth flecked with tiny bits of tobacco.

Thomas called Nancy on the way and filled her in on the meeting and their change of location. Once he got off the phone, Thomas and his friend chatted about business on the farm and in the shop. Jeb asked about his leg and gave apologies about the house. They were almost to the shop when the driver asked Thomas if he was selling the farm.

"Where'd you hear that?"

There was something in Thomas' voice that seemed different. As if he was trying very hard to seem casual, but if you knew him well, you could certainly tell the question hit a nerve. Was he planning on selling the farm? Because of his leg?

"Just drunk bar talk around town. Heard some company was trying to offer over market for the land." Jeb pulled the truck into the lot, oblivious to the change in his friend. He may not see it, but Mina certainly could.

Now sitting here in the shop watching as he flipped through a magazine too fast to really be seeing the pages, she was bothered by the fact he never answered the question.

She leaned into him and kept her voice low. "Are you selling the farm?"

He stared at the pages on his lap for a few seconds before taking a deep breath. "No." He closed the magazine and flopped it on the table beside him. "There is somebody who wants to buy it, but I'm not really interested."

Mina was relieved. She felt attached to the farm. For so long running past it was the highlight of her day. Well. Running past the farmer tending it was the highlight of her day.

She suddenly remembered something Paul said. "Are you the sole owner?"

"No."

* * * *

The great mood Thomas woke up in this morning was quickly turning sour.

Being there to wake Mina up and make her breakfast after helping get the kids off to school was everything he thought it would be. He wanted every morning to be like this morning.

The rest of the day however, was going to total shit.

Getting this meeting about Don over with would have meant one big thing off Mina's mind and pushed them one step closer to the quiet domestic life he'd dreamed of for years. But the minute they left the house it had been one long downhill slide, with no brakes.

The brakes were no big deal, just another thing he had to deal with on a constantly growing list. The bigger deal was Don and his ability to strong arm at least a couple of city guys. He would be calling Mina's contact at the city and find out what the hell was going on.

His little stunt today wasn't going to do Don any favors. He was probably going to lose his job at this point. That meant Mina wouldn't have to deal with him anymore, eventually. Until then it was one more problem they had to deal with.

He hoped to hear from Jerry this morning, at least get some idea what was really happening with Mina's ex-husband. Hopefully somebody somewhere had an idea where he was. Hell, for all he knew the guy had already been picked up and was back in jail.

"You okay?" Mina looked at him over Charlie's head as it bobbed along with the movement of the car, her brows drawn together.

Thomas cracked his window. This damn car was a sauna. "I'm okay. Just a little warm." The heat was adding to his agitation.

He had a mental list started of everything he needed to do once they got to Mina's house. He had to do something. He couldn't keep spending every day worrying about ex-husbands and building inspectors.

Once he got insurance squared away, he had a house to build and before he knew it, spring would be right around the corner and the farm would eat up all his spare time. What if this thing with Mina's ex wasn't resolved before then? Working the farm meant long hours away from her. How could he keep his sanity if he left her every morning not knowing what could be lurking around just waiting for the opportunity to take her from him?

Thomas rubbed his temples. He was getting a headache. And a little car sick from riding in the backseat of a hot car. They were only a couple minutes from the house, then he could stretch his cramped leg and cool off outside while he made some calls.

The first would have to be to Rich.

They didn't have a chance to finish their conversation at the bar yesterday before Thomas ran out to find Mina. It hadn't gone well up until that point and he didn't expect it to go well today. Hopefully he could convince Rich to keep the farm. If not...

Just as they turned onto Mina's street his phone began to vibrate in his pocket. He glanced at the screen surprised to see the car shop's number. They worked fast.

"Hello?"

"Hey Thomas. I got a problem with this truck."

Another problem to add to his list. Wonderful.

His truck was old and he wasn't surprised they found more issues, but he was really hoping they could get it back on the road pretty quick. "What's the problem?"

"Man, I'm not sure what's going on. Have you pissed anybody off lately?"

Thomas looked at Mina out of the corner of his eye. She was chatting happily with his mom and Maddie in the front seat. He tucked his head and lowered his voice. "What's going on?"

"Your break lines didn't just go out. Somebody cut them."

Thomas felt his face go cold. It took everything he had not to start yelling at the top of his lungs and firing questions into the phone. He took a deep breath trying to calm down. Once he felt confident in his ability to control the tone and volume of his voice he told Jeb he would call him back in a little bit.

He hung up the phone just as his mom pulled down the driveway, parking next to Mina's van. Mina's van that was parked right next to his truck. Shit.

He helped get everyone unloaded trying his best to seem fine even though he was ready to explode. Had he heard anything last night? He had spent most of the night lying on the couch staring at the ceiling, resisting the urge to creep down the hall and slip into bed beside Mina and hold her close. Knowing someone was out there who might want to hurt her was beginning to make him crazy. Now, someone might have actually tried to hurt her.

As soon as he had everyone safe inside the house, he marched back outside and headed straight for the van. He knew even before he slid underneath, the cold gravel driveway biting into his back, what he would find.

"Damn it." He inched his way back out and sat up leaning his back against the body of the van. He called the number of the shop.

"Her van's lines are cut too."

"Shit man. Call the cops. Want me to wait to fix the truck till you talk to them?"

"No. They can come look at the van if they want to. I'm sure there's no prints or anything. Probably slid right under and clipped." He shifted his head from side to side trying to ease the tension and the headache it was causing. "When do you think the truck'll be done?"

"I got what I need to fix it. I can have it ready tomorrow if you want."

"Thanks man. I really appreciate it."

"I'll try to come get the van in the next couple of days and get it fixed up for ya."

"That'd be great." Thomas gave him the address before thanking him again and disconnecting.

He sat for a minute contemplating what to do next. He rubbed his hand back and forth across his head as he wracked his brain. The hair was finally getting long enough to turn from raspy to soft.

After ten minutes of running different scenarios in his mind, he kept coming to the same conclusion. He had to tell Mina. There was just no way around it.

He didn't want to scare her, but he needed to keep her safe and the only way to do that was to be honest with her. They were just going to have to be even more diligent and be absolutely positive they did everything possible to keep her and the kids safe. It wasn't lost on him that whoever did this obviously knew about him and had no problem taking him out as well.

He pulled his phone back out and dialed Jerry's number. It rang a few times and went to voicemail.

"It's Thomas. The brake lines on our cars were cut last night. My truck's at the shop but Mina's van is still here at the house if the guys want to check it over. Call me when you get this. If you can't get me, call Mina." He left Mina's number and hung up. He considered calling Rich, but he just didn't have the energy.

He still had to call the city and tell Mina about their brakes. That was gonna be fun.

TWENTY-SIX

THOMAS STAYED UP half the night cleaning and reorganizing the garage. He wanted to get Mina's van inside once the brake lines were fixed. He also needed to blow off some steam and manual labor had always done the trick for him. He needed to be calm and confident for Mina and right now he wasn't feeling either of those.

Everything had gone from wonderful to out of control in what seemed like a few days. One minute he was planning the rest of his life with Mina, the next it became a real possibility that might end up being true, only a much shorter life than he anticipated.

He'd never had an enemy in his life, and suddenly, someone was okay with killing him. And there wasn't only one potential culprit. There were two people he could think of, one he'd never even met, that might be okay with killing him.

Thank God they didn't seem to be very good at it. They were in the flat farmlands of Indiana. Pretty much anybody who could work an emergency brake could stop a car without brakes around here. Hell, gravity would eventually stop a car with no brakes around here. Maybe they knew that and just wanted to scare them.

That would make sense if it was Don, and he prayed it was. Don was a lot of things. An ass, arrogant, obsessive, aggressive, but he was too maniacal to be smart and careful.

That's what he was worried about. Someone smart. Someone with a plan. What if Mina's husband thought he would be able to get off or at least a greatly reduced sentence if she couldn't testify? He'd had a couple years to sit and think about what he would do if he ever got out. Come up with a way to get rid of her that could never be traced back to him.

Thomas worked on the garage until almost two in the morning, when he physically couldn't do any more. His body was tired. His leg hurt and he was mentally and physically exhausted. He crept inside to take a shower, using the hall bath to avoid waking Mina. He'd come out to find her waiting in the hall for him, eyes watery, hair everywhere and just as beautiful as always.

She stepped into him silently, pressing her face to his chest and wrapping her arms around his waist. They stood like that until he couldn't hold her up anymore. "Come on Angel, let's get you back to bed." He scooped her up and carried her back to her room, laying her on the still warm mattress.

She grabbed his t-shirt and pulled. "I need you to stay with me. Please."

He brushed the hair off her face feeling dampness left from tears.

"Please." She mouthed the word at him, her eyes pleading.

He was so tired. He didn't have it left in him to argue about anything, especially something he needed so much himself.

He slid between the covers beside her and pulled her tightly against him, her body sinking into his. It felt so good to be here with her, holding her in the night. Knowing she came to him seeking comfort and security made his heart swell with pride and love.

He spent years mourning the loss of his first marriage. Only now, after just a short time with this woman did he really understand exactly what he lost. Nothing.

Never had he felt for Mary what he felt for Mina. Never had Mary made him feel the way Mina did. And he knew Mary never felt for him the way his angel did. He could see it in her eyes every time she looked at him. He told her he loved her yesterday. She didn't say it back. She didn't have to. He knew. He felt it when she touched him.

So many crazy and terrible things were happening all around him, but lying here with Mina in his arms and her kids sleeping safely down the hall, he was the happiest he'd ever been in his life.

It only took a few minutes for her to fall back asleep, her breath warming his skin through the fabric of his shirt. He wanted to stay awake, listen to the sound of her breathing. Memorize the feel of her in his arms. Commit everything about this night, the first night they really spent together, to memory. But he couldn't.

Everything about this moment, everything he wanted to remember were the same things helping his overwhelmed body and mind relax and finally find peace. He was where he was meant to be. Where he wanted to be. In that quiet moment before he slipped away he knew everything would be okay.

* * * *

Mina awoke to the muffled sounds of the kids and Nancy talking downstairs. She stretched, trying to work up the desire to get out of bed. She needed to get down there and help Nancy with the kids.

Nancy was the best friend she'd ever had. Was she really her friend? The way she came in and picked up where Mina couldn't was like a mother. She treated her kids like a grandmother. She was so much more than a friend.

Which was why it was time for Mina to stop taking advantage and get it together. She rolled over and snuggled up against Thomas, glad she had been able to finally get him in her bed. The couch was no place for a man doing so much for her.

She tucked her face against his shoulder and inhaled deeply. The clean smell of his shirt and the fresh scent of his shower gel couldn't cover up what she initially thought was cologne, but turned out to just be him.

There was something about the woodsy smell that calmed her. It probably had less to do with the smell and more to do with the man, but one was always followed by the other, ending up with her brain not knowing the difference.

"Good morning."

She tilted her head up from where it rested against his shoulder to find him looking at her, a smile on his face.

"How'd you sleep?"

She wasn't going to lie. Maybe the truth would result in this becoming a habit. "The best I have slept in a very, very long time." She wrapped her arm across his chest, sliding her hand over his body as she went snuggling in close.

He leaned his head down kissing her forehead as his arm came across to wrap around her, cradling her head against him. There was so much she wanted to tell him, so many things that needed to be said, but all of them would have to wait until they were on the other side of all that was happening. All of them but one.

Pulling far enough away from him so she could look at his face, she brought her hand to his cheek, stroking the soft hair of the beard she now almost couldn't remember him without.

She moved her hand to his head. The hair was growing back well except for the slash across the back. She slid her fingers across the smooth skin of the scar remembering the morning he'd gotten it. He almost died. He almost died in her arms. At the time she was devastated. Now, it was unthinkable.

"Thank you." She blinked trying to keep it together.

She had decided to run head on into everything from here on out and crying like a baby now wasn't going to be a promising start. She swallowed hard and took a deep breath trying to get her emotions under control. She probably shouldn't have thought about him almost dying.

"Thank you for doing things you didn't have to do." She leaned forward giving him a soft kiss. She pulled back, but just a little. "I don't know what I would have done without you and your mom." She chewed her lip, wanting to say more but not sure how.

Yesterday morning he'd caught her a little off guard when he told her he loved her. After the brakeless ride her mind wasn't really working. She hadn't actually realized what he said until she was almost inside and she'd been kicking herself ever since.

337

Before she had a chance to say anything else, he pulled her tightly against him, whispering against her hair. "You don't have to thank me." She felt him gently kiss her head. "I promised I would take care of you and I plan to do it."

The tears she'd worked so hard to hold in broke free, but for the first time in days, they weren't tears of fear or anger. They were tears of happiness. In spite of everything, right this moment, she was the happiest she could remember ever being. "Thomas," she whispered against his chest, "I love you."

He wrapped his arms tightly around her, encircling her in their warmth. "I know angel."

* * * *

"The kids and I will go home and get started on homework and snacks. Hopefully we can have it all wrapped up by the time you two get back and we can all have a good dinner and relax." Nancy pulled into the parking lot of the auto shop and put the car in park.

"Do you want anything special from the store?" Mina held the list in her lap, jotting additional items as she thought of them. She hadn't been prepared to feed two additional adults and they were running low on just about everything. When then guy from the shop called to say the truck was done, it was kind of perfect timing.

"I think my son has monopolized every meal for the next week."

It was true. She'd asked him the same question earlier and he had taken full advantage. If she wasn't so sure he loved her, she would think he was just there for the food.

"You always told me to marry a woman who could cook."

Nancy spun in her seat, probably coming close to giving herself whiplash. "Are you going to marry her?"

Thomas' face went a little white as his eyes darted between her and Nancy. As much as he was worried about protecting her, he was turning out to need her to save him an awful lot.

"That is probably a conversation for another day." She gave him a wink before jumping out of the car. She leaned back in through her still open door to look at her friend. "Don't give him a heart attack. He's been under a lot of stress lately and it probably won't take much." She blew Nancy a kiss as she shut the door.

Thomas was out of the car and standing behind her, so close she could feel the heat coming off his body through her coat. She waved as Nancy drove away unable to focus on anything besides the man behind her. He put his hands on her hips and used his grip to spin her to face him.

"When are you going to let me open your doors?"

"When you can move faster than I can." She grinned as she brushed past him, headed to the warmth of the shop. She yelped as a firm grip on the back of her coat, yanked hard, pulling her against the wall of Thomas' body.

"Guess, I'll just have to improvise until then." Lacing his fingers between hers before tucking their joined hands into the pocket of his coat, he held her at his side, making sure he reached the doors first.

Mina smiled the whole way. She'd never had a man open a door for her outside the random older grandpa types when the kids were small, let alone a man who insisted he be allowed to open her doors.

As they headed inside, Mina recognized Thomas' friend from yesterday walking in from a back door wiping his hands on a rag. "Saw you guys pull in. Got one of my guys pulling the truck around." He fished an invoice out of the pile on the front desk and slid it across so Thomas could see it, using his finger as he slid down the row of charges explaining each one.

After they'd settled up, he looked at Mina. "How are you holding up?"

"Okay." She smiled. Last time something like this happened, people avoided her like the plague. Nobody asked how she was, if she needed anything and these were people she'd known her whole life. Here she was, relatively new to town and people she'd hardly even met were concerned and offering help, not to mention the people she knew well.

"I'll be out for your van tomorrow if that's okay."

She felt those damn happy tears from earlier tingling in her eyes threatening a repeat performance. "That'd be great. Thank you for all your help."

"Not a problem. We'll get you taken care of." He reached out his hand, giving Thomas' a shake. "Call me if you need anything." He didn't let go and looked Thomas in the eye. "I mean anything."

Thomas looked back at him, both men suddenly serious. "I will."

Mina looked from man to man. She was fairly certain Jeb just offered to help Thomas kill her ex husband... or Don. At the very least help dispose of the body. Bodies. How in the world did she end up living a life where one person potentially wanted to hurt her, let alone two?

An hour later, after hitting the grocery and filling up the rear seat of Thomas' extended cab with enough food to hopefully last a week, they were headed back to Mina's. As promised, Nancy and the kids were there, homework finished, piled on the couch watching cartoons.

Everyone came out to help unload the truck making it an easy job. While Nancy and Mina put everything away, Thomas hung out with Maddie and Charlie. Mina stole a few glances into the family room, watching her kids, especially Charlie, get to spend some time with a man who would always have their best interests at heart.

"He's always wanted a family you know." Nancy stood beside her watching as Thomas and Charlie talked sports and video games. "Wanted a chance to be the kind of dad he never had. Give his kids what he was always missing." Nancy wrapped her arm around Mina's waist. "I think he's found the kids who need it as much as he does."

The two women watched a few more minutes before Thomas stood and headed their way. "I'm gonna take the truck and park it in the barn. Hopefully keep it from being messed with again until we figure out what happened."

He grabbed his coat off the chair and swung it on. "I'll probably get some more clothes while I'm there and check on the house, make sure everything looks okay. Can one of you come get me in a little while?"

"Sure." Nancy was wiping down the counters and putting away the last of the groceries. Mina heard Thomas' phone ringing across the kitchen and hurried to grab it so he didn't have to try to rush. She picked it up off the counter and saw Rich's name across the screen. She watched Thomas' face as he answered the call, waving to them as he headed out of the house.

"I'm on my way to mom's. I should be there for a while. That's-" He closed the door behind him.

Nancy looked around the kitchen. "Well if you don't need anything from me right this minute, I have a couple errands I could run before I go grab him. Give you three a little time to yourselves." She winked at Mina as she grabbed her purse and keys off the counter. Mina threw her arms around her and squeezed her tight.

"I can't thank you enough for all this."

Nancy squeezed her back. "Honey, I am more than happy to help. I've been where you are and I know what it's like. It is helping me to help you."

She let her go and before Nancy turned away to leave, Mina was almost positive she saw her wipe a couple tears. "I've gotta go or he'll try to walk back here to get to you."

They both laughed because they knew it was the truth. Nancy blew her a kiss as she headed into the newly parkable garage.

Mina and the kids piled under a blanket on the couch and were finishing up the second episode of Teen Titans when her phone rang. Probably Thomas making sure she was okay. She rushed across the house to where she'd left it in the kitchen. A local number she didn't recognize made her stomach flip a little.

"Hello?"

"Mina? It's Jerry. Is Thomas with you?" The tone of his voice made Mina's skin go cold and her palms start to sweat. Something was wrong.

"No. He's at Nancy's. What's wrong?"

"I don't know that anything's wrong. I tried to call him a couple times and it went to voicemail. He gave me your number if I couldn't reach him." He hesitated.

"Thomas asked me to see if I could find anything out about your ex and his whereabouts so I called around and talked with some of the guys who work around where you're from."

He took a deep breath she could hear through the phone. "I should tell you in person, but there's a lot that has me worried so I need to tell you now. Is that okay?"

If a cop was worried, she knew that meant she should be terrified. Which was good, because she was. "Okay." She took a deep breath, trying to keep it together until she heard what he had to say.

"I just got two calls I'd been waiting for. The first was from one of the officer's I've been in contact with. They found your ex-husband. He was dead. He'd been dead a long time, probably since right after he took off."

Dead? Since he disappeared? That was weeks ago. Relief washed over her body, but it was short lived.

"The second call was the fire marshal. That fire at Thomas' house wasn't an accident. Somebody tampered with the gas line. With it being cold, the house was shut up tight and it just built up until something set it off."

Somebody blew up Thomas' house on purpose. Was Don capable of something like that? Was anybody she knew?

Her stomach turned, bile making her throat burn as she identified a feeling she hadn't quite been able to put her finger on. Until now.

What if none of this, none of what happened was ever about her? What if she wasn't the one who was supposed to get hurt? Nothing was an accident. Not the brakes, not the fire, not-

"You need to send everyone you can think of to Nancy's right now Jerry. Tell them to go as fast as they can. Hurry!"

She hung up the phone and she dialed Nancy's number.

"Answer. Please answer." She could hear the pitch of her voice rising as panic consumed her body. The phone rang, each one seeming to take longer than the last.

Nancy's voicemail played in her ear. "Maddie!" Mina grabbed her running coat off the rack by the door. "Get your phone and call Nancy till she answers. Tell her to get to her house as fast a she can."

"Mom?" Maddie stood off the couch, eyes wide. "What's wrong? Where are you going?"

"You guys are safe, but Thomas is not. I have to go now." She yanked the door open and looked back one last time hoping she would be able to save someone that had become so important to all of them.

"Keep calling. I will call you as soon as I can." She pulled the door closed and took off, praying her time off wouldn't slow her down. If she'd ever needed to run in her life it was now. She switched her phone to silent and zipped it into her pocket as she went, praying she wouldn't be too late.

TWENTY-SEVEN

THOMAS CAREFULLY PULLED his truck through the sliding door. It was the first time he'd been in the barn since his fall. It felt like years instead of just under two months. So much had changed in that time. His body. His life. Himself.

The day of the fall he was living a life stunted by fear. He was scared. Scared of the future. Scared of the past. Afraid he would end up alone. Wanting everything to change so much, but unwilling to give up the control to allow it to happen.

That day, he lost all control over his life in a matter of minutes. As terrible as it was, it was the best thing that could have happened to him. He'd learned just how weak and just how strong he was. Or how strong he could be with the right motivation.

RUN

All it took was one golden eyed angel and he felt like he could handle anything that came his way. Even if it was only for her.

He got out of the truck and walked over to a dark patch covering a large area of the concrete floor. He scuffed the sole of his boot across the spot, pushing loose a thin crust of dust caked with his dried blood. He should clean this up. Even though everything turned out okay, it would probably upset his mom if she walked out here and saw it.

He grabbed a shop broom from the corner of the barn and used the last of the quickly fading light to sweep the loose layer off the spot into a pile. As he bent with a dustpan to brush the pile up, he saw the broken section of ladder propped against the tractor he'd been attempting to siphon the gas out of that morning.

He didn't know whether to be mad the ladder had given out or grateful. If the ladder was still standing, where would he be? Would he have changed on his own? Or would he still be spending every morning waiting to let a beautiful woman to run right past him?

He picked the ladder up from its resting spot. Maybe he should keep it. Give it to Mina as a wedding present someday. Someday soon.

As he was looking at it, something about the broken rung caught his eye. Before he could get a good look, the blinding light from a set of headlights filled the darkening barn. He headed up the side of the truck, carrying the ladder with him. It was time to have a conversation he should have had a long time ago.

He used his free arm to shield his eyes as he got to the back of his truck. "Are those your brights?"

He leaned back against the tailgate as he waited for the lights to switch off. The door of the other truck opened and closed. "I don't mind the dark man, you can shut the lights off."

"I won't be here long." He heard Rich before he could see him. The lights made it almost impossible to see anything between him and them.

"You got plans?"

"I guess you could say that." Rich stepped in front of the lights, blocking just enough of the beam so Thomas could see him. "You ready to sell the farm?" He stood between his truck and Thomas' truck, arms folded across his chest.

Thomas knew this conversation was going to end one of two ways. Rich would either agree to let Thomas buy the farm for a fair price or their relationship would be over.

His cousin had become increasingly agitated about the sale of the farm and Thomas was pretty sure Rich was dead set on selling and was going to do everything he could to make that happen. Thomas was ready to fight to make sure the farm stayed where it belonged.

"Yes or no? I'm tired of dragging this out."

Thomas squinted against the brightness of the lights trying to get a good look at Rich. He did look tired. He'd been looking worse and worse every time Thomas saw him.

"No."

Rich began to pace back and forth between the beams of light, his eyes boring into Thomas, never leaving him as he moved.

"God you're a pain in the ass. You just can't make anything easy can you?" Rich's voice was filled with an icy rage. "All you ever had to do was sign a little fuckin' paper and everything would have been fine." He stopped in between the headlights and reached behind his back to pull a gun from the waistband of his jeans.

"You haven't left me any options. I tried. I tried and I tried to make you understand, but you just wouldn't. So I had to find another way." His eyes fell to the ladder still in Thomas' hand.

Thomas went cold. He looked down at the ladder and in the light was finally able to clearly see the saw marks eaten into one of the rungs.

"You did this?" He held up the rigged ladder in disbelief. They were family. They were going to work this whole thing with the farm out. Tonight. That's why they were here. That's why

Thomas was here. Now Rich was going to kill him over what? Money? "You almost killed me."

"So close. I was so close so many damn times, but that little bitch you found kept fuckin' everything up." Rich was flailing as he ranted, the gun in his hand catching the light as he waved his arms.

"Why would you do this? Just for the money?" It was incomprehensible. Rich tried to kill him and from the situation at hand, intended to accomplish what he started, all over money?

"I had to do something. You're too stupid and hardheaded to see an opportunity of a lifetime. 'I can't sell grandpa's farm. It's a part of our family.'" Rich mocked him. "What about my family, huh? I got a wife's always got one foot out the door and the bank breathing down my neck. They're already trying to take the goddamn house. I gotta keep the cars all locked up so the motherfuckers don't take em." He ran his hand through the wild hair sticking up off his head. "That money was gonna fix everything for me."

Rich staggered a little then leaned against the front of his truck. "All I wanted was for you to sell it but you just wouldn't fucking give up. Look at you." He used the gun in his hand to motion at Thomas' leg. "Can't even work the farm and you still won't let it go."

Sweat beaded his brow and Thomas could smell the stink of liquor even twenty feet away. "Then I got to thinking how much all the money could do for me. I could save the house, the cars, all of it. So I figured maybe you should just be out of the equation. I tried every way I could think of to get rid of you. You're like a God damned cat. Got nine lives."

He pushed himself off the car and headed toward Thomas. "But it looks like you're on your last one brother."

"I'm not your fucking brother."

Rich stopped fifteen feet in front of him and laughed. He was so close Thomas could see the wildness in his glassy eyes. "You don't know? You're mama never told you? Hell, maybe she doesn't know."

Rich stood silent for a moment almost as if he'd lost his train of thought. Thomas held his breath as he tried to think of a way out. If Rich was as drunk as he suspected, he might be able to make it if he ran.

Before he could move, Rich's face seemed to clear. "Don't think about running. I go to the range enough to know I could hit you trying to run on a bum leg." He swiped the sweat on his face with his sleeve. "Turns out our piece of shit daddy was fuckin' your mother and mine for years."

It couldn't be true. If it was, he hoped his mother never found out.

"How do you know?" He needed to keep Rich talking. He needed time to think. He was not going to die. Not here, not now. He was going home to Mina one way or another.

"I found my mama's diary when we were kids. He was all she ever wrote about. When he died, she lost it. Went crazy and took off."

"And left you to be raised by her sister? Her dead boyfriend's wife?"

"Your mother is a saint! She saved me. Took care of me. Loved me like her own." Rich was on the move again, closing the gap between them. "She deserves a better son than you. You don't deserve her. You've never appreciated her the way I have. Always took her for granted." He stopped just short of ten feet away, gun pointed at Thomas' face. "I guess that stops now, huh?"

Like hell Rich appreciated her. He'd put Nancy through more than his father, their father, ever had, but Thomas wasn't stupid enough to think pointing that out would do him any favors. "What do you think it will do to her when she finds out you're the one who did this?" Rich might be too selfish to realize how shitty of a son he'd been, but Thomas didn't doubt the love he had for Nancy. Maybe thinking of how this would affect her would at least give him time to come up with some sort of plan.

"She's not gonna. Your girl's husband is on the loose remember? Everybody knows a man hates it when another man messes with what's his." Rich smirked. "It's been nice having a heart to heart with you, but I've got to get out of here."

Time stopped. This was it. There was nowhere to go, nothing to do. He wanted to close his eyes and picture Mina's face, not wanting Rich's bloated, unshaven face to be the last thing he saw. But he couldn't. He watched, frozen as Rich's finger twitched against the trigger. He wondered who would find him. *Please don't let it be Mina.*

The pain of loss radiated through his body. He was so close. If only he hadn't been so wrapped up in his own problems he could have had more time. More time with Mina. More time with the kids. He'd wasted it being an ass and now he would never be able to get it back.

"Bye brother. It's been nice knowing you."

Thomas held his breath and waited for the inevitable sound of the shot that would end his dreams and his life. The noise that came was not the pop of a hand gun firing, but a dull metallic thud mixed with a sickening crack. He stared in horror as Rich's head jerked to the side at an unnatural angle, his eyes bulging from their sockets before glassing over as his body crumpled to the ground.

Standing just behind him, staring down at the unmoving body at her feet was Mina, a shovel still gripped in her fists and held over her shoulder, ready to strike again.

Thomas stood, shock freezing his mind and muscles, and stared. Mina's chest was heaving, her hair and eyes wild, a deep red flush covering her face. After a few seconds, she crept to where the gun had fallen and carefully picked it up, switching on the safety. She stayed bent over, watching Rich intently. When she finally turned to look at Thomas there were tears running down her face.

"He's not breathing." She wiped her cheek against her shoulder. "I didn't know what to do. I didn't mean to..." The words barely tumbled out of her mouth before sobs wracked her body, finally snapping Thomas into action.

He took the shovel from her and tossed it away, then unwrapped her fingers from the gun that nearly ended his life and tucked it in the back of his waistband. He pulled her into his arms and held her as he tried to process what just happened.

Less than a minute later, he heard sirens that quickly grew louder and louder. Gravel spewed from the driveway as car after car came peeling in.

"Tom!" Jerry's voice came from behind Rich's truck.

"We're here. Everything's okay." That wasn't true.

He held Mina tight unable to look down. See the man he'd thought of as a brother, was his brother, dead at his feet.

355

"Mina and I are okay but we might need an ambulance for… for Rich." He knew an ambulance wouldn't help anything, but knowing it and admitting it were two different things.

Uniformed and plain clothes cops swarmed the barn, guns drawn. Jerry knelt down next to Rich's lifeless body and felt for a pulse before saying something Thomas couldn't hear into his radio.

Activity swirled around him but he felt disconnected from it all. He closed his eyes and focused on something that a few short minutes ago, he thought he may never have the chance to do again. He held Mina in his arms and made her a silent promise. One he would cherish every minute of keeping.

TWENTY-EIGHT

"ARE WE GONNA order pizza?"

"Honey, I don't know. You'll have to ask when we get there."

"Are you and Thomas staying?"

"We are going to dinner."

"Like a date?" Charlie was full of questions as they drove to Nancy's house.

"Yup. Exactly like that."

"Is he gonna keep staying at our house?"

Mina took a deep breath. She really wished he could be staying at their house, but Nancy was struggling with being alone at her house since-

"Cause I'd probably like it if he did. He was really good at video games and helping me with my homework." Charlie looked at his lap. "Kinda like a dad, but better."

The sound of his little voice broke her heart.

It was a miracle it was still beating after all the heartbreak of the past few days. It broke when she had to tell the kids their father was dead. It broke again when she heard Thomas tell Nancy about Rich. It broke when Thomas recounted all Rich said in the barn. Now it was breaking again for her sweet little boy.

Charlie didn't remember his dad before drugs and money ruined him. He'd never had a really good man in his life and after experiencing it just a short time, he was desperate for more.

Mina smiled at him in the rearview mirror. "Well, Nancy needs him very much right now, but I'm very sure one day soon, he will be coming to our house a lot."

"Yeah he will." Maddie wiggled her eyebrows and made kissy faces at her from the passenger seat.

Mina rolled her eyes. No point in arguing. It was true.

She pulled the van onto the gravel driveway, unable to stop herself from looking at the barn. In that barn she had saved Thomas' life. Twice. The second time, only succeeding by taking someone else's.

As they stopped in front of the white farmhouse the front door opened and Thomas stepped out onto the porch. Both kids jumped out, overnight bags slung over their shoulders and ran to the house. Maddie threw him a smile as she slipped past him, but Charlie hit him full tilt. Thomas' eyes were wide with surprise at the bear hug the little boy gave him. She got to the porch just as Charlie let go and started dragging Thomas inside to show him whatever cool things he'd packed with him.

Thomas looked back over his shoulder at her. "Mom's upstairs. We've gotta leave in twenty minutes."

She nodded and closed the door behind her before heading up the narrow staircase. Only one light was on, making it easy to find Nancy where she sat in the middle of her bed, surrounded by the contents of an old cardboard box that sat on the floor.

She hadn't seen her friend since the night she'd stopped Rich from killing Thomas. It was easier to think of it that way as opposed to the night she killed Rich.

Thomas, Mina and Nancy sat with the police as Thomas explained what happened. She thought Rich being dead would be the worst of it, but it wasn't, not really. As a mother, which Nancy was to him, finding out your child was capable of the things Rich had done would be devastating. Add to that an ultimate betrayal by her sister, and Mina wasn't expecting what she saw in front of her.

Nancy looked beautiful. Her hair was down, slung over one shoulder, still wavy from the braid she must have recently taken out. Her face was scrubbed clean, her cheeks rosy from the warmth of the house.

"Hey." Mina didn't know what to say. She loved Nancy so much and knowing she'd done something to cause her pain had been eating her up.

Nancy looked up and smiled. "Hi honey." She patted a spot on the bed beside her. "Come sit with me."

Mina did as she was told and sat down, eyeing the items covering the blanket.

"I went looking for that diary." She picked up a small bound journal. The cover was printed with rainbows that had faded over years spent in an old box in an attic. "He was telling the truth. Looks like Sam was with her almost the whole time he was with me." Nancy opened the book and flipped through the pages, sadness dulling the blue of her eyes. "I should have known I guess. Looking back I can see it." She tossed the book into the box on the floor. "You only see what you want to I guess."

She turned to Mina and reached for her hands. "I never thanked you for saving my son. Both times."

"I don't know that you should thank me, at least not for the second time." Mina felt a tear run down her cheek. She knew it would take a long time for her to come to terms with what she had done. She had expected it to be the same for Nancy.

"You did what had to be done and proved me right. Thomas did need someone very special. If you hadn't been there, Thomas would be dead and Rich would be in prison. I would have lost them both." Nancy squeezed her hands, her gaze holding Mina's. "And I've lost so much in my life. Some of it my own fault." Nancy stared across the room and Mina couldn't shake the feeling her friend was talking about a different kind of loss.

Nancy shook her head and blinked a few times before turning her attention back to Mina. "I wish things were different. I tried so hard to help him. I did everything I knew to do." She released Mina's hands and began gathering the folded pieces of paper around her.

She took the stack and put it in the box beside the diary. "Sam wrote all these to my sister. I couldn't read the first one. Maybe someday."

"I'm so sorry." Her voice quivered with the strain of holding in tears.

"You have nothing to be sorry for." Nancy paused to look at her thoughtfully.

"How did you know?"

Could she tell her she'd known from the first moment she met Rich he was bad? The way he spoke, tried to control the room. The dullness in his eyes, even when he was smiling. They were all things she'd seen before and promised herself she wouldn't ignore the next time.

"Sweetheart?" Mina spun around at Thomas' voice in the doorway. "We've got to go if you want to make it to the movie."

She turned back to Nancy. "Are you sure it's all right? We could all stay here and order pizza and watch a movie."

"No way. I have looked forward to getting those kiddos to myself all day." She lowered her voice. "And I think he's needing you all to his self."

They laughed as Thomas leaned against the door frame with one eyebrow raised, tapping his watch. Mina threw her arms around Nancy's neck. "I love you."

"Oh honey. You know I love you too."

She threw the last of the letters into the box and set it on her dresser. "I better get downstairs and see what these kids want to do tonight." She breezed past Thomas and headed down the stairs calling to the kids as she went.

"Ready?" Thomas held his hand out to her. She reached for it and instead of leading her down the stairs like she expected, he pulled her hard against him, wrapping one arm around her waist and using the other to tilt her face up to look at his. "Thank you."

She looked up at him, not sure she deserved the thanks she kept getting and unsure what to say even if she did. Does one say 'you're welcome' for killing someone? "You don't have to thank me. You would have done the same thing."

"You're right. I would do it a million times over if I had to. And I wouldn't feel bad about it." He gently rubbed the space between her eyebrows she hadn't even realized she'd crinkled up. "But you do."

"How do you not feel bad about something like that? I took a husband from his wife and a father from his children." She rested her forehead against his chest trying to breathe through the pangs of guilt squeezing the air from her lungs.

"I think Rich reminded you of someone you knew well. Ready and willing to do whatever it took to get what he wanted, taking out anyone or anything in his way." Thomas ran his hand down the back of her head, using his fingertips to gently massage her scalp as he moved. "Just remember that when you start feeling like you've done something wrong."

She stepped closer, wrapping her arms around him, and turned her head so she could hear his heart beating slow and steady in her ear. "I think what I feel the worst about are the times I'm almost happy he's dead. Because if he wasn't..." Her voice caught.

"I would be." He cupped her face in his hands bringing her eyes to his. "You saved my life doing what you did."

"Again."

"Yes again." Thomas laughed pulling her back against him.

"I love you so much." He kissed the top of her head, her eyes, her cheeks, and then finally her mouth. A soft slow kiss that reminded her, just in case she needed it, of just what she had protected. The only person who had ever made her feel safe, loved, cherished. "And not just because you keep showing up to save my ass."

Thank you so much for reading Run!

If you loved it and want to know more check out my website at www.janicemwhiteaker.com for all the latest news.

You can also join my readers group on Facebook to get the first peek at covers and exclusive excerpts you won't find anywhere else.

Hopefully I'll see you soon!

xoxo,

Janice

Made in the USA
Middletown, DE
02 August 2025